G

RICHARD DALBY is a freelance writer and leading authority on ghost stories and supernatural fiction. He has edited single-author collections by Bram Stoker, Richard Marsh, E. F. Benson, and S. Baring-Gould; and several anthologies including *The Virago Book of Ghost Stories* (3 volumes), *The Mammoth Book of Ghost Stories* (2 volumes), *The Mammoth Book of Victorian and Edwardian Ghost Stories*, and six volumes of Christmas tales.

Oxford Twelves

Twelve Mystery Stories
JACK ADRIAN

Twelve Tales of Murder
JACK ADRIAN

Twelve English Detective Stories
MICHAEL COX

Twelve Tales of the Supernatural
MICHAEL COX

Twelve Victorian Ghost Stories
MICHAEL COX

Twelve Irish Ghost Stories
PATRICIA CRAIG

Twelve Gothic Tales
RICHARD DALBY

Twelve American Crime Stories
ROSEMARY HERBERT

Twelve American Detective Stories
EDWARD D. HOCH

Twelve Women Detective Stories
LAURA MARCUS

12

GOTHIC
TALES

Selected and introduced by

RICHARD DALBY

Oxford   New York

OXFORD UNIVERSITY PRESS

1998

Oxford University Press, Great Clarendon Street, Oxford OX2 6DP

Oxford New York

Athens Auckland Bangkok Bogota Buenos Aires
Calcutta Cape Town Chennai Dar es Salaam Delhi Florence Hong Kong Istanbul
Karachi Kuala Lumpur Madrid Melbourne Mexico City Mumbai
Nairobi Paris Singapore Taipei Tokyo Toronto Warsaw

and associated companies in
Berlin Ibadan

Oxford is a registered trade mark of Oxford University Press

© Selection, introduction, and biographical notes
Richard Dalby 1998
The moral rights of the author have been asserted

First published as an Oxford University Press paperback 1998

British Library Cataloguing in Publication Data

Data available

Library of Congress Cataloging in Publication Data

12 gothic tales / selected and introduced by Richard Dalby.
Includes bibliographical references.
Contents : Leixlip Castle / Charles R. Maturin—The dream / Mary Shelley—Metzengerstein /
Edgar Allan Poe—Master Sacristan Eberhart / Sabine Baring-Gould—Dickon the Devil /
J. Sheridan Le Fanu—The secret of the growing gold / Bram Stoker—In Kropfsberg keep /
Ralph Adams Cram—The dead smile / F. Marion Crawford—By one, by two, and by
three / Stephen Hall—The Buckross ring / L.A.G. Strong—The knocker at the portico /
Basil Copper—The entrance / Gerald Durrell.
1. Horror tales, English.   2. Horror tales, American.   3. Gothic revival (Literature)   I. Dalby, Richard.
PR1309. H6A122 1998   823'.0872908—dc21   98–23332

ISBN 0–19–288094–2 (Pbk.)

1 3 5 7 9 10 8 6 4 2

Typeset by Jayvee, Trivandrum, India
Printed in Great Britain by
Cox & Wyman
Reading, England

CONTENTS

Contents

INTRODUCTION

The phrase 'Gothic Fiction' immediately conjures up a vision of wild desolate landscapes, haunted abbeys, windswept graveyards, and ancient grand houses with secret rooms, treacherous stairways, creepy vaults—and purple passages—all essential ingredients in antiquarian tales of the macabre, fantastic, and supernatural.

Gothic mood, with all its conventional furniture of spooky ruins and castles (usually ghastly *and* ghostly—and haunted not only by ghosts but also by past deeds), with a frequent setting of Germanic or Italianate mystery, was seen at its best in the monumental classics of Horace Walpole (*The Castle of Otranto*, 1764), Clara Reeve (*The Champion of Virtue*, 1777 / *The Old English Baron*, 1778), Ann Radcliffe (*The Mysteries of Udolopho*, 1794), Mary Shelley (*Frankenstein*, 1818), and Charles R. Maturin (*Melmoth the Wanderer*, 1820), while William Beckford (*Vathek*, 1786) and Matthew G. Lewis (*The Monk*, 1796) effectively added the elements of sex and sadism.

A typical statement from one of Ann Radcliffe's heroines says: 'When I entered the portals of this gothic structure a chill purely prophetic chilled my veins, pressed upon my heart and scarcely allowed me to breathe.'

Many subsequent writers from Edgar Allan Poe to Sabine Baring-Gould, Ralph Adams Cram, and L. A. G. Strong (all represented in this anthology) cut their earliest literary teeth on Gothic fiction, before moving on to other areas.

Whereas Poe set his first story, 'Metzengerstein' (1832), with all the old trappings of Gothic horror, in an ancient castle with its insane occupants, he soon broke away into his own original style maintaining that 'terror is not of Germany, but of the soul'.

Although the Gothic literary style was humorously mocked in *Nightmare Abbey* and other novels by Thomas Love Peacock, and in *Northanger Abbey* by Jane Austen, a strong Gothic strain survived in the historical novels of Walter Scott, W. Harrison Ainsworth, and many others—and also in several mainstream works, notably in those of the Brontës (*Wuthering Heights*, *Villette*, and *Jane Eyre*).

The genre was magnificently sustained in the Victorian era by Joseph Sheridan Le Fanu and Wilkie Collins, and to a lesser extent in the novels of Charles Dickens, while the more sensational Gothic horrors survived for a long period in mass-produced 'penny dreadfuls'. These greatly influenced writers at the decadent end of the century, such as Robert Louis Stevenson, Oscar Wilde, Vincent O'Sullivan, James Platt, Arthur Machen, and especially Bram Stoker with his Gothic masterpiece *Dracula* (1897).

Gothic tales have continued to flourish throughout the twentieth century in popular fiction, by a multitude of writers as diverse as William Faulkner, Joyce Carol Oates, Anne Rice, Angela Carter, and Iain Sinclair; in addition to countless 'dark' romantic thrillers like *Rebecca*, often reissued today as 'paperback Gothics'.

The present anthology covers the cream of a period of more than 150 years, concentrating chiefly on the century from 1825 to 1925, with the addition of two exceptional modern examples by Basil Copper and Gerald Durrell.

A few classics are inevitably included, but several are currently unavailable elsewhere—and some (like Baring-Gould and Strong) have never been anthologized before.

RICHARD DALBY
December 1997

1

CHARLES R. MATURIN

Leixlip Castle

An Irish Family Legend

The incidents of the following tale are not merely *founded* on fact, they are facts themselves, which occurred at no very distant period in my own family. The marriage of the parties, their sudden and mysterious separation, and their total alienation from each other until the last period of their mortal existence, are all *facts*. I cannot vouch for the truth of the supernatural solution given to all these mysteries; but I must still consider the story as a fine specimen of Gothic horrors, and can never forget the impression it made on me when I heard it related for the first time among many other thrilling traditions of the same description.

The tranquillity of the Catholics of Ireland during the disturbed periods of 1715 and 1745, was most commendable, and somewhat extraordinary; to enter into an analysis of their probable motives, is not at all the object of the writer of this tale, as it is pleasanter to state the fact of their honour, than at this distance of time to assign dubious and unsatisfactory reasons for it. Many of them, however, showed a kind of secret disgust at the existing state of affairs, by quitting their family residences, and wandering about like persons who were uncertain of their homes, or possibly expecting better from some near and fortunate contingency.

Among the rest was a Jacobite Baronet, who, sick of his uncongenial situation in a Whig neighbourhood, in the north—where he heard of nothing but the heroic defence of Londonderry; the barbarities of the French generals; and the resistless exhortations of the godly Mr Walker, a Presbyterian clergyman, to whom the citizens gave the title

1

of 'Evangelist';—quitted his paternal residence, and about the year 1720 hired the Castle of Leixlip for three years (it was then the property of the Conollys, who let it to triennial tenants); and removed thither with his family, which consisted of three daughters—their mother having long been dead.

The Castle of Leixlip, at that period, possessed a character of romantic beauty and feudal grandeur, such as few buildings in Ireland can claim, and which is now, alas, totally effaced by the destruction of its noble woods; on the destroyers of which the writer would wish 'a minstrel's malison were said'. Leixlip, though about seven miles from Dublin, has all the sequestered and picturesque character that imagination could ascribe to a landscape a hundred miles from, not only the metropolis but an inhabited town. After driving a dull mile (an *Irish* mile) in passing from Lucan to Leixlip, the road—hedged up on one side of the high wall that bounds the demesne of the Veseys, and on the other by low enclosures, over whose rugged tops you have no view at all—at once opens on Leixlip Bridge, at almost a right angle, and displays a luxury of landscape on which the eye that has seen it even in childhood dwells with delighted recollection. Leixlip Bridge, a rude but solid structure, projects from a high bank of the Liffey, and slopes rapidly to the opposite side, which there lies remarkably low. To the right the plantations of the Vesey's demesne—no longer obscured by walls—almost mingle their dark woods in its stream, with the opposite ones of Marshfield and St Catharine's. The river is scarcely visible, overshadowed as it is by the deep, rich and bending foliage of the trees. To the left it bursts out in all the brilliancy of light, washes the garden steps of the houses of Leixlip, wanders round the low walls of its churchyard, plays with the pleasure-boat moored under the arches on which the summer-house of the Castle is raised, and then loses itself among the rich woods that once skirted those grounds to its very brink. The contrast on the other side, with the luxuriant vegetation, the lighter and more diversified arrangement of terraced walks, scattered shrubberies, temples seated on pinnacles, and thickets that conceal from you the sight of the river until you are on its banks, that mark the character of the grounds which are now the property of Colonel Marly, is peculiarly striking.

Visible above the highest roofs of the town, though a quarter of a mile distant from them, are the ruins of Confy Castle, a right good old predatory tower of the stirring times when blood was shed like water; and as you pass the bridge you catch a glimpse of the waterfall (or salmon-leap, as it is called) on whose noon-day lustre, or moonlight beauty, probably the rough livers of that age when Confy Castle was 'a tower of strength', never glanced an eye or cast a thought, as they clattered in their harness over Leixlip Bridge, or waded through the stream before that convenience was in existence.

Whether the solitude in which he lived contributed to tranquillize Sir Redmond Blaney's feelings, or whether they had begun to rust from want of collision with those of others, it is impossible to say, but certain it is, that the good Baronet began gradually to lose his tenacity in political matters; and except when a Jacobite friend came to dine with him, and drink with many a significant 'nod and beck and smile', the King over the water—or the parish priest (good man) spoke of the hopes of better times, and the final success of the *right* cause, and the old religion—or a Jacobite servant was heard in the solitude of the large mansion whistling 'Charlie is my darling', to which Sir Redmond involuntarily responded in a deep bass voice, somewhat the worse for wear, and marked with more emphasis than good discretion—except, as I have said, on such occasions, the Baronet's politics, like his life, seemed passing away without notice or effort. Domestic calamities, too, pressed sorely on the old gentleman: of his three daughters, the youngest, Jane, had disappeared in so extraordinary a manner in her childhood, that though it is but a wild, remote family tradition, I cannot help relating it:

The girl was of uncommon beauty and intelligence, and was suffered to wander about the neighbourhood of the castle with the daughter of a servant, who was also called Jane, as a *nom de caresse*. One evening Jane Blaney and her young companion went far and deep into the woods; their absence created no uneasiness at the time, as these excursions were by no means unusual, till her playfellow returned home alone and weeping, at a very late hour. Her account was, that, in passing through a lane at some distance from the castle, an old woman, in the *Fingallian* dress (a red petticoat and a long green jacket), suddenly started out of a thicket, and took Jane Blaney by the arm: she had in her hand two rushes, one of which she threw over her shoulder, and giving the other to the child, motioned to her to do the same. Her young companion, terrified at what she saw, was running away, when Jane Blaney called after her—'Goodbye, goodbye, it is a long time before you will see me again.' The girl said they then disappeared, and she found her way home as she could. An indefatigable search was immediately commenced—woods were traversed, thickets were explored, ponds were drained—all in vain. The pursuit and the hope were at length given up.

Ten years afterwards, the housekeeper of Sir Redmond, having remembered that she left the key of a closet where sweetmeats were kept, on the kitchen-table, returned to fetch it. As she approached the door, she heard a childish voice murmuring—'Cold—cold—cold how long it is since I have felt a fire!'—She advanced, and saw, to her amazement, Jane Blaney, shrunk to half her usual size, and covered with rags, crouching over the embers of the fire. The housekeeper flew in terror from the spot, and roused the servants, but the vision had fled. The child was reported to have been seen several times afterwards, as diminutive in form, as though she had not grown an inch since she was ten years of age, and always crouching over a fire, whether in the turret-room or kitchen, complaining of cold and hunger, and apparently covered with rags. Her existence is still said to be protracted under these dismal circumstances, so unlike those of Lucy Gray in Wordsworth's beautiful ballad:

> Yet some will say, that to this day
>   She is a living child—
> That they have met sweet Lucy Gray
>   Upon the lonely wild;
> O'er rough and smooth she trips along,
>   And never looks behind;
> And hums a solitary song
>   That whistles in the wind.

The fate of the eldest daughter was more melancholy, though less extraordinary; she was addressed by a gentleman of competent fortune and unexceptionable character: he was a Catholic, moreover; and Sir Redmond Blaney signed the marriage articles, in full satisfaction of the security of his daughter's soul, as well as of her jointure. The marriage was celebrated at the Castle of Leixlip; and, after the bride and bridegroom had retired, the guests still remained drinking to their future happiness, when suddenly, to the great alarm of Sir Redmond and his friends, loud and piercing cries were heard to issue from the part of the castle in which the bridal chamber was situated.

Some of the more courageous hurried upstairs; it was too late—the wretched bridegroom had burst, on that fatal night, into a sudden and most horrible paroxysm of insanity. The mangled form of the unfortunate and expiring lady bore attestation to the mortal virulence with which the disease had operated on the wretched husband, and died a victim to it himself after the involuntary murder of his bride. The bodies were interred, as soon as decency would permit, and the story hushed up.

Sir Redmond's hopes of Jane's recovery were diminishing every day, though he still continued to listen to every wild tale told by the domestics; and all his care was supposed to be now directed towards his only surviving daughter. Anne living in solitude, and partaking only of the very limited education of Irish females of that period, was left very much to the servants, among whom she increased her taste for superstitious and supernatural horrors, to a degree that had a most disastrous effect on her future life.

Among the numerous menials of the Castle, there was one 'withered crone', who had been nurse to the late Lady Blaney's mother, and whose memory was a complete *Thesaurus terrorum*. The mysterious fate of Jane first encouraged her sister to listen to the wild tales of this hag, who avouched, that at one time she saw the fugitive standing before the portrait of her late mother in one of the apartments of the Castle, and muttering to herself—'Woe's me, woe's me! how little my mother thought her wee Jane would ever come to be what she is!' But as Anne grew older she began more 'seriously to incline' to the hag's promises that she could show her her future bridegroom, on the performance of certain ceremonies, which she at first revolted from as horrible and impious; but, finally, at the repeated instigation of the old woman, consented to act a part in.

The period fixed upon for the performance of these unhallowed rites, was now approaching—it was near the 31st of October—the eventful night, when such ceremonies were, and still are supposed, in the North of Ireland, to be most potent in their effects. All day long the

Crone took care to lower the mind of the young lady to the proper key of submissive and trembling credulity, by every horrible story she could relate; and she told them with frightful and supernatural energy. This woman was called *Collogue* by the family, a name equivalent to Gossip in England, or Cummer in Scotland (though her real name was Bridget Dease); and she verified the name, by the exercise of an unwearied loquacity, an indefatigable memory, and a rage for communicating and inflicting terror, that spared no victim in the household, from the groom, whom she sent shivering to his rug, to the Lady of the Castle, over whom she felt she held unbounded sway.

The 31st of October arrived—the Castle was perfectly quiet before eleven o'clock; half an hour afterwards, the Collogue and Anne Blaney were seen gliding along a passage that led to what is called King John's Tower, where it said that monarch received the homage of the Irish princes as Lord of Ireland, and which, at all events, is the most ancient part of the structure. The Collogue opened a small door with a key which she had secreted about her, and urged the young lady to hurry on. Anne advanced to the postern, and stood there irresolute and trembling like a timid swimmer on the bank of an unknown stream. It was a dark autumnal evening; a heavy wind sighed among the woods of the Castle, and bowed the branches of the lower trees almost to the waves of the Liffey, which, swelled by recent rains, struggled and roared amid the stones that obstructed its channel. The steep descent from the Castle lay before her, with its dark avenue of elms; a few lights still burned in the little village of Leixlip—but from the lateness of the hour it was probable they would soon be extinguished.

The lady lingered—'And must I go alone?' said she, foreseeing that the terrors of her fearful journey could be aggravated by her more fearful purpose.

'Ye must, or all will be spoiled,' said the hag, shading the miserable light, that did not extend its influence above six inches on the path of the victim. 'Ye must go alone—and I will watch for you here, dear, till you come back, and then see what will come to you at twelve o' clock.'

The unfortunate girl paused. 'Oh! Collogue, Collogue, if you would but come with me. Oh! Collogue, come with me, if it be but to the bottom of the castle-hill.'

'If I went with you, dear, we should never reach the top of it alive again, for there are them near that would tear us both in pieces.'

'Oh! Collogue, Collogue—let me turn back then, and go to my own room—I have advanced too far, and I have done too much.'

'And that's what you have, dear, and so you must go further, and do more still, unless, when you return to your own room, you would see the likeness of *someone* instead of a handsome young bridegroom.'

The young lady looked about her for a moment, terror and wild hope trembling at her heart—then, with a sudden impulse of supernatural courage, she darted like a bird from the terrace of the Castle, the fluttering of her white garments was seen for a few moments, and then the hag who had been shading the flickering light with her hand, bolted the postern, and, placing the candle before a glazed loophole, sat down on a stone seat in the recess of the tower, to watch the event of the spell. It was an hour before the young lady returned; when her face was as pale, and her eyes as fixed, as those of a dead body, but she held in her grasp *a dripping garment*, a proof that her errand had been performed. She flung it into her companion's hands, and then stood panting and gazing wildly about her as if she knew not where she was. The hag herself grew terrified at the insane and breathless state of her victim, and hurried her to her chamber; but here the preparations for the terrible ceremonies of the night were the first objects that struck her, and, shivering at the sight, she covered her eyes with her hands, and stood immovably fixed in the middle of the room.

It needed all the hag's persuasions (aided even by mysterious menaces), combined with the returning faculties and reviving curiosity of the poor girl, to prevail on her to go through the remaining business of the night. At length she said, as if in desperation, 'I *will* go through with it: but be in the next room; and if what I dread should happen, I will ring my father's little silver bell which I have secured for the night—and as you have a soul to be saved, Collogue, come to me at its very first sound.'

The hag promised, gave her last instructions with eager and jealous minuteness, and then retired to her own room, which was adjacent to that of the young lady. Her candle had burned out, but she stirred up the embers of her turf fire, and sat nodding over them, and smoothing her pallet from time to time, but resolved not to lie down while there was a chance of a sound from the lady's room, for which she herself, withered as her feelings were, waited with a mingled feeling of anxiety and terror.

It was now long past midnight, and all was silent as the grave throughout the Castle. The hag dozed over the embers till her head touched her knees, then started up as the sound of the bell seemed to tinkle in her ears, then dozed again, and again started as the bell appeared to tinkle more distinctly—suddenly she was roused, not by the bell, but by the most piercing and horrible cries from the neighbouring chamber. The Crone, aghast for the first time, at the possible consequences of the mischief she might have occasioned, hastened to the room. Anne was in convulsions, and the hag was compelled reluctantly to call up the housekeeper (removing meanwhile the implements of the ceremony), and assist in applying all the specifics known at that day, burnt feathers, etc., to restore her. When they had at length succeeded, the housekeeper was dismissed, the door was bolted, and the Collogue was left alone with Anne; the subject of their conference might have been guessed at, but was not known until many years afterwards; but Anne that night held in her hand, in the shape of a weapon with the use of which neither of them was acquainted, an evidence that her chamber had been visited by a being of no earthly form.

This evidence the hag importuned her to destroy, or to remove, but she persisted with fatal tenacity in keeping it. She locked it up, however, immediately, and seemed to think she had acquired a right, since she had grappled so fearfully with the mysteries of futurity, to know all the secrets of which that weapon might yet lead to the disclosure. But from that night it was observed that her character, her manner, and even her countenance, became altered. She grew stern and solitary, shrunk at the sight of her former associates, and imperatively forbade the slightest allusion to the circumstances which had occasioned this mysterious change.

It was a few days subsequent to this event that Anne, who after dinner had left the Chaplain reading the life of St Francis Xavier to Sir Redmond, and retired to her own room to work, and, perhaps, to muse, was surprised to hear the bell at the outer gate ring loudly and repeatedly—a sound she had never heard since her first residence in the Castle; for the few guests who resorted there came and departed as noiselessly as humble visitors at the house of a great man generally do. Straightway there rode up the avenue of elms, which we have already mentioned, a stately gentleman, followed by four servants, all mounted, the two former having pistols in their holsters, and the two latter carrying saddle-bags before them: though it was the first week in November, the dinner hour being one o'clock, Anne had light enough to notice all these circumstances. The arrival of the stranger seemed to cause much, though not unwelcome tumult in the Castle; orders were loudly and hastily given for the accommodation of the servants and horses—steps were heard traversing the numerous passages for a full hour—then all was still; and it was said that Sir Redmond had locked with his own hand the door of the room where he and the stranger sat, and desired that no one should dare to approach it.

About two hours afterwards, a female servant came with orders from her master, to have a plentiful supper ready by eight o'clock, at which he desired the presence of his daughter. The family establishment was on a handsome scale for an Irish house, and Anne had only to descend to the kitchen to order the roasted chickens to be well strewed with brown sugar according to the unrefined fashion of the day, to inspect the mixing of the bowl of sago with its allowance of a bottle of port wine and a large handful of the richest spices, and to order particularly that the pease pudding should have a huge lump of cold salt butter stuck in its centre; and then, her household cares being over, to retire to her room and array herself in a robe of white damask for the occasion.

At eight o'clock she was summoned to the supper-room. She came in, according to the fashion of the times, with the first dish; but as she passed through the ante-room, where the servants were holding lights and bearing the dishes, her sleeve was twitched, and the ghastly face of the Collogue pushed close to hers; while she muttered 'Did not I say *he would come for you*, dear?' Anne's blood ran cold, but she advanced, saluted her father and the stranger with two low and distinct reverences, and then took her place at the table. Her feelings of awe and perhaps terror at the whisper of her associate, were not diminished by the appearance of the stranger; there was a singular and mute solemnity in his manner during the meal. He ate nothing. Sir Redmond appeared constrained, gloomy and thoughtful. At length, starting, he said (without naming the stranger's name), 'You will drink my daughter's health?' The stranger intimated his willingness to have that honour, but absently filled his glass with water; Anne put a few drops of wine into hers, and bowed towards him. At that moment, for the first time since they had met, she beheld his face—it was pale as that of a corpse. The deadly whiteness of his cheeks and lips, the hollow and distant sound of his voice, and the strange lustre of his large dark moveless eyes, strongly fixed on her, made her pause and even tremble as she raised the glass to her lips; she set it down, and then with another silent reverence retired to her chamber.

There she found Bridget Dease, busy in collecting the turf that burned on the hearth, for there was no grate in the apartment. 'Why are you here?' she said, impatiently.

The hag turned on her, with a ghastly grin of congratulation, 'Did not I tell you that *he* would come for you?'

'I believe he has,' said the unfortunate girl, sinking into the huge wicker chair by her bedside; 'for never did I see mortal with such a look.'

'But is not he a fine stately gentleman?' pursued the hag.

'He looks as if he were not of this world,' said Anne.

'Of this world, or of the next,' said the hag, raising her bony forefinger, 'mark my words—so sure as the—(here she repeated some of the horrible formularies of the 31st of October)—so sure he will be your bridegroom.'

'Then I shall be the bride of a corpse,' said Anne; 'for he I saw tonight is no living man.'

A fortnight elapsed, and whether Anne became reconciled to the features she had thought so ghastly, by the discovery that they were the handsomest she had ever beheld—and that the voice, whose sound at first was so strange and unearthly, was subdued into a tone of plaintive softness when addressing her—or whether it is impossible for two young persons with unoccupied hearts to meet in the country, and meet often, to gaze silently on the same stream, wander under the same trees, and listen together to the wind that waves the branches, without experiencing an assimilation of feeling rapidly succeeding an assimilation of taste; or whether it was from all these causes combined, but in less than a month Anne heard the declaration of the stranger's passion with many a blush, though without a sigh. He now avowed his name and rank. He stated himself to be a Scottish Baronet, of the name of Sir Richard Maxwell; family misfortunes had driven him from his country, and for ever precluded the possibility of his return: he had transferred his property to Ireland, and purposed to fix his residence there for life. Such was his statement. The courtship of those days was brief and simple. Anne became the wife of Sir Richard, and, I believe, they resided with her father till his death, when they removed to their estate in the North.

There they remained for several years, in tranquillity and happiness, and had a numerous family. Sir Richard's conduct was marked by but two peculiarities: he not only shunned the intercourse, but the sight of any of his countrymen, and, if he happened to hear that a Scotsman had arrived in the neighbouring town, he shut himself up till assured of the stranger's departure. The other was his custom of retiring to his own chamber, and remaining invisible to his family on the anniversary of the 30th of October. The lady, who had her own associations connected with that period, only questioned him once on the subject of this seclusion, and was then solemnly and even sternly enjoined never to repeat her enquiry. Matters stood thus, somewhat mysteriously, but not unhappily, when on a sudden, without any cause assigned or assignable, Sir Richard and Lady Maxwell parted, and never more met in this world, nor was she ever permitted to see one of her children to her dying hour. He continued to live at the family mansion, and she fixed her residence with a distant relative in a remote part of the country. So total was the disunion, that the name of either was never heard to pass the other's lips, from the moment of separation until that of dissolution.

Lady Maxwell survived Sir Richard forty years, living to the great age of 96; and, according to a promise, previously given, disclosed to a descendant with whom she had lived, the following extraordinary circumstances.

She said that on the night of the 30th of October, about seventy-five years before, at the instigation of her ill-advising attendant, she had washed one of her garments in a place where four streams met, and

performed other unhallowed ceremonies under the direction of the
Collogue, in the expectation that her future husband would appear to
her in her chamber at twelve o'clock that night. The critical moment
arrived, but with it no lover-like form. A vision of indescribable horror
approached her bed, and flinging at her an iron weapon of a shape and
construction unknown to her, bade her 'recognize her future husband by *that*'. The terrors of this visit soon deprived her of her senses;
but on her recovery, she persisted, as has been said, in keeping the fearful pledge of the reality of the vision, which, on examination,
appeared to be encrusted with blood. It remained concealed in the
inmost drawer of her cabinet till the morning of her separation.

On that morning, Sir Richard Maxwell rose before daylight to join
a hunting party—he wanted a knife for some accidental purpose, and,
missing his own, called to Lady Maxwell, who was still in bed, to lend
him one. The lady, who was half asleep, answered, that in such a
drawer of her cabinet he would find one. He went, however, to
another, and the next moment she was fully awakened by seeing her
husband present the terrible weapon to her throat, and threaten her
with instant death unless she disclosed how she came by it. She sup-
plicated for life, and then, in an agony of horror and contrition, told
the tale of that eventful night. He gazed at her for a moment with a
countenance which rage, hatred, and despair converted, as she
avowed, into a living likeness of the demon-visage she had once
beheld (so singularly was the fated resemblance fulfilled), and then
exclaiming, 'You won me by the devil's aid, but you shall not keep me
long,' left her—to meet no more in this world. Her husband's secret
was not unknown to the lady, though the means by which she became
possessed of it were wholly unwarrantable. Her curiosity had been
strongly excited by her husband's aversion to his countrymen, and it
was so stimulated by the arrival of a Scottish gentleman in the neighbourhood some time before, who professed himself formerly
acquainted with Sir Richard, and spoke mysteriously of the causes
that drove him from his country—that she contrived to procure an
interview with him under a feigned name, and obtained from him the
knowledge of circumstances which embittered her after-life to its
latest hour. His story was this:

Sir Richard Maxwell was at deadly feud with a younger brother; a family feast was proposed to reconcile them, and as the use of knives and forks was then unknown in the Highlands, the company met armed with their dirks for the purpose of carving. They drank deeply; the feast, instead of harmonizing, began to inflame their spirits; the topics of old strife were renewed; hands, that at first touched their weapons in defiance, drew them at last in fury, and in the fray, Sir Richard mortally wounded his brother. His life was with difficulty saved from the vengeance of the clan, and he was hurried towards the sea-coast, near which the house stood, and concealed there till a vessel could be procured to convey him to Ireland. He embarked *on the night of the 30th of October*, and while he was traversing the deck in unutterable agony of spirit, his hand accidentally touched the dirk which he had unconsciously worn ever since the fatal night. He drew it, and, praying 'that the guilt of his brother's blood might be as far from his soul, as he could fling that weapon from his body', sent it with all his strength into the air. This instrument he found secreted in the lady's cabinet, and whether he really believed her to have become possessed of it by supernatural means, or whether he feared his wife was a secret witness of his crime, has not been ascertained, but the result was what I have stated.

The reparation took place on the discovery: for the rest,

> I know not how the truth may be,
> I tell the Tale as 'twas told to me.

2

MARY SHELLEY

The Dream

The time of the occurrence of the little legend about to be narrated, was that of the commencement of the reign of Henry IV of France, whose accession and conversion, while they brought peace to the kingdom whose throne he ascended, were inadequate to heal the deep wounds mutually inflicted by the inimical parties. Private feuds, and the memory of mortal injuries, existed between those now apparently united; and often did the hands that had clasped each other in seeming friendly greeting, involuntarily, as the grasp was released, clasp the dagger's hilt, as fitter spokesman to their passions than the words of courtesy that had just fallen from their lips. Many of the fiercer Catholics retreated to their distant provinces; and while they concealed in solitude their rankling discontent, not less keenly did they long for the day when they might show it openly.

In a large and fortified château built on a rugged steep overlooking the Loire, not far from the town of Nantes, dwelt the last of her race, and the heiress of their fortunes, the young and beautiful Countess de Villeneuve. She had spent the preceding year in complete solitude in her secluded abode; and the mourning she wore for a father and two brothers, the victims of the civil wars, was a graceful and good reason why she did not appear at court, and mingle with its festivities. But the orphan countess inherited a high name and broad lands; and it was soon signified to her that the king, her guardian, desired that she should bestow them, together with her hand, upon some noble whose birth and accomplishments should entitle him to the gift. Constance, in reply, expressed her intention of taking vows, and retiring to a convent. The king earnestly and resolutely forbade this act, believing such an idea to be the result of sensibility overwrought by sorrow, and relying on the hope that, after a time, the genial spirit of youth would break through this cloud.

A year passed, and still the countess persisted; and at last Henry, unwilling to exercise compulsion—desirous, too, of judging for himself of the motives that led one so beautiful, young, and gifted with fortune's favours, to desire to bury herself in a cloister—announced his intention, now that the period of her mourning was expired, of visiting her château; and if he brought not with him, the monarch said, inducement sufficient to change her design, he would yield his consent to its fulfilment.

Many a sad hour had Constance passed—many a day of tears, and many a night of restless misery. She had closed her gates against every visitant; and, like the Lady Olivia in 'Twelfth Night', vowed herself to loneliness and weeping. Mistress of herself, she easily silenced the entreaties and remonstrances of underlings, and nursed her grief as it had been the thing she loved. Yet it was too keen, too bitter, too burning, to be a favoured guest. In fact, Constance, young, ardent, and vivacious, battled with it, struggled and longed to cast it off; but all that was joyful in itself, or fair in outward show, only served to renew it; and she could best support the burden of her sorrow with patience, when, yielding to it, it oppressed but did not torture her.

Constance had left the castle to wander in the neighbouring grounds. Lofty and extensive as were the apartments of her abode, she felt pent up within their walls, beneath their fretted roofs. The spreading uplands and the antique wood, associated to her with every dear recollection of her past life, enticed her to spend hours and days beneath their leafy coverts. The motion and change eternally working, as the wind stirred among the boughs, or the journeying sun rained its beams through them, soothed and called her out of that dull sorrow which clutched her heart with so unrelenting a pang beneath her castle roof.

There was one spot on the verge of the well-wooded park, one nook of ground, whence she could discern the country extended beyond, yet which was in itself thick set with tall umbrageous trees—a spot which she had forsworn, yet whither unconsciously her steps for ever tended, and where now again, for the twentieth time that day, she had unaware found herself. She sat upon a grassy mound, and looked wistfully on the flowers she had herself planted to adorn the verdurous recess—to her the temple of memory and love. She held the letter from the king which was the parent to her of so much despair. Dejection sat upon her features, and her gentle heart asked fate why, so young, unprotected, and forsaken, she should have to struggle with this new form of wretchedness.

'I but ask,' she thought, 'to live in my father's halls—in the spot familiar to my infancy—to water with my frequent tears the graves of those I loved; and here in these woods, where such a mad dream of happiness was mine, to celebrate for ever the obsequies of Hope!'

A rustling among the boughs now met her ear—her heart beat quick—all again was still.

'Foolish girl!' she half muttered; 'dupe of thine own passionate fancy: because here we met; because seated here I have expected, and sounds like these have announced, his dear approach; so now every coney as it stirs, and every bird as it awakens silence, speaks of him. O Gaspar!—mine once—never again will this beloved spot be made glad by thee—never more!'

Again the bushes were stirred, and footsteps were heard in the brake. She rose; her heart beat high; it must be that silly Manon, with her impertinent entreaties for her to return. But the steps were firmer and slower than would be those of her waiting-woman; and now emerging from the shade, she too plainly discerned the intruder. Her first impulse was to fly: but once again to see him—to hear his voice: once again before she placed eternal vows between them, to stand together, and find the wide chasm filled which absence had made, could not injure the dead, and would soften the fatal sorrow that made her cheek so pale.

And now he was before her, the same beloved one with whom she had exchanged vows of constancy. He, like her, seemed sad; nor could she resist the imploring glance that entreated her for one moment to remain.

'I come, lady,' said the young knight, 'without a hope to bend your inflexible will. I come but once again to see you, and to bid you farewell before I depart for the Holy Land. I come to beseech you not to immure yourself in the dark cloister to avoid one as hateful as myself—one you will never see more. Whether I die or live, France and I are parted for ever!'

'That were fearful, were it true,' said Constance; 'but King Henry will never so lose his favourite cavalier. The throne you helped to build, you still will guard. Nay, as I ever had power over thought of thine, go not to Palestine.'

'One word of yours could detain me—one smile—Constance'— and the youthful lover knelt before her; but her harsher purpose was recalled by the image once so dear and familiar, now so strange and so forbidden.

'Linger no longer here!' she cried. 'No smile, no word of mine will ever again be yours. Why are you here—here, where the spirits of the dead wander, and claiming these shades as their own, curse the false girl who permits their murderer to disturb their sacred repose?'

'When love was young and you were kind,' replied the knight, 'you taught me to thread the intricacies of these woods—you welcomed me to this dear spot, where once you vowed to be my own—even beneath these ancient trees.'

'A wicked sin it was,' said Constance, 'to unbar my father's doors to the son of his enemy, and dearly is it punished!'

The young knight gained courage as she spoke; yet he dared not move, lest she, who, every instant, appeared ready to take flight, should be startled from her momentary tranquillity; but he slowly replied: 'Those were happy days, Constance, full of terror and deep joy, when evening brought me to your feet; and while hate and vengeance were as its atmosphere to yonder frowning castle, this leafy, starlit bower was the shrine of love.'

'*Happy*?—miserable days!' echoed Constance; 'when I imagined good could arise from failing in my duty, and that disobedience would be rewarded of God. Speak not of love, Gaspar!—a sea of blood divides us for ever! Approach me not! The dead and the beloved stand even now between us: their pale shadows warn me of my fault, and menace me for listening to their murderer.'

'That am not I!' exclaimed the youth. 'Behold, Constance, we are each the last of our race. Death has dealt cruelly with us, and we are alone. It was not so when first we loved—when parent, kinsman, brother, nay, my own mother breathed curses on the house of

Villeneuve; and in spite of all I blessed it. I saw thee, my lovely one, and blessed it. The God of peace planted love in our hearts, and with mystery and secrecy we met during many a summer night in the moonlit dells; and when daylight was abroad, in this sweet recess we fled to avoid its scrutiny, and here, even here, where now I kneel in supplication, we both knelt and made our vows. Shall they be broken?'

Constance wept as her lover recalled the images of happy hours. 'Never,' she exclaimed, 'O never! Thou knowest, or wilt soon know, Gaspar, the faith and resolves of one who dare not be yours. Was it for us to talk of love and happiness, when war, and hate, and blood were raging around! The fleeting flowers our young hands strewed were trampled by the deadly encounter of mortal foes. By your father's hand mine died; and little boots it to know whether, as my brother swore, and you deny, your hand did or did not deal the blow that destroyed him. You fought among those by whom he died. Say no more—no other word: it is impiety towards the unreposing dead to hear you. Go, Gaspar; forget me. Under the chivalrous and gallant Henry your career may be glorious; and some fair girl will listen, as once I did, to your vows, and be made happy by them. Farewell! May the Virgin bless you! In my cell and cloister-home I will not forget the best Christian lesson—to pray for our enemies. Gaspar, farewell!'

She glided hastily from the bower: with swift steps she threaded the glade and sought the castle. Once within the seclusion of her own apartment she gave way to the burst of grief that tore her gentle bosom like a tempest; for hers was that worst sorrow which taints past joys, making remorse wait upon the memory of bliss, and linking love and fancied guilt in such fearful society as that of the tyrant when he bound a living body to a corpse. Suddenly a thought darted into her mind. At first she rejected it as puerile and superstitious; but it would not be driven away. She called hastily for her attendant, 'Manon,' she said, 'didst thou ever sleep on St Catherine's couch?'

Manon crossed herself. 'Heaven forefend! None ever did, since I was born, but two: one fell into the Loire and was drowned; the other only looked upon the narrow bed, and returned to her own home without a word. It is an awful place; and if the votary have not led a pious and good life, woe betide the hour when she rests her head on the holy stone!'

Constance crossed herself also. 'As for our lives, it is only through our Lord and the blessed saints that we can any of us hope for right-eousness. I will sleep on that couch tomorrow night!'

'Dear, my lady! and the king arrives tomorrow.'

'The more need that I resolve. It cannot be that misery so intense should dwell in any heart, and no cure be found. I had hoped to be the bringer of peace to our houses; and if the good work to be for me a crown of thorns Heaven shall direct me. I will rest tomorrow night on St Catherine's bed: and if, as I have heard, the saint deigns to direct her votaries in dreams, I will be guided by her; and, believing that I act according to the dictates of Heaven, I shall feel resigned even to the worst.'

The king was on his way to Nantes from Paris, and he slept on this night at a castle but a few miles distant. Before dawn a young cavalier was introduced into his chamber. The knight had a serious, nay, a sad aspect; and all beautiful as he was in feature and limb, looked way-worn and haggard. He stood silent in Henry's presence, who, alert and gay, turned his lively blue eyes upon his guest, saying gently, 'So thou foundest her obdurate, Gaspar?'

'I found her resolved on our mutual misery. Alas! my liege, it is not, credit me, the least of my grief, that Constance sacrifices her own happiness when she destroys mine.'

'And thou believest that she will say nay to the gaillard chevalier whom we ourselves present to her?'

'Oh, my liege, think not that thought! it cannot be. My heart deeply, most deeply, thanks you for your generous condescension. But she whom her lover's voice in solitude—whose entreaties, when memory and seclusion aided the spell—could not persuade, will resist even your majesty's commands. She is bent upon entering a cloister; and I, so please you, will now take my leave:—I am henceforth a soldier of the cross.'

'Gasper,' said the monarch, 'I know woman better than thou. It is not by submission nor tearful plaints she is to be won. The death of her relatives naturally sits heavy at the young countess's heart; and nourishing in solitude her regret and her repentance, she fancies that Heaven itself forbids your union. Let the voice of the world reach her—the voice of earthly power and earthly kindness—the one commanding, the other pleading, and both finding response in her own heart—and by my say and the Holy Cross, she will be yours. Let our plan still hold. And now to horse: the morning wears, and the sun is risen.'

The king arrived at the bishop's palace, and proceeded forthwith to mass in the cathedral. A sumptuous dinner succeeded, and it was afternoon before the monarch proceeded through the town beside the Loire to where, a little above Nantes, the Chateau Villeneuve was situated. The young countess received him at the gate. Henry looked in vain for the cheek blanched by misery, the aspect of downcast despair which he had been taught to expect. Her cheek was flushed, her manner animated, her voice scarce tremulous. 'She loves him not,' thought Henry, 'or already her heart has consented.'

A collation was prepared for the monarch; and after some little hesitation, arising from the cheerfulness of her mien, he mentioned the name of Gaspar. Constance blushed instead of turning pale, and replied very quickly, 'Tomorrow, good my liege; I ask for a respite but until tomorrow—all will then be decided—tomorrow I am vowed to God—or—'

She looked confused, and the king, at once surprised and pleased, said, 'Then you hate not young De Vaudemont; you forgive him for the inimical blood that warms his veins.'

'We are taught that we should forgive, that we should love our enemies,' the countess replied, with some trepidation.

'Now, by Saint Denis, that is a right welcome answer for the novice,' said the king, laughing. 'What ho! my faithful serving-man, Don Apollo in disguise! come forward, and thank your lady for her love.'

In such disguise as had concealed him from all, the cavalier had hung behind, and viewed with infinite surprise the demeanour and calm countenance of the lady. He could not hear her words: but was this even she whom he had seen trembling and weeping the evening before?—this she whose very heart was torn by conflicting passion?—who saw the pale ghosts of parent and kinsman stand between her and the lover whom more than her life she adored? It was a riddle hard to solve. The king's call was in unison with his impatience, and he sprang forward. He was at her feet; while she, still passion-driven overwrought by the very calmness she had assumed, uttered one cry as she recognized him, and sank senseless on the floor.

All this was very unintelligible. Even when her attendants had brought her to life, another fit succeeded; and then passionate floods of tears; while the monarch, waiting in the hall, eyeing the half-eaten collation, and humming some romance in commemoration of woman's waywardness, knew not how to reply to Vaudemont's look of bitter disappointment and anxiety. At length the countess' chief attendant came with an apology: 'Her lady was ill, very ill. The next day she would throw herself at the king's feet, at once to solicit his excuse, and to disclose her purpose.'

'Tomorrow—again tomorrow!—Does tomorrow bear some charm, maiden?' said the king. 'Can you read us the riddle, pretty one? What strange tale belongs to tomorrow, that all rests on its advent?'

Manon coloured, looked down, and hesitated. But Henry was no tyro in the art of enticing ladies' attendants to disclose their ladies' council. Manon was besides frightened by the countess' scheme, on which she was still obstinately bent, so she was the more readily induced to betray it. To sleep in St Catherine's bed, to rest on a narrow ledge overhanging the deep rapid Loire, and if, as was most probable, the luckless dreamer escaped from falling into it, to take the disturbed visions that such uneasy slumber might produce for the dictate of Heaven, was a madness of which even Henry himself could scarcely deem any woman capable. But could Constance, her whose beauty was so highly intellectual, and whom he had heard perpetually praised for her strength of mind and talents, could *she* be so strangely infatuated! And can passion play such freaks with us?—like death, levelling even the aristocracy of the soul, and bringing noble and peasant, the wise and foolish, under one thraldom? It was strange—yes she must have her way. That she hesitated in her decision was much; and it was to be hoped that St Catherine would play no ill-natured part. Should it be otherwise, a purpose to be swayed by a dream might be influenced by other waking thoughts. To the more material kind of danger some safeguard should be brought.

There is no feeling more awful than that which invades a weak human heart bent upon gratifying its ungovernable impulses in contradiction to the dictates of conscience. Forbidden pleasures are said to be the most agreeable; it may be so to rude natures, to those who love to struggle, combat, and contest; who find happiness in a fray, and joy in the conflict of passion. But softer and sweeter was the gentle spirit of Constance; and love and duty contending crushed and tortured her poor heart. To commit her conduct to the inspirations of religion, or, if it was so to be named, of superstition, was a blessed relief. The very perils that threatened her undertaking gave zest to it—to dare for his sake was happiness—the very difficulty of the way that led to the completion of her wishes at once gratified her love and distracted her thoughts from her despair. Or if it was decreed that she must sacrifice all, the risk of danger and of death were of trifling import in comparison with the anguish which would then be her portion for ever.

The night threatened to be stormy, the raging wind shook the casements, and the trees waved their huge shadowy arms, as giants might in fantastic dance and mortal broil. Constance and Manon, unattended, quitted the château by a postern, and began to descend the hillside. The moon had not yet risen; and though the way was familiar to both, Manon tottered and trembled; while the countess, drawing her silken cloak around her, walked with a firm step down the steep. They came to the river's side, where a small boat was moored, and one man was in waiting. Constance stepped lightly in, and then aided her fearful companion. In a few moments they were in the middle of the stream. The warm, tempestuous, animating, equinoctial wind swept over them. For the first time since her mourning, a thrill of pleasure swelled the bosom of Constance. She hailed the emotion with double joy. It cannot be, she thought, that Heaven will forbid me to love one so brave, so generous, and so good as the noble Gaspar. Another I can never love; I shall die if divided from him; and this heart, these limbs, so alive with glowing sensation, are they already predestined to an early grave? Oh no! life speaks aloud within them. I shall live to love. Do not all things love?—the winds as they whisper to the rushing waters? the waters as they kiss the flowery banks, and speed to mingle with the sea? Heaven and earth are sustained by, and live through, love; and shall Constance alone, whose heart has ever been a deep, gushing, overflowing well of true affection, be compelled to set a stone upon the fount to lock it up for ever?

These thoughts bade fair for pleasant dreams; and perhaps the countess, an adept in the blind god's lore, therefore indulged them the more readily. But as thus she was engrossed by soft emotions, Manon caught her arm—'Lady, look,' she cried; 'it comes—yet the oars have no sound. Now the Virgin shield us! Would we were at home!'

A dark boat glided by them. Four rowers, habited in black cloaks, pulled at oars which, as Manon said, gave no sound; another sat at the helm: like the rest, his person was veiled in a dark mantle, but he wore no cap; and though his face was turned from them, Constance recognized her lover. 'Gaspar,' she cried aloud, 'dost thou live?'—but the figure in the boat neither turned its head nor replied, and quickly it was lost in the shadowy waters.

How changed now was the fair countess' reverie! Already Heaven had begun its spell, and unearthly forms were around, as she strained her eyes through the gloom. Now she saw and now she lost view of the bark that occasioned her terror; and now it seemed that another was there, which held the spirits of the dead; and her father waved to her from shore, and her brothers frowned on her.

Meanwhile they neared the landing. Her bark was moored in a little cove, and Constance stood upon the bank. Now she trembled, and half yielded to Manon's entreaty to return; till the unwise *suivante* mentioned the king's and De Vaudemont's name, and spoke of the answer to be given tomorrow. What answer, if she turned back from her intent?

She now hurried forward up the broken ground of the bank, and then along its edge, till they came to a hill which abruptly hung over the tide. A small chapel stood near. With trembling fingers the countess drew forth the key and unlocked its door. They entered. It was dark—save that a little lamp, flickering in the wind, showed an uncertain light from before the figure of Saint Catherine. The two women knelt; they prayed; and then rising, with a cheerful accent the countess bade her attendant good-night. She unlocked a little low iron door. It opened on a narrow cavern. The roar of waters was heard beyond. 'Thou mayest not follow, my poor Manon,' said Constance—'nor dost thou much desire—this adventure is for me alone.'

It was hardly fair to leave the trembling servant in the chapel alone, who had neither hope nor fear, nor love, nor grief to beguile her; but, in those days, esquires and waiting-women often played the part of subalterns in the army, gaining knocks and no fame. Besides, Manon was safe in holy ground. The countess meanwhile pursued her way groping in the dark through the narrow tortuous passage. At length what seemed light to her long darkened sense gleamed on her. She reached an open cavern in the overhanging hill's side, looking over the rushing tide beneath. She looked out upon the night. The waters of the Loire were speeding, as since that day have they ever sped— changeful, yet the same; the heavens were thickly veiled with clouds, and the wind in the trees was as mournful and ill-omened as if it rushed round a murderer's tomb. Constance shuddered a little, and looked upon her bed—a narrow ledge of earth and a moss-grown stone bordering on the very verge of the precipice. She doffed her mantle—such was one of the conditions of the spell—she bowed her head, and loosened the tresses of her dark hair; she bared her feet; and thus, fully prepared for suffering to the utmost the chill influence of the cold night, she stretched herself on the narrow couch that scarce afforded room for her repose, and whence, if she moved in sleep, she must be precipitated into the cold waters below.

At first it seemed to her as if she never should sleep again. No great wonder that exposure to the blast and her perilous position should forbid her eyelids to close. At length she fell into a reverie so soft and soothing that she wished even to watch; and then by degrees her senses became confused; and now she was on St Catherine's bed—the Loire rushing beneath, and the wild wind sweeping by—and now— oh whither?—and what dreams did the saint send, to drive her to despair, or to bid her be blest for ever?

Beneath the rugged hill, upon the dark tide, another watched, who feared a thousand things, and scarce dared hope. He had meant to pre- cede the lady on her way, but when he found that he had outstayed his time, with muffled oars and breathless haste he had shot by the bark that contained his Constance, nor even turned at her voice, fearful to incur her blame, and her commands to return. He had seen her emerge from the passage, and shuddered as she leant over the cliff. He saw her step forth, clad as she was in white, and could mark her as she lay on the ledge beetling above. What a vigil did the lovers keep!—she given up to visionary thoughts, he knowing—and the consciousness thrilled his bosom with strange emotion—that love, and love for him, had led her to that perilous couch; and that while dangers surrounded her in every shape, she was alive only to the small still voice that whispered to her heart the dream which was to decide their destinies. She slept perhaps—but he waked and watched; and night wore away, as now praying, now entranced by alternating hope and fear, he sat in his boat, his eyes fixed on the white garb of the slumberer above.

Morning—was it morning that struggled in the clouds? Would morning ever come to waken her? And had she slept? and what dreams of weal or woe had peopled her sleep? Gaspar grew impatient. He commanded his boatmen still to wait, and he sprang forward, intent on clambering the precipice. In vain they urged the danger, nay, the impossibility of the attempt; he clung to the rugged face of the hill, and found footing where it would seem no footing was. The acclivity, indeed, was not high; the dangers of St Catherine's bed arising from the likelihood that anyone who slept on so narrow a couch would be precipitated into the waters beneath. Up the steep ascent Gaspar continued to toil, and at last reached the roots of a tree that grew near the summit. Aided by its branches, he made good his stand at the very extremity of the ledge, near the pillow on which lay the uncovered head of his beloved. Her hands were folded on her bosom; her dark hair fell round her throat and pillowed her cheek: her face was serene: sleep was there in all its innocence and in all its helplessness; every wilder emotion was hushed, and her bosom heaved in regular breathing. He could see her heart beat as it lifted her fair hands crossed above. No statue hewn of marble in monumental effigy was ever half so fair; and within that surpassing form dwelt a soul true, tender, self-devoted, and affectionate as ever warmed a human breast.

With what deep passion did Gaspar gaze, gathering hope from the placidity of her angel countenance! A smile wreathed her lips; and he too involuntarily smiled, as he hailed the happy omen; when suddenly her cheek was flushed, her bosom heaved, a tear stole from her dark lashes, and then a whole shower fell, as starting up she cried, 'No!—he shall not die!—I will unloose his chains!—I will save him!' Gaspar's hand was there. He caught her light form ready to fall from the perilous couch. She opened her eyes and beheld her lover, who had watched over her dream of fate, and who had saved her.

Manon also had slept well, dreaming or not, and was startled in the morning to find that she waked surrounded by a crowd. The little desolate chapel was hung with tapestry—the altar adorned with golden chalices—the priest was chanting mass to a goodly array of kneeling knights. Manon saw that King Henry was there; and she looked for another whom she found not, when the iron door of the cavern passage opened, and Gaspar de Vaudemont entered from it, leading the fair form of Constance; who, in her white robes and dark dishevelled hair, with a face in which smiles and blushes contended with deeper emotion, approached the altar, and, kneeling with her lover, pronounced the vows that united them for ever.

It was long before the happy Gaspar could win from his lady the secret of her dream. In spite of the happiness she now enjoyed, she had suffered too much not to look back even with terror to those days when she thought love a crime, and every event connected with them wore an awful aspect. Many a vision, she said, she had that fearful night. She had seen the spirits of her father and brothers in Paradise; she had beheld Gaspar victoriously combating among the infidels; she had beheld him in King Henry's court, favoured and beloved; and she herself—now pining in a cloister, now a bride, now grateful to Heaven for the full measure of bliss presented to her, now weeping away her sad days—till suddenly she thought herself in Paynim land; and the saint herself, St Catherine, guiding her unseen through the city of the infidels. She entered a palace, and beheld the miscreants rejoicing in victory; and then, descending to the dungeons beneath, they groped their way through damp vaults, and low, mildewed passages, to one cell, darker and more frightful than the rest. On the floor lay one with soiled and tattered garments, with unkempt locks and wild, matted beard. His cheek was worn and thin; his eyes had lost their fire; his form was a mere skeleton; the chains hung loosely on the fleshless bones.

'And was it my appearance in that attractive state and winning costume that softened the hard heart of Constance?' asked Gaspar, smiling at this painting of what would never be.

'Even so,' replied Constance; 'for my heart whispered me that this was my doing; and who could recall the life that waned in your pulses—who restore, save the destroyer? My heart never warmed to

26

my living, happy knight as then it did to his wasted image as it lay, in the visions of night, at my feet. A veil fell from my eyes; a darkness was dispelled from before me. Methought I then knew for the first time what life and what death was. I was bid believe that to make the living happy was not to injure the dead; and I felt how wicked and how vain was that false philosophy which placed virtue and good in hatred and unkindness. You should not die; I would loosen your chains and save you, and bid you live for love. I sprung forward, and the death I deprecated for you would, in my presumption, have been mine—then, when first I felt the real value of life—but that your arm was there to save me, your dear voice to bid me be blest for evermore.'

3

EDGAR ALLAN POE

Metzengerstein

Pestis eram vivus—moriens tua mors ero.

MARTIN LUTHER

Horror and fatality have been stalking abroad in all ages. Why then give a date to the story I have to tell? Let it suffice to say, that at the period of which I speak, there existed, in the interior of Hungary, a settled although hidden belief in the doctrines of the Metempsychosis. Of the doctrines themselves—that is, of their falsity, or of their probability—I say nothing. I assert, however, that much of our incredulity (as La Bruyère says of all our unhappiness) *'vient de ne pouvoir être seuls'*.[1]

But there were some points in the Hungarian superstition which were fast verging to absurdity. They—the Hungarians—differed very essentially from their Eastern authorities. For example. *'The soul'*, said the former—I give the words of an acute and intelligent Parisian—*'ne demeure qu'une seule fois dans un corps sensible: au reste—un cheval, un chien, un homme même, n'est que la ressemblance peu tangible de ces animaux'*.

The families at Berlifitzing and Metzengerstein had been at variance for centuries. Never before were two houses, so illustrious, mutually embittered by hostility so deadly. The origin of this enmity seems to be found in the words of an ancient prophecy—'A lofty name

---

[1] Mercier, in *L'An deux mille quatre cent quarante*, seriously maintains the doctrines of the Metempsychosis, and J. D'Israeli says that 'no system is so simple and so little repugnant to the understanding'. Colonel Ethan Allen, the 'Green Mountain Boy', is also said to have been a serious metempsychosist.

shall have a fearful fall when, as the rider over his horse, the mortality of Metzengerstein shall triumph over the immortality of Berlifitzing.'

To be sure, the words themselves had little or no meaning. But more trivial causes have given rise—and that no long while ago—to consequences equally eventful. Besides, the estates, which were contiguous, had long exercised a rival influence in the affairs of a busy government. Moreover, near neighbours are seldom friends; and the inhabitants of the Castle Berlifitzing might look from their lofty buttresses into the very windows of the Palace Metzengerstein. Least of all had the more than feudal magnificence, thus discovered, a tendency to allay the irritable feelings of the less ancient and less wealthy Berlifitzings. What wonder, then, that the words, however silly, of that prediction, should have succeeded in setting and keeping at variance two families already predisposed to quarrel by every instigation of hereditary jealousy? The prophecy seemed to imply—if it implied anything—a final triumph on the part of the already more powerful house; and was of course remembered with the more bitter animosity by the weaker and less influential.

Wilhelm, Count Berlifitzing, although loftily descended, was, at the epoch of this narrative, an infirm and doting old man, remarkable for nothing but an inordinate and inveterate personal antipathy to the family of his rival, and so passionate a love of horses, and of hunting, that neither bodily infirmity, great age, nor mental incapacity, prevented his daily participation in the dangers of the chase.

Frederick, Baron Metzengerstein, was, on the other hand, not yet of age. His father, the Minister G——, died young. His mother, the Lady Mary, followed him quickly. Frederick was, at that time, in his eighteenth year. In a city, eighteen years are no long period; but in a wilderness—in so magnificent a wilderness as that old principality, the pendulum vibrates with a deeper meaning.

From some peculiar circumstances attending the administration of his father, the young Baron, at the decease of the former, entered immediately upon his vast possessions. Such estates were seldom held before by a nobleman of Hungary. His castles were without number. The chief in point of splendour and extent was the 'Palace Metzengerstein'. The boundary line of his dominions was never clearly defined; but his principal park embraced a circuit of fifty miles.

Upon the succession of a proprietor so young, with a character so well known, to a fortune so unparalleled, little speculation was afloat in regard to his probable course of conduct. And, indeed, for the space of three days the behaviour of the heir out-Heroded Herod, and fairly surpassed the expectations of his most enthusiastic admirers. Shameful debaucheries—flagrant treacheries—unheard-of atrocities—gave his trembling vassals quickly to understand that no servile submission on their part—no punctilios of conscience on his own—were thenceforward to prove any security against the remorseless fangs of a petty Caligula. On the night of the fourth day, the stables of the Castle Berlifitzing were discovered to be on fire; and the unanimous opinion of the neighbourhood added the crime of the incendiary to the already hideous list of the Baron's misdemeanours and enormities.

But during the tumult occasioned by this occurrence, the young nobleman himself sat apparently buried in meditation, in a vast and desolate upper apartment of the family palace of Metzengerstein. The rich although faded tapestry hangings which swung gloomily upon the walls represented the shadowy and majestic forms of a thousand illustrious ancestors. *Here*, rich-ermined priests and pontifical dignitaries, familiarly seated with the autocrat and the sovereign, put a veto on the wishes of a temporal king, or restrained with the fiat of papal supremacy the rebellious sceptre of the Arch-enemy. *There*, the dark, tall statures of the Princes Metzengerstein—their muscular warcoursers plunging over the carcasses of fallen foes—startled the steadiest nerves with their vigorous expression; and *here*, again, the voluptuous and swan-like figures of the dames of days gone by floated away in the mazes of an unreal dance to the strains of imaginary melody.

But as the Baron listened, or affected to listen, to the gradually increasing uproar in the stables of Berlifitzing—or perhaps pondered upon some more novel, some more decided act of audacity—his eyes were turned unwittingly to the figure of an enormous, and unnaturally coloured horse, represented in the tapestry as belonging to a Saracen ancestor of the family of his rival. The horse itself, in the foreground of the design, stood motionless and statue-like—while, further back, its discomfited rider perished by the dagger of a Metzengerstein.

On Frederick's lip arose a fiendish expression, as he became aware of the direction which his glance had, without his consciousness, assumed. Yet he did not remove it. On the contrary, he could by no means account for the overwhelming anxiety which appeared falling like a pall upon his senses. It was with difficulty that he reconciled his dreamy and incoherent feelings with the certainty of being awake. The longer he gazed the more absorbing became the spell—the more impossible did it appear that he could ever withdraw his glance from the fascination of that tapestry. But the tumult without becoming suddenly more violent, with a compulsory exertion he diverted his attention to the glare of ruddy light thrown full by the flaming stables upon the windows of the apartment.

The action, however, was but momentary; his gaze returned mechanically to the wall. To his extreme horror and astonishment, the head of the gigantic steed had, in the meantime, altered its position. The neck of the animal, before arched, as if in compassion, over the prostrate body of its lord, was now extended at full length, in the direction of the Baron. The eyes, before invisible, now wore an energetic and human expression, while they gleamed with a fiery and unusual red; and the distended lips of the apparently enraged horse left in full view his sepulchral and disgusting teeth.

Stupefied with terror, the young nobleman tottered to the door. As he threw it open, a flash of red light, streaming far into the chamber, flung his shadow with a clear outline against the quivering tapestry; and he shuddered to perceive that shadow—as he staggered awhile upon the threshold—assuming the exact position, and precisely filling up the contour, of the relentless and triumphant murderer of the Saracen Berlifitzing.

To lighten the depression of his spirits, the Baron hurried into the open air. At the principal gate of the palace he encountered three equerries. With much difficulty, and at the imminent peril of their lives, they were restraining the convulsive plunges of a gigantic and fiery-coloured horse.

'Whose horse? Where did you get him?' demanded the youth, in a querulous and husky tone, as he became instantly aware that the mysterious steed in the tapestried chamber was the very counterpart of the furious animal before his eyes.

'He is your own property, sire,' replied one of the equerries, 'at least he is claimed by no other owner. We caught him flying, all smoking and foaming with rage, from the burning stables of the Castle Berlifitzing. Supposing him to have belonged to the old Count's stud of foreign horses, we led him back as an estray. But the grooms there disclaim any title to the creature; which is strange, since he bears evident marks of having made a narrow escape from the flames.'

'The letters W. V. B. are also branded very distinctly on his forehead,' interrupted a second equerry; 'I suppose them, of course, to be the initials of William Von Berlifitzing—but all at the castle are positive in denying any knowledge of the horse.'

'Extremely singular!' said the young Baron, with a musing air, and apparently unconscious of the meaning of his words. 'He is, as you say, a remarkable horse—a prodigious horse! although, as you very justly observe, of a suspicious and untractable character; let him be mine, however,' he added, after a pause, 'perhaps a rider like Frederick of Metzengerstein may tame even the devil from the stables of Berlifitzing.'

'You are mistaken, my lord; the horse, as I think we mentioned, is *not* from the stables of the Count. If such had been the case, we know our duty better than to bring him into the presence of a noble of your family.'

'True!' observed the Baron, dryly; and at that instant a page of the bedchamber came from the palace with a heightened colour, and a precipitate step. He whispered into his master's ear an account of the sudden disappearance of a small portion of the tapestry, in an apartment which he designated; entering, at the same time, into particulars of a minute and circumstantial character; but from the low tone of voice in which these latter were communicated, nothing escaped to gratify the excited curiosity of the equerries.

The young Frederick, during the conference, seemed agitated by a variety of emotions. He soon, however, recovered his composure, and an expression of determined malignancy settled upon his countenance, as he gave peremptory orders that the apartment in question should be immediately locked up, and the key placed in his own possession.

'Have you heard of the unhappy death of the old hunter, Berlifitzing?' said one of his vassals to the Baron, as, after the departure of the page, the huge steed which that nobleman had adopted as his own, plunged and curveted, with redoubled fury, down the long avenue which extended from the palace to the stables of Metzengerstein.

'No!' said the Baron, turning abruptly toward the speaker, 'dead! say you?'

'It is indeed true, my lord; and, to the noble of your name, will be. I imagine, no unwelcome intelligence.'

A rapid smile shot over the countenance of the listener. 'How died he?'

'In his rash exertions to rescue a favourite portion of the hunting stud, he has himself perished miserably in the flames.'

'I—n—d—e—e—d—!' ejaculated the Baron, as if slowly and deliberately impressed with the truth of some exciting idea.

'Indeed,' repeated the vassal.

'Shocking!' said the youth, calmly, and turned quietly into the palace.

From this date a marked alteration took place in the outward demeanour of the dissolute young Baron Frederick Von Metzengerstein. Indeed, his behaviour disappointed every expectation, and proved little in accordance with the views of many a manœuvring mamma; while his habits and manner, still less than formerly, offered anything congenial with those of the neighbouring aristocracy. He was never to be seen beyond the limits of his own domain, and, in this wide and social world, was utterly companionless—unless, indeed, that unnatural, impetuous, and fiery-coloured horse, which he henceforward continually bestrode, had any mysterious right to the title of his friend.

Numerous invitations on the part of the neighbourhood for a long time, however, periodically came in. 'Will the Baron honour our festivals with his presence?' 'Will the Baron join us in a hunting of the boar?'—'Metzengerstein does not hunt'; 'Metzengerstein will not attend', were the haughty and laconic answers.

These repeated insults were not to be endured by an imperious nobility. Such invitations became less cordial—less frequent—in time they ceased altogether. The widow of the unfortunate Count Berlifitzing was even heard to express a hope 'that the Baron might be at home when he did not wish to be at home, since he disdained the company of his equals; and ride when he did not wish to ride, since he preferred the society of a horse'. This, to be sure, was a very silly explosion of hereditary pique; and merely proved how singularly unmeaning our sayings are apt to become, when we desire to be unusually energetic.

The charitable, nevertheless, attributed the alteration in the conduct of the young nobleman to the natural sorrow of a son for the untimely loss of his parents;—forgetting, however, his atrocious and reckless behaviour during the short period immediately succeeding that bereavement. Some there were, indeed, who suggested a too haughty idea of self-consequence and dignity. Others again (among whom may be mentioned the family physician) did not hesitate in speaking of morbid melancholy, and hereditary ill-health; while dark hints, of a more equivocal nature, were current among the multitude.

Indeed, the Baron's perverse attachment to his lately acquired charger—an attachment which seemed to attain new strength from every fresh example of the animal's ferocious and demon-like propensities—at length became, in the eyes of all reasonable men, a hideous and unnatural fervour. In the glare of noon—at the dead hour of night—in sickness or in health—in calm or in tempest—the young Metzengerstein seemed riveted to the saddle of that colossal horse, whose intractable audacities so well accorded with his own spirit.

There were circumstances, moreover, which, coupled with late events, gave an unearthly and portentous character to the mania of the rider, and to the capabilities of the steed. The space passed over in a single leap had been accurately measured, and was found to exceed, by an astounding difference, the wildest expectations of the most imaginative. The Baron, besides, had no particular *name* for the animal, although all the rest in his collection were distinguished by characteristic appellations. His stable, too, was appointed at a distance from the rest; and, with regard to grooming and other necessary offices, none but the owner in person had ventured to officiate, or even to enter the enclosure of that horse's particular stall. It was also to be observed, that although the three grooms, who had caught the steed as he fled from the conflagration at Berlifitzing, had succeeded in arresting his course by means of a chain-bridle and noose—yet not one of the three could with any certainty affirm that he had, during that dangerous struggle, or at any period thereafter, actually placed his hand upon the body of the beast. Instances of peculiar intelligence in the demeanour of a noble and high-spirited horse are not to be supposed capable of exciting unreasonable attention, but there were certain circumstances which intruded themselves perforce upon the most sceptical and phlegmatic; and it is said there were times when the animal caused the gaping crowd who stood around to recoil in horror from the deep and impressive meaning of his terrible stamp—times when the young Metzengerstein turned pale and shrunk away from the rapid and searching expression of his human-looking eye.

Among all the retinue of the Baron, however, none were found to doubt the ardour of that extraordinary affection which existed on the part of the young nobleman for the fiery qualities of his horse; at least, none but an insignificant and misshapen little page, whose deformities were in everybody's way, and whose opinions were of the least possible importance. He (if his ideas are worth mentioning at all) had the effrontery to assert that his master never vaulted into the saddle without an unaccountable and almost imperceptible shudder; and that, upon his return from every long-continued and habitual ride, an expression of triumphant malignity distorted every muscle in his countenance.

One tempestuous night, Metzengerstein, awaking from a heavy slumber, descended like a maniac from his chamber, and, mounting in hot haste, bounded away into the mazes of the forest. An occurrence so common attracted no particular attention, but his return was looked for with intense anxiety on the part of his domestics, when, after some hours' absence, the stupendous and magnificent battlements of the Palace Metzengerstein were discovered crackling and rocking to their very foundation, under the influence of a dense and livid mass of ungovernable fire.

As the flames, when first seen, had already made so terrible a progress that all efforts to save any portion of the building were evidently futile, the astonished neighbourhood stood idly around in silent if not apathetic wonder. But a new and fearful object soon riveted the attention of the multitude, and proved how much more intense is the excitement wrought in the feelings of a crowd by the contemplation of human agony, than that brought about by the most appalling spectacles of inanimate matter.

Up the long avenue of aged oaks which led from the forest to the main entrance of the Palace Metzengerstein, a steed, bearing an unbonneted and disordered rider, was seen leaping with an impetuosity which outstripped the very Demon of the Tempest.

The career of the horseman was indisputably, on his own part, uncontrollable. The agony of his countenance, the convulsive struggle of his frame, gave evidence of superhuman exertion; but no sound, save a solitary shriek, escaped from his lacerated lips, which were bitten through and through in the intensity of terror. One instant, and the clattering of hoofs resounded sharply and shrilly above the roaring of the flames and the shrieking of the winds—another, and, clearing at a single plunge the gateway and the moat, the steed bounded far up the tottering staircases of the palace, and, with its rider, disappeared amid the whirlwind of chaotic fire.

The fury of the tempest immediately died away, and a dead calm sullenly succeeded. A white flame still enveloped the building like a shroud, and, streaming far away into the quiet atmosphere, shot forth a glare of preternatural light; while a cloud of smoke settled heavily over the battlements in the distinct colossal figure of—*a horse*.

4

SABINE BARING-GOULD

Master Sacristan Eberhart

The much respected Master Eberhart, Sacristan of the ancient church of S. Sebaldus, lived, as others of his profession have done before, and do still on the continent, in the tower, above the big bells. His office was to keep his keen eye upon the villages around; and, should he detect the rising smoke and flame from a house on fire, to sound the alarum on a separate bell in the turret above his chamber.

This chamber, by the way, requires description. It formed one stage in the square tower; four windows commanded the points of the compass, glazed with the coarse old-fashioned glass, called in some places, 'bull's eye', with the exception of one light in each, that was filled with quarries, and that was just the one to peep through. In the corner of this room rose a crazy wooden stair, leading to the leads; below it, descended another to the belfry. There was a table of common deal, a large slope-backed armchair, and another chair for visitors, if they should come, but they didn't. Against the wall, as is the custom with pious people abroad, there hung a crucifix. Now, the Sacristan was a pious man, though he was odd too—at least, 'the people down below' called him so—*I* think he was very sensible, but as we may differ on the point, I leave you to judge for yourself. The good old man lived very much to himself up there in the windy old steeple, and very seldom descended into the wicked world, except to hear Mass of a morning, and to fetch his bread and milk; and these were brought for him as far as to the tower door. No one ever thought of going up the three hundred and sixty-five steps leading to the Sacristan's room, except the bell-ringers just occasionally; and they tried the old man's temper dreadfully—they were so earthy; and the Priest called now and then, but Master Eberhart, although he respected and honoured him (I said before he was very pious)—yet from being only associated with the birds and the old gargoyles—(those are the old carved spouts) he talked to him, not as if he were flesh and blood, but as if he were a stone man; not a gargoyle exactly, but a church monument. I don't think the Priest quite liked that.

Master Eberhart had a way of making friends too; but then they were not the ordinary friends 'people down below' make. You shall hear who they were. On the top of the tower below the broach of the spire, were four carved figures, life-size; one was a horse, another a dragon, a third an eagle, the fourth a monk, and the frost had taken his nose off. These statues had their mouths wide open, and were intended to spout the water off from the spire; but they never did, the rain always ran off another way down an ugly lead pipe. Yellow lichens marbled these grotesques all over, even over their faces. The monk turned west, and at sunset a red light covered him. He looked very terrible then, as if dipped in blood. It was not to be expected that Master Eberhart should care much for the three animals, at least not more than the people below would for their horses—they haven't got dragons or eagles—or for their guinea-pigs and fancy pigeons. But it was quite another matter with regard to the monk: the Sacristan loved him dearly, and had long conversations with him—only the talking was all on one side, but that was the pleasanter. On a sunny day, it was so agreeable to sit on the leads, leaning against the battlements, right over against the monk, and discuss the world below: a genial light ir-radiated the stone face, and it looked quite smiling; if it had not lost the nose, it would have been even handsome. On a moon-bright night also, when the lights were going out, one after another, in the win-dows far below, like sparks on a bit of tinder, the Sacristan loved to kneel in the shadow of the stone man, whose cowl and mutilated face would be cutting the moon's disc, and chant clearly some beautiful psalm, finishing with his hymn '*Te lucis ante terminum*'. The old man thought sometimes that the shooting lips of the figure moved; but, of course, we who live on the earth, know well enough that it was only his fancy. For a long time Master Eberhart did not know his friend's name, as he had never told him, but he found it out at last; for one day the Priest of S. Sebaldus came up to visit him, bringing under his arm a big book bound in hogskin, and having a quantity of leaves in it. The Sacristan had never seen more; he thought there must be about a thousand five hundred and something over. The Priest talked to the old man a great deal, chiefly about some Egyptian saint whose life he was going to read to him. The Sacristan loved stories, so he listened with all his ears; the life was that of S. Simon Stylites, who lived—I don't know how long—on the top of a pillar, ate nothing but leeks, and was never once blown off, however high the wind was. As he heard the account, a clear gleam of light shot into the old man's brain, and looking up through the little door at the top of the stairs, at the monk who was just visible, nodded friendly to him, with a 'Good morrow, Father Simon!' After that day, the Sacristan always called the gargoyle man 'Father Simon'.

Master Eberhart had his notions concerning things in general; they were bright and expansive, as the view from his belfry; but as in that he looked over the rising gables of the church below, each topped with a cross, so in every view he took of earthly matters, the cross was in them. It was quite wonderful how clear and panoramic his ideas were; quaint fancies surrounded them, and they were like the gargoyles, from among which he saw the earth. We do not get these broad theories below, for somehow, a neighbour's garden wall, or a granary gable, or sometimes merely a twig, debars us from taking a general sweep of the horizon.

The old man was one day sitting on the leads, looking up to his stone monk. 'I think,' said he, 'that the people down below are very self-sufficient, they fancy that all Creation is made to do them service; for that purpose called into being, and may be trimmed and pruned just as suits their wayward fancies; as if the handiwork of God were not made first to do Him praise and glory, and only secondly to rejoice the heart of man. I wish the folk down on earth would know their Benedicite a little better, and remember that all God's works praise him! Do you not agree with me, Father Simon? I know you do; why— a scud of rain cannot break over this fair spire, and the water trickle down these runnels, but the men down there think it is sent just to clear their gutters and sewers; as if there were not first the yellow lichen stain to rejoice and the pretty moss to make glad before ever it reaches them.' A ripple of golden sunlight ran over the weathered face of the gargoyle: 'Heaven knows,' sighed the old man, 'I do not, the exact way in which all the works of God praise Him; perhaps it may be in being always cheerful; perhaps in fulfilling what their mission is; perhaps in having no thought of themselves; but being beautiful; they work so steadily till they have done all they can, and till they are perfectly beautiful—and how cheerful they always are! There are those men down below! They seek their own interests, their self-advancement, and, if they be the least religious, their own feelings, forgetting all about the duty of praise; and that lifeless—I mean what *they* would call lifeless—things which cannot praise any other way, praise by doing their duty.' A bird perched on the monk's cowl, and sent forth a stream of song; 'There! there!' exclaimed the Sacristan—and he was undoubtedly going on to moralize, when, for the first time, he noticed a long crack at the back of the old carved spout. 'Bless me,' gasped the good man in alarm, 'Father Simon is breaking from the spire: what shall I do? The next high wind or frost, and he will be off—horrible! into the naughty world below. I will save him from that: what shall I do?' Master Eberhart rushed down the stairs; and catching the rope, sent forth peal after peal on the alarm bell. The folk on earth said, 'There surely must be a whole village on fire somewhere'—but it was only the gargoyle that was cracked. Up the stairs ran the sexton to know what was the matter; and the terrified Sacristan implored him to send a mason and his men at once, that his friend the monk might be saved. The sexton growled and went down the tower, he was quite disappointed that *that* was all; he had made up his mind that Alt-dorf was in flames. What men we are!

Well!—next day there came the mason and one man; and they pulled down the stone man, and laid him on the leads. 'You had better bring him into my room,' said Master Eberhart. 'What shall we do next?' asked the mason, when he had done so. 'Put him in my visitor's chair, wait—one moment—let me move my cash box.' The Sacristan pulled a tin coffer containing all his savings, from the seat, and laid it on the table; then the gargoyle was lifted into the place. 'When shall he be put up again?' asked the old man. 'Put up,' exclaimed the mason, 'He ain't worth the expense. What's the good of an ugly bit of stone like that, up aloft? Why, he might have tumbled and welcome, but that people feared for their heads.'

'Not put back again!' groaned the Sacristan; 'Never mind my box, leave it alone,' said he sharply, to the mason's man, who was lifting it. 'I don't care what it costs, I'll pay for him; and if I haven't enough, why the monk will wait till my death, and all my savings shall go to put him back again; he shall be my monument.' The mason laughed, and would have brought his hammer down on the head of the monk, but the Sacristan withheld his hand.

'You haven't got enough to pay for replacing that thing,' said the mason's man.

'I do not know that,' answered the old man, 'What would it cost?'

'Why there's a new block to be let into the spire, and the figure to be rivetted with iron clamps—'

'Iron clamps!' moaned the Sacristan.

'Don't know what it would come to exactly,' replied the mason; 'Good evening, master.'

Eberhart sat down to supper, in his slope-backed chair, on one side of the table; on the other, in the visitor's chair, the stone Friar squatted on his haunches, hands on knees, head thrust forward, the mouth protruding and wide open, the cowl half drawn over the dull eyes; the nose, I said before, was gone. The wind moaned at the window, but that it always did; the little fire burned brightly; and Master Eberhart looked lovingly and with a serene brow on his guest. 'I never have a meal quite to myself,' said he. 'There's a mouse or two generally comes out at supper time, and a robin is at the window of a morning; it is very strange that my mice do not come tonight! I cannot eat all by myself, I should feel as if doing wrong, not to share with some creature. Father Simon, will you have some?' he laid a piece of bread before him, but the courtesy passed without any acknowledgement.

'I always say my prayers after supper,' said the Sacristan, 'and then to bed; would that you could join!' Then he cleared the victuals from his table, moved to it his book of devotions, swept away the crumbs, and knelt down. Long and earnestly did the old man pray, his silver hair trailing over his thin fingers. He said his prayers aloud and sang a psalm or two on his knees, then remained silent for a moment or two. A shadow fell along his book—something cold touched his head—he felt two heavy hands on his hair—like a priest's, blessing him; then they were withdrawn and Master Eberhart rose joyously from his knees. 'That is just as it ought to have been,' murmured he in his happy heart. Afterwards he undressed and went to bed. It might have been three hours after this that the old man awoke; hearing a heavy tread about the floor, he opened his eyes. The moon lighted up the interior of the room, shining in at one of the four windows: in the corner stood Father Simon, going down the staircase into the belfry. Shortly after, Master Eberhart heard him groping among the bells, every touch of his fingers sounding on them, for those fingers were stone; then up he came again. The old man chuckled, and said to himself—'Friend Simon is curious to know how the bells are hung and worked; he has heard them so very long without having seen them.' The figure was again in the room, crossed it and coming up to the bedside laid itself down on it. The old Sacristan did feel a little startled, the weight seemed so great, bending down the outer side of the bed; and, as he put his hand to the figure, it was so cold, so bitterly cold; but he drove away these foolish fears, and said, 'Father, if you are chilly take the coverlid'; the statue remained immovable, so the old man sitting up, folded the counterpane over his bedfellow, then turning his face to the wall, tried to sleep. Now and then, however, he cast a furtive back-glance at the monk. The moon was on his face—that was cold, white and rigid with deep shadows in the eye sockets, the monstrous mouth gaping wide.

Master Eberhart dozed off, and when morning dawned, the figure was crouching in the visitor's chair, looking before it out of the opposite window. The day passed, as days usually passed in the tower top; at half-past seven the old man went down to hear Mass, after which he received his bread, milk, and leeks at the door. Breakfast followed; but the bird was not at the window ledge, as was its wont; nor did the mice appear all day. In the evening, the fire was lighted, and Master Eberhart warmed himself at the blaze; he would have moved the monk to the fire, only he was not strong enough. At nine a bell rung in a distant church tower; they had no clock in S. Sebaldus' steeple, but that of S. Lorenz had one. The Sacristan wiped his table, brought out his book and said his evening prayers. Again the shadow fell across the page, and two cold hands were laid in benediction on his head. Strengthened heart and soul, the old man rose from his knees, undressed by the fire; for some time he remained sitting before it, meditating, till at last he grew sleepy (people generally do get sleepy sitting over the grate), and crept to bed. Ten o'clock struck faintly and sweetly in the distant tower, and then the chimes began to play 'Willkommen, du seliger Abend,' plaintively, 'I am thankful we have no chimes in S. Sebaldus,' muttered the Sacristan, half dozing. 'They are like emperors playing spellikens. Bells were made to be pealed, not to be hammered about with little knockers.' Somehow, now that he was in bed, he could not sleep. First he turned his face to the wall, then the other way; then with great misgivings tried his back. In that position he may have slept for half an hour or an hour; I do not know, nor did he; but he was again awake, and his eyes opening fell on the fireplace. Then he brisked up thoroughly, for he saw, seated before the hearth, the monk, his hands on his knees, the crimson glare of the embers seeming to saturate his maimed face, cowl, and robe with blood, red, red blood. He had the blue grey of the room for a background, and through the window, the indigo sky, in which sparkled one bright frosty star. The foregoing night, Eberhart had felt but little fear; but now, a cold shudder quivered his old flesh; it was so awful, the face of his friend was changed, the brow seemed to be contracted over eyes no longer dull, but burning as iron from a forge; the vast mouth was closed and the lips firmly set. The features were no longer grotesque, but resolute, inflexible, determined; that was what paralysed the Sacristan. The monk had some errand to perform; he saw it in that unwavering face, on which the reflection of the embers was steady, however it might flicker on cowl and robe. The clock of S. Lorenz struck twelve, and then the chimes played a simple hymn, now sounding clearly as the wind bore the notes, then feebler as it died away. A falling star glided past the opposite window without haste. The bright star was beyond the window frame, another appeared. A slight clatter from below reached the Sacristan's ears; an owl must have got in among the bells; but for that stone figure he would have risen to drive the bird out. Slowly the monk rose from his seat and walked deliberately to the head of the stair ladder, stationing himself a little on one side, slightly back. On the other side there was but a narrow strip of flooring to the wall, sufficiently wide for a chest to stand, on which was placed the Sacristan's cash box. Again a noise below. 'Well,' said the old man, half audibly, 'Father Simon will not hurt me, I know; and I must see what is going on among the bells; those owls and jackdaws'—he put one leg out of bed, 'No—! I hear a step on the stair.' The monk turned his head cautiously round and beckoned with his stone finger. Master Eberhart understood his meaning and settled himself in bed again. There *was* a stealthy tread on the stair. Surprised and terrified the old man sat up in bed. Thirteen—fourteen—fifteen; whoever it might be, he must be near the top: there!—a head rose through an opening in the floor, and Eberhart recognized the mason's man by the firelight. The shadow of the slope-backed armchair crossed the corner where the old man sat so as to conceal him. The fellow crept nearly to the top; a large knife was in one of his hands; his eyes roved about the room, seeking something in the obscurity: in an instant they kindled up; he saw, and put out his hand to grasp the money coffer. A heavy tread behind him made him turn sharply round, and a fearful shriek broke from him, as his eyes encountered the stone monk leaning towards him, the cold eyes fixed on his, the granite hands extended, the knees bent as if for a leap. The mason stood benumbed with horror—the knife fell from his fingers and clattered down the steps, till it struck a bell. The gargoyle stooped further forward, sloping towards him; the cold hand touched his throat—in a moment those fingers collapsed; the figure became rigid; there was a gurgle, a fall, a furious bounding and crashing down the ladder; one wild jangle on a tenor bell, droning off fainter, fainter, faint, lost.

Not a sound to be heard, but the breath of the wind on the window panes, and its hum through traceried battlements overhead, an Æolian wail. Then, scarcely audible, came the horn of the watch from the great square; a bat dashed against the glass; all was still again. One o'clock struck far off in S. Lorenz tower: something moved on the bed, it was only a mouse, it scrambled down the coverlid and trotted across the floor. The last embers grew cold. A moth fluttered against the window top, and would not be still; the death watch ticked in an old beam; the cinders fell together in the grate! Morning came at last: 'Thank God' sighed the Sacristan. The chair was in front of the extinguished fire; the cash box safe; no gargoyle-monk to be seen. 'It cannot have been a dream,' faltered Master Eberhart. Then he rose from his pallet, slowly dressed, said his prayers, and hesitated at the top of the stairs, for he feared to descend. First he peeped down, but there was only sufficient light to distinguish huge rounded shapes of bells and massive rafters. 'I will wait until it is a little lighter,' muttered he.

The sun rose, bars of yellow shone through the luffer-boards on the bells. 'I must go and ring for Mass,' said the old man; 'that is a duty, I *must* go now'; so down he went. In the belfry, under one of the largest bells, lay a heap—the stone monk on top, crouching, one hand on his knee, the other clenched at the mason's throat, the large mouth gaping as of old; and the man—he lay, his feet doubled under his back, his hands clutching the stone arm, the head slung unnaturally on one side, for his neck was broken. The gargoyle, too, was snapped in half.

The old man said gravely to himself, 'I daresay that all creatures in nature, or in art, whatever they may be, cheerful flowers, happy birds, or only bits of stone, may become to us angels of good, if we only love them with true heart and reverence; but then we must love them because they are true, and good, and not because we may see in them reflections of our own selves, our feelings, and passions.'

5

J. SHERIDAN LE FANU

Dickon the Devil

About thirty years ago I was selected by two rich old maids to visit a property in that part of Lancashire which lies near the famous forest of Pendle, with which Mr Ainsworth's 'Lancashire Witches' has made us so pleasantly familiar. My business was to make partition of a small property, including a house and demesne, to which they had a long time before succeeded as co-heiresses.

The last forty miles of my journey I was obliged to post, chiefly by crossroads, little known, and less frequented, and presenting scenery often extremely interesting and pretty. The picturesqueness of the landscape was enhanced by the season, the beginning of September, at which I was travelling.

I had never been in this part of the world before; I am told it is now a great deal less wild, and, consequently, less beautiful.

At the inn where I had stopped for a relay of horses and some dinner—for it was then past five o'clock—I found the host, a hale old fellow of five-and-sixty, as he told me, a man of easy and garrulous benevolence, willing to accommodate his guests with any amount of talk, which the slightest tap sufficed to set flowing, on any subject you pleased.

I was curious to learn something about Barwyke, which was the name of the demesne and house I was going to. As there was no inn within some miles of it, I had written to the steward to put me up there, the best way he could, for a night.

The host of the 'Three Nuns', which was the sign under which he entertained wayfarers, had not a great deal to tell. It was twenty years, or more, since old Squire Bowes died, and no one had lived in the Hall ever since, except the gardener and his wife.

46

'Tom Wyndsour will be as old a man as myself; but he's a bit taller, and not so much in flesh, quite,' said the fat innkeeper.

'But there were stories about the house,' I repeated, 'that they said, prevented tenants from coming into it?'

'Old wives' tales; many years ago, that will be, sir; I forget 'em; I forget 'em all. Oh yes, there always will be, when a house is left so; foolish folk will always be talkin'; but I hadn't heard a word about it this twenty year.'

It was vain trying to pump him; the old landlord of the 'Three Nuns', for some reason, did not choose to tell tales of Barwyke Hall, if he really did, as I suspected, remember them.

I paid my reckoning, and resumed my journey, well pleased with the good cheer of that old-world inn, but a little disappointed.

We had been driving for more than an hour, when we began to cross a wild common; and I knew that, this passed, a quarter of an hour would bring me to the door of Barwyke Hall.

The peat and furze were pretty soon left behind; we were again in the wooded scenery that I enjoyed so much, so entirely natural and pretty, and so little disturbed by traffic of any kind. I was looking from the chaise-window, and soon detected the object of which, for some time, my eye had been in search. Barwyke Hall was a large, quaint house, of that cage-work fashion known as 'black-and-white', in which the bars and angles of an oak framework contrast, black as ebony, with the white plaster that over-spreads the masonry built into its interstices. This steep-roofed Elizabethan house stood in the midst of park-like grounds of no great extent, but rendered imposing by the noble stature of the old trees that now cast their lengthening shadows eastward over the sward, from the declining sun.

The park-wall was grey with age, and in many places laden with ivy. In deep grey shadow, that contrasted with the dim fires of evening reflected on the foliage above it, in a gentle hollow, stretched a lake that looked cold and black, and seemed, as it were, to skulk from observation with a guilty knowledge.

I had forgot that there was a lake at Barwyke; but the moment this caught my eye, like the cold polish of a snake in the shadow, my instinct seemed to recognize something dangerous, and I knew that the lake was connected, I could not remember how, with the story I had heard of this place in my boyhood.

I drove up a grass-grown avenue, under the boughs of these noble trees, whose foliage, dyed in autumnal red and yellow, returned the beams of the western sun gorgeously.

We drew up at the door. I got out, and had a good look at the front of the house; it was a large and melancholy mansion, with signs of long neglect upon it; great wooden shutters, in the old fashion, were barred, outside, across the windows; grass, and even nettles, were growing thick on the courtyard, and a thin moss streaked the timber beams; the plaster was discoloured by time and weather, and bore great russet and yellow stains. The gloom was increased by several grand old trees that crowded close about the house.

I mounted the steps, and looked round; the dark lake lay near me now, a little to the left. It was not large; it may have covered some ten or twelve acres; but it added to the melancholy of the scene. Near the centre of it was a small island, with two old ash trees, leaning toward each other, their pensive images reflected in the stirless water. The only cheery influence in this scene of antiquity, solitude, and neglect was that the house and landscape were warmed with the ruddy western beams. I knocked, and my summons resounded hollow and ungenial in my ear; and the bell, from far away, returned a deep-mouthed and surly ring, as if it resented being roused from a score years' slumber.

A light-limbed, jolly-looking old fellow, in a barracan jacket and gaiters, with a smile of welcome, and a very sharp, red nose, that seemed to promise good cheer, opened the door with a promptitude that indicated a hospitable expectation of my arrival.

There was but little light in the hall, and that little lost itself in darkness in the background. It was very spacious and lofty, with a gallery running round it, which, when the door was open, was visible at two or three points. Almost in the dark my new acquaintance led me across this wide hall into the room destined for my reception. It was spacious, and wainscoted up to the ceiling. The furniture of this capacious chamber was old-fashioned and clumsy. There were curtains still to the windows, and a piece of Turkey carpet lay upon the floor; those windows were two in number, looking out, through the trunks of the trees close to the house, upon the lake. It needed all the fire, and all the pleasant associations of my entertainer's red nose, to light up this melancholy chamber. A door at its farther end admitted to the room that was prepared for my sleeping apartment. It was wainscoted, like the other. It had a four-post bed, with heavy tapestry curtains, and in other respects was furnished in the same old-world and ponderous style as the other room. Its windows, like those of that apartment, looked out upon the lake.

Sombre and sad as these rooms were, they were yet scrupulously clean. I had nothing to complain of; but the effect was rather dispiriting. Having given some directions about supper—a pleasant incident to look forward to—and made a rapid toilet, I called on my friend with the gaiters and red nose (Tom Wyndsour) whose occupation was that of a 'bailiff', or under-steward, of the property, to accompany me, as we had still an hour or so of sun and twilight, in a walk over the grounds.

It was a sweet autumn evening, and my guide, a hardy old fellow, strode at a pace that tasked me to keep up with.

Among clumps of trees at the northern boundary of the demesne we lighted upon the little antique parish church. I was looking down upon it, from an eminence, and the park-wall interposed; but a little way down was a stile affording access to the road, and by this we approached the iron gate of the churchyard. I saw the church door open; the sexton was replacing his pick, shovel, and spade, with which he had just been digging a grave in the churchyard, in their little repository under the stone stair of the tower. He was a polite, shrewd little hunchback, who was very happy to show me over the church. Among the monuments was one that interested me; it was erected to commemorate the very Squire Bowes from whom my two old maids had inherited the house and estate of Barwyke. It spoke of him in terms of grandiloquent eulogy, and informed the Christian reader that he had died, in the bosom of the Church of England, at the age of seventy-one.

I read this inscription by the parting beams of the setting sun, which disappeared behind the horizon just as we passed out from under the porch.

'Twenty years since the Squire died,' said I, reflecting as I loitered still in the churchyard.

'Ay, sir; 'twill be twenty year the ninth o' last month.'

'And a very good old gentleman?'

'Good-natured enough, and an easy gentleman he was, sir; I don't think while he lived he ever hurt a fly,' acquiesced Tom Wyndsour. 'It ain't always easy sayin' what's in 'em though, and what they may take or turn to afterwards; and some o' them sort, I think, goes mad.'

'You don't think he was out of his mind?' I asked.

'He? La! no; not he, sir; a bit lazy, perhaps, like other old fellows; but a knew devilish well what he was about.'

Tom Wyndsour's account was a little enigmatical; but, like old Squire Bowes, I was 'a bit lazy' that evening, and asked no more questions about him.

We got over the stile upon the narrow road that skirts the churchyard. It is overhung by elms more than a hundred years old, and in the twilight, which now prevailed, was growing very dark. As side-by-side we walked along this road, hemmed in by two loose stone-like walls, something running towards us in a zig-zag line passed us at a wild pace, with a sound like a frightened laugh or a shudder, and I saw, as it passed, that it was a human figure. I may confess now, that I was a little startled. The dress of this figure was, in part, white: I know I mistook it at first for a white horse coming down the road at a gallop. Tom Wyndsour turned about and looked after the retreating figure.

'He'll be on his travels tonight,' he said, in a low tone. 'Easy served with a bed, *that* lad be; six foot o' dry peat or heath, or a nook in a dry ditch. That lad hasn't slept once in a house this twenty year, and never will while grass grows.'

'Is he mad?' I asked.

'Something that way, sir; he's an idiot, an awpy; we call him "Dickon the devil", because the devil's almost the only word that's ever in his mouth.'

It struck me that this idiot was in some way connected with the story of old Squire Bowes.

'Queer things are told of him, I dare say?' I suggested.

'More or less, sir; more or less. Queer stories, some.'

'Twenty years since he slept in a house? That's about the time the Squire died,' I continued.

'So it will be, sir; and not very long after.'

'You must tell me all about that, Tom, tonight, when I can hear it comfortably, after supper.'

Tom did not seem to like my invitation; and looking straight before him as we trudged on, he said:

'You see, sir, the house has been quiet, and nout's been troubling folk inside the walls or out, all round the woods of Barwyke, this ten year, or more; and my old woman, down there, is clear against talking about such matters, and thinks it best—and so do I—to let sleepin' dogs be.'

He dropped his voice towards the close of the sentence, and nodded significantly.

We soon reached a point where he unlocked a wicket in the park wall, by which we entered the grounds of Barwyke once more.

The twilight deepening over the landscape, the huge and solemn trees, and the distant outline of the haunted house, exercised a sombre influence on me, which, together with the fatigue of a day of travel, and the brisk walk we had had, disinclined me to interrupt the silence in which my companion now indulged.

A certain air of comparative comfort, on our arrival, in great measure dissipated the gloom that was stealing over me. Although it was by no means a cold night, I was very glad to see some wood blazing in the grate; and a pair of candles aiding the light of the fire, made the room look cheerful. A small table, with a very white cloth, and preparations for supper, was also a very agreeable object.

I should have liked very well, under these influences, to have listened to Tom Wyndsour's story; but after supper I grew too sleepy to attempt to lead him to the subject; and after yawning for a time, I found there was no use in contending against my drowsiness, so I betook myself to my bedroom, and by ten o'clock was fast asleep.

What interruption I experienced that night I shall tell you presently. It was not much, but it was very odd.

By next night I had completed my work at Barwyke. From early morning till then I was so incessantly occupied and hard-worked, that I had no time to think over the singular occurrence to which I have just referred. Behold me, however, at length once more seated at my little supper-table, having ended a comfortable meal. It had been a sultry day, and I had thrown one of the large windows up as high as it would go. I was sitting near it, with my brandy and water at my elbow, looking out into the dark. There was no moon, and the trees that are grouped about the house make the darkness round it supernaturally profound on such nights.

'Tom,' said I, so soon as the jug of hot punch I had supplied him with began to exercise its genial and communicative influence; 'you must tell me who beside your wife and you and myself slept in the house last night.'

Tom, sitting near the door, set down his tumbler, and looked at me askance, while you might count seven, without speaking a word.

'Who else slept in the house?' he repeated, very deliberately. 'Not a living soul, sir'; and he looked hard at me, still evidently expecting something more.

'That *is* very odd,' I said, returning his stare, and feeling really a little odd. 'You are sure *you* were not in my room last night?'

'Not till I came to call you, sir, this morning; *I* can make oath of that.'

'Well', said I, 'there was someone there, *I* can make oath of that. I was so tired I could not make up my mind to get up; but I was waked by a sound that I thought was someone flinging down the two tin boxes in which my papers were locked up violently on the floor. I heard a slow step on the ground, and there was light in the room, although I remembered having put out my candle. I thought it must have been you, who had come in for my clothes, and upset the boxes by accident. Whoever it was, he went out and the light with him. I was about to settle again, when, the curtain being a little open at the foot of the bed, I saw a light on the wall opposite; such as a candle from outside would cast if the door were very cautiously opening. I started up in the bed, drew the side curtain, and saw that the door *was* opening, and admitting light from outside. It is close, you know, to the head of the bed. A hand was holding on the edge of the door and pushing it open; not a bit like yours; a very singular hand. Let me look at yours.'

He extended it for my inspection.

'Oh no; there's nothing wrong with your hand. This was differently shaped; fatter; and the middle finger was stunted, and shorter than the rest, looking as if it had once been broken, and the nail was crooked like a claw. I called out 'Who's there?' and the light and the hand were withdrawn, and I saw and heard no more of my visitor.'

'So sure as you're a living man, that was him!' exclaimed Tom

Wyndsour, his very nose growing pale, and his eyes almost starting out of his head.

'Who?' I asked.

'Old Squire Bowes; 'twas *his* hand you saw; the Lord a' mercy on us!' answered Tom. 'The broken finger, and the nail bent like a hoop. Well for you, sir, he didn't come back when you called, that time. You came here about them Miss Dymocks' business, and he never meant they should have a foot o' ground in Barwyke; and he was making a will to give it away quite different, when death took him short. He never was uncivil to no one; but he couldn't abide them ladies. My mind misgave me when I heard 'twas about their business you were coming; and now you see how it is; he'll be at his old tricks again!'

With some pressure and a little more punch, I induced Tom Wyndsour to explain his mysterious allusions by recounting the occurrences which followed the old Squire's death.

'Squire Bowes of Barwyke died without making a will, as you know,' said Tom. 'And all the folk round were sorry; that is to say, sir, as sorry as folk will be for an old man that has seen a long tale of years, and has no right to grumble that death has knocked an hour too soon at his door. The Squire was well liked; he was never in a passion, or said a hard word; and he would not hurt a fly; and that made what happened after his decease the more surprising.

'The first thing these ladies did, when they got the property was to buy stock for the park.

'It was not wise, in any case, to graze the land on their own account. But they little knew all they had to contend with.

'Before long something went wrong with the cattle; first one, and then another, took sick and died, and so on, till the loss began to grow heavy. Then, queer stories, little by little, began to be told. It was said, first by one, then by another, that Squire Bowes was seen, about evening time, walking, just as he used to do when he was alive, among the old trees, leaning on his stick; and, sometimes when he came up with the cattle, he would stop and lay his hand kindly like on the back of one of them; and that one was sure to fall sick next day, and die soon after.

'No one ever met him in the park, or in the woods, or ever saw him, except a good distance off. But they knew his gait and his figure well, and the clothes he used to wear; and they could tell the beast he laid his hand on by its colour—white, dun, or black; and that beast was sure to sicken and die. The neighbours grew shy of taking the path over the park; and no one liked to walk in the woods, or come inside the bounds of Barwyke: and the cattle went on sickening and dying as before.

'At that time there was one Thomas Pyke; he had been a groom to the old Squire; and he was in care of the place, and was the only one that used to sleep in the house.

'Tom was vexed, hearing these stories; which he did not believe the half on 'em; and more especial as he could not get man or boy to herd the cattle; all being afeared. So he wrote to Matlock in Derbyshire, for his brother, Richard Pyke, a clever lad, and one that knew nout o' the story of the old Squire walking.

'Dick came; and the cattle was better; folk said they could still see the old Squire, sometimes, walking, as before, in openings of the wood, with his stick in his hand; but he was shy of coming nigh the cattle, whatever his reason might be, since Dickon Pyke came; and he used to stand a long bit off, looking at them, with no more stir in him than a trunk o' one of the old trees, for an hour at a time, till the shape melted away, little by little, like the smoke of a fire that burns out.

'Tom Pyke and his brother Dickon, being the only living souls in the house, lay in the big bed in the servants' room, the house being fast barred and locked, one night in November.

'Tom was lying next the wall, and he told me, as wide awake as ever he was at noonday. His brother Dickon lay outside, and was sound asleep.

'Well, as Tom lay thinking, with his eyes turned toward the door, it opens slowly, and who should come in but old Squire Bowes, his face lookin' as dead as he was in his coffin.

'Tom's very breath left his body; he could not take his eyes off him; and he felt his hair rising up on his head.

'The Squire came to the side of the bed, and put his arms under Dickon, and lifted the boy—in a dead sleep all the time—and carried him out so, at the door.

'Such was the appearance, to Tom Pyke's eyes, and he was ready to swear to it, anywhere.

'When this happened, the light, wherever it came from, all on a sudden went out, and Tom could not see his own hand before him.

'More dead than alive, he lay till daylight.

'Sure enough his brother Dickon was gone. No sign of him could he discover about the house; and with some trouble he got a couple of the neighbours to help him to search the woods and grounds. Not a sign of him anywhere.

'At last one of them thought of the island in the lake; the little boat was moored to the old post at the water's edge. In they got, though with small hope of finding him there. Find him, nevertheless, they did, sitting under the big ash tree, quite out of his wits; and to all their questions he answered nothing but one cry—"Bowes, the devil! See him; see him; Bowes, the devil!" An idiot they found him; and so he will be till God sets all things right. No one could ever get him to sleep under roof-tree more. He wanders from house to house while day-light lasts; and no one cares to lock the harmless creature in the work-house. And folk would rather not meet him after nightfall, for they think where he is there may be worse things near.'

A silence followed Tom's story. He and I were alone in that large room; I was sitting near the open window, looking into the dark night air. I fancied I saw something white move across it; and I heard a sound like low talking that swelled into a discordant shriek—'Hoo-oo-oo! Bowes, the devil! Over your shoulder. Hoo-oo-oo! ha! ha! ha!' I started up, and saw, by the light of the candle with which Tom strode to the window, the wild eyes and blighted face of the idiot, as, with a sudden change of mood, he drew off, whispering and tittering to himself, and holding up his long fingers, and looking at the tips like a 'hand of glory'.

Tom pulled down the window. The story and its epilogue were over. I confess I was rather glad when I heard the sound of the horses' hoofs on the courtyard, a few minutes later; and still gladder when, having bidden Tom a kind farewell, I had left the neglected house of Barwyke a mile behind me.

BRAM STOKER

The Secret of the Growing Gold

When Margaret Delandre went to live at Brent's Rock the whole neighbourhood awoke to the pleasure of an entirely new scandal. Scandals in connection with either the Delandre family or the Brents of Brent's Rock, were not few; and if the secret history of the county had been written in full both names would have been found well represented. It is true that the status of each was so different that they might have belonged to different continents—or to different worlds for the matter of that—for hitherto their orbits had never crossed. The Brents were accorded by the whole section of the country an unique social dominance, and had ever held themselves as high above the yeoman class to which Margaret Delandre belonged, as a blue-blooded Spanish hidalgo out-tops his peasant tenantry.

The Delandres had an ancient record and were proud of it in their way as the Brents were of theirs. But the family had never risen above yeomanry; and although they had been once well-to-do in the good old times of foreign wars and protection, their fortunes had withered under the scorching of the free trade sun and the 'piping times of peace'. They had, as the elder members used to assert, 'stuck to the land', with the result that they had taken root in it, body and soul. In fact, they, having chosen the life of vegetables, had flourished as vegetation does—blossomed and thrived in the good season and suffered in the bad. Their holding, Dander's Croft, seemed to have been worked out, and to be typical of the family which had inhabited it. The latter had declined generation after generation, sending out now and again some abortive shoot of unsatisfied energy in the shape of a soldier or sailor, who had worked his way to the minor grades of the services and had there stopped, cut short either from unheeding gallantry in action or from that destroying cause to men without breeding or youthful care—the recognition of a position above them which they feel unfitted to fill. So, little by little, the family dropped lower and lower, the men brooding and dissatisfied, and drinking themselves into the grave, the women drudging at home, or marrying beneath them—or worse. In process of time all disappeared, leaving only two in the Croft, Wykham Delandre and his sister Margaret. The man and woman seemed to have inherited in masculine and feminine form respectively the evil tendency of their race, sharing in common the principles, though manifesting them in different ways, of sullen passion, voluptuousness and recklessness.

The history of the Brents had been something similar, but showing the causes of decadence in their aristocratic and not their plebeian forms. They, too, had sent their shoots to the wars; but their positions had been different, and they had often attained honour—for without flaw they were gallant, and brave deeds were done by them before the selfish dissipation which marked them had sapped their vigour.

The present head of the family—if family it could now be called when one remained of the direct line—was Geoffrey Brent. He was almost a type of a worn-out race, manifesting in some ways its most brilliant qualities, and in others its utter degradation. He might be fairly compared with some of those antique Italian nobles whom the painters have preserved to us with their courage, their unscrupulousness, their refinement of lust and cruelty—the voluptuary actual with the fiend potential. He was certainly handsome, with that dark, aquiline, commanding beauty which women so generally recognize as dominant. With men he was distant and cold; but such a bearing never deters womankind. The inscrutable laws of sex have so arranged that even a timid woman is not afraid of a fierce and haughty man. And so it was that there was hardly a woman of any kind or degree, who lived within view of Brent's Rock, who did not cherish some form of secret admiration for the handsome wastrel. The category was a wide one, for Brent's Rock rose up steeply from the midst of a level region and for a circuit of a hundred miles it lay on the horizon, with its high old towers and steep roofs cutting the level edge of wood and hamlet, and far-scattered mansions.

So long as Geoffrey Brent confined his dissipations to London and Paris and Vienna—anywhere out of sight and sound of his home—opinion was silent. It is easy to listen to far off echoes unmoved, and we can treat them with disbelief, or scorn, or disdain, or whatever attitude of coldness may suit our purpose. But when the scandal came close home it was another matter; and the feelings of independence and integrity which is in people of every community which is not utterly spoiled, asserted itself and demanded that condemnation should be expressed. Still there was a certain reticence in all, and no more notice was taken of the existing facts than was absolutely necessary. Margaret Delandre bore herself so fearlessly and so openly—she accepted her position as the justified companion of Geoffrey Brent so naturally that people came to believe that she was secretly married to him, and therefore thought it wiser to hold their tongues lest time should justify her and also make her an active enemy.

The one person who, by his interference, could have settled all doubts was debarred by circumstances from interfering in the matter. Wykham Delandre had quarrelled with his sister—or perhaps it was that she had quarrelled with him—and they were on terms not merely of armed neutrality but of bitter hatred. The quarrel had been antecedent to Margaret going to Brent's Rock. She and Wykham had almost come to blows. There had certainly been threats on one side and on the other; and in the end Wykham overcome with passion, had ordered his sister to leave his house. She had risen straightway, and, without waiting to pack up even her own personal belongings, had walked out of the house. On the threshold she had paused for a moment to hurl a bitter threat at Wykham that he would rue in shame and despair to the last hour of his life his act of that day. Some weeks had since passed; and it was understood in the neighbourhood that Margaret had gone to London, when she suddenly appeared driving out with Geoffrey Brent, and the entire neighbourhood knew before nightfall that she had taken up her abode at the Rock. It was no subject of surprise that Brent had come back unexpectedly, for such was his usual custom. Even his own servants never knew when to expect him, for there was a private door, of which he alone had the key, by which he sometimes entered without anyone in the house being aware of his coming. This was his usual method of appearing after a long absence.

Wykham Delandre was furious at the news. He vowed vengeance—and to keep his mind level with his passion drank deeper than ever. He tried several times to see his sister, but she contemptuously refused to meet him. He tried to have an interview with Brent and was refused by him also. Then he tried to stop him in the road, but without avail, for Geoffrey was not a man to be stopped against his will. Several actual encounters took place between the two men, and many more were threatened and avoided. At last Wykham Delandre settled down to a morose, vengeful acceptance of the situation.

Neither Margaret nor Geoffrey was of a pacific temperament, and it was not long before there began to be quarrels between them. One thing would lead to another, and wine flowed freely at Brent's Rock. Now and again the quarrels would assume a bitter aspect, and threats would be exchanged in uncompromising language that fairly awed the listening servants. But such quarrels generally ended where domestic altercations do, in reconciliation, and in a mutual respect for the fighting qualities proportionate to their manifestation. Fighting for its own sake is found by a certain class of persons, all the world over, to be a matter of absorbing interest, and there is no reason to believe that domestic conditions minimize its potency. Geoffrey and Margaret made occasional absences from Brent's Rock, and on each of these occasions Wykham Delandre also absented himself; but as he generally heard of the absence too late to be of any service, he returned home each time in a more bitter and discontented frame of mind than before.

At last there came a time when the absence from Brent's Rock became longer than before. Only a few days earlier there had been a quarrel, exceeding in bitterness anything which had gone before; but this, too, had been made up, and a trip on the Continent had been mentioned before the servants. After a few days Wykham Delandre also went away, and it was some weeks before he returned. It was noticed that he was full of some new importance—satisfaction, exaltation—they hardly knew how to call it. He went straightway to Brent's Rock, and demanded to see Geoffrey Brent, and on being told that he had not yet returned, said, with a grim decision which the servants noted:

'I shall come again. My news is solid—it can wait!' and turned away. Week after week went by, and month after month; and then there came a rumour, certified later on, that an accident had occurred in the Zermatt valley. Whilst crossing a dangerous pass the carriage containing an English lady and the driver had fallen over a precipice, the gentleman of the party, Mr Geoffrey Brent, having been fortunately saved as he had been walking up the hill to ease the horses. He gave information, and search was made. The broken rail, the excoriated roadway, the marks where the horses had struggled on the decline before finally pitching over into the torrent—all told the sad tale. It was a wet season, and there had been much snow in the winter, so that the river was swollen beyond its usual volume, and the eddies of the stream were packed with ice. All search was made, and finally the wreck of the carriage and the body of one horse were found in an eddy of the river. Later on the body of the driver was found on the sandy, torrent-swept waste near Täsch; but the body of the lady, like that of the other horse, had quite disappeared, and was—what was left of it by that time—whirling amongst the eddies of the Rhone on its way down to the Lake of Geneva.

Wykham Delandre made all the enquiries possible, but could not find any trace of the missing woman. He found, however, in the books of the various hotels the name of 'Mr and Mrs Geoffrey Brent'. And he had a stone erected at Zermatt to his sister's memory, under her married name, and a tablet put up in the church at Bretten, the parish in which both Brent's Rock and Dander's Croft were situated.

There was a lapse of nearly a year, after the excitement of the matter had worn away, and the whole neighbourhood had gone on its accustomed way. Brent was still absent, and Delandre more drunken, more morose, and more revengeful than before.

Then there was a new excitement. Brent's Rock was being made ready for a new mistress. It was officially announced by Geoffrey himself in a letter to the Vicar, that he had been married some months before to an Italian lady, and that they were then on their way home. Then a small army of workmen invaded the house; and hammer and plane sounded, and a general air of size and paint pervaded the atmosphere. One wing of the old house, the south, was entirely redone; and then the great body of the workmen departed, leaving only materials for the doing of the old hall when Geoffrey Brent should have returned, for he had directed that the decoration was only to be

done under his own eyes. He had brought with him accurate drawings of a hall in the house of his bride's father, for he wished to repro-
duce for her the place to which she had been accustomed. As the
moulding had all to be re-done, some scaffolding poles and boards
were brought in and laid on one side of the great hall, and also a great
wooden tank or box for mixing the lime, which was laid in bags beside it.

When the new mistress of Brent's Rock arrived the bells of the
church rang out, and there was a general jubilation. She was a beautiful creature, full of the poetry and fire and passion of the South; and
the few English words which she had learned were spoken in such a
sweet and pretty broken way that she won the hearts of the people
almost as much by the music of her voice as by the melting beauty of
her dark eyes.

Geoffrey Brent seemed more happy than he had ever before
appeared; but there was a dark, anxious look on his face that was new
to those who knew him of old, and he started at times as though at
some noise that was unheard by others.

And so months passed and the whisper grew that at last Brent's
Rock was to have an heir. Geoffrey was very tender to his wife, and the
new bond between them seemed to soften him. He took more interest in his tenants and their needs than he had ever done; and works of
charity on his part as well as on his sweet young wife's were not lacking. He seemed to have set all his hopes on the child that was coming,
and as he looked deeper into the future the dark shadow that had
come over his face seemed to die gradually away.

All the time Wykham Delandre nursed his revenge. Deep in his
heart had grown up a purpose of vengeance which only waited an
opportunity to crystallize and take a definite shape. His vague idea
was somehow centred in the wife of Brent, for he knew that he could
strike him best through those he loved, and the coming time seemed
to hold in its womb the opportunity for which he longed. One night
he sat alone in the living-room of his house. It had once been a handsome room in its way, but time and neglect had done their work and it
was now little better than a ruin, without dignity or picturesqueness
of any kind. He had been drinking heavily for some time and was
more than half stupefied. He thought he heard a noise as of someone
at the door and looked up. Then he called half savagely to come in; but

there was no response. With a muttered blasphemy he renewed his potations. Presently he forgot all around him, sank into a daze, but suddenly awoke to see standing before him someone or something like a battered, ghostly edition of his sister. For a few moments there came upon him a sort of fear. The woman before him, with distorted features and burning eyes seemed hardly human, and the only thing that seemed a reality of his sister, as she had been, was her wealth of golden hair, and this was now streaked with grey. She eyed her brother with a long, cold stare; and he, too, as he looked and began to realize the actuality of her presence, found the hatred of her which he had had, once again surging up in his heart. All the brooding passion of the past year seemed to find a voice at once as he asked her:

'Why are you here? You're dead and buried.'

'I am here, Wykham Delandre, for no love of you, but because I hate another even more than I do you!' A great passion blazed in her eyes.

'Him?' he asked, in so fierce a whisper that even the woman was for an instant startled till she regained her calm.

'Yes, him!' she answered. 'But make no mistake, my revenge is my own; and I merely use you to help me to it.' Wykham asked suddenly:

'Did he marry you?'

The woman's distorted face broadened out in a ghastly attempt at a smile. It was a hideous mockery, for the broken features and seamed scars took strange shapes and strange colours, and queer lines of white showed out as the straining muscles pressed on the old cicatrices.

'So you would like to know! It would please your pride to feel that your sister was truly married! Well, you shall not know. That was my revenge on you, and I do not mean to change it by a hair's breadth. I have come here tonight simply to let you know that I am alive, so that if any violence be done me where I am going there may be a witness.'

'Where are you going?' demanded her brother.

'That is my affair! and I have not the least intention of letting you know!' Wykham stood up, but the drink was on him and he reeled and fell. As he lay on the floor he announced his intention of following his sister; and with an outburst of splenetic humour told her that he would follow her through the darkness by the light of her hair, and of her beauty. At this she turned on him, and said that there were others beside him that would rue her hair and her beauty too. 'As he will,' she hissed; 'for the hair remains though the beauty be gone. When he withdrew the lynch-pin and sent us over the precipice into the torrent, he had little thought of my beauty. Perhaps his beauty would be scarred like mine were he whirled, as I was, among the rocks of the Visp, and frozen on the ice pack in the drift of the river. But let him beware! His time is coming!' and with a fierce gesture she flung open the door and passed out into the night.

Later on that night, Mrs Brent, who was but half-asleep, became suddenly awake and spoke to her husband:

'Geoffrey, was not that the click of a lock somewhere below our window?'

But Geoffrey—though she thought that he, too, had started at the noise—seemed sound asleep, and breathed heavily. Again Mrs Brent dozed; but this time awoke to the fact that her husband had arisen and was partially dressed. He was deadly pale, and when the light of the lamp which he had in his hand fell on his face, she was frightened at the look in his eyes.

'What is it, Geoffrey? What dost thou?' she asked.

'Hush! little one,' he answered, in a strange, hoarse voice. 'Go to sleep. I am restless, and wish to finish some work I left undone.'

'Bring it here, my husband,' she said; 'I am lonely and I fear when thou art away.'

For reply he merely kissed her and went out, closing the door behind him. She lay awake for awhile, and then nature asserted itself, and she slept.

Suddenly she started broad awake with the memory in her ears of a smothered cry from somewhere not far off. She jumped up and ran to the door and listened, but there was no sound. She grew alarmed for her husband, and called out: 'Geoffrey! Geoffrey!'

After a few moments the door of the great hall opened, and Geoffrey appeared at it, but without his lamp.

'Hush!' he said, in a sort of whisper, and his voice was harsh and stern. 'Hush! Get to bed! I am working, and must not be disturbed. Go to sleep, and do not wake the house!'

With a chill in her heart—for the harshness of her husband's voice was new to her—she crept back to bed and lay there trembling, too frightened to cry, and listened to every sound. There was a long pause of silence, and then the sound of some iron implement striking muffled blows! Then there came a clang of a heavy stone falling, followed by a muffled curse. Then a dragging sound, and then more noise of stone on stone. She lay all the while in an agony of fear, and her heart beat dreadfully. She heard a curious sort of scraping sound; and then there was silence. Presently the door opened gently, and Geoffrey appeared. His wife pretended to be asleep; but through her eyelashes she saw him wash from his hands something white that looked like lime.

In the morning he made no allusion to the previous night, and she was afraid to ask any question.

From that day there seemed some shadow over Geoffrey Brent. He neither ate nor slept as he had been accustomed, and his former habit of turning suddenly as though someone were speaking from behind him revived. The old hall seemed to have some kind of fascination for him. He used to go there many times in the day, but grew impatient if anyone, even his wife, entered it. When the builder's foreman came to enquire about continuing his work Geoffrey was out driving; the man went into the hall, and when Geoffrey returned the servant told him of his arrival and where he was. With a frightful oath he pushed the servant aside and hurried up to the old hall. The workman met him almost at the door; and as Geoffrey burst into the room he ran against him. The man apologized:

'Beg pardon, sir, but I was just going out to make some enquiries. I directed twelve sacks of lime to be sent here, but I see there are only ten.'

'Damn the ten sacks and the twelve too!' was the ungracious and incomprehensible rejoinder.

The workman looked surprised, and tried to turn the conversation.

'I see, sir, there is a little matter which our people must have done; but the governor will of course see it set right at his own cost.'

'What do you mean?'

'That 'ere 'arth-stone, sir: Some idiot must have put a scaffold pole on it and cracked it right down the middle, and it's thick enough you'd think to stand hanythink.' Geoffrey was silent for quite a minute, and then said in a constrained voice and with much gentler manner:

'Tell your people that I am not going on with the work in the hall at present. I want to leave it as it is for a while longer.'

'All right sir. I'll send up a few of our chaps to take away these poles and lime bags and tidy the place up a bit.'

'No! No!' said Geoffrey, 'leave them where they are. I shall send and tell you when you are to get on with the work.' So the foreman went away, and his comment to his master was:

'I'd send in the bill, sir, for the work already done. 'Pears to me that money's a little shaky in that quarter.'

Once or twice Delandre tried to stop Brent on the road, and, at last, finding that he could not attain his object rode after the carriage, calling out:

'What has become of my sister, your wife.' Geoffrey lashed his horses into a gallop, and the other, seeing from his white face and from his wife's collapse almost into a faint that his object was attained, rode away with a scowl and a laugh.

That night when Geoffrey went into the hall he passed over to the great fireplace, and all at once started back with a smothered cry. Then with an effort he pulled himself together and went away, returning with a light. He bent down over the broken hearth-stone to see if the moonlight falling through the storied window had in any way deceived him. Then with a groan of anguish he sank to his knees.

There, sure enough, through the crack in the broken stone were protruding a multitude of threads of golden hair just tinged with grey!

He was disturbed by a noise at the door, and looking round, saw his wife standing in the doorway. In the desperation of the moment he took action to prevent discovery, and lighting a match at the lamp, stooped down and burned away the hair that rose through the broken stone. Then rising nonchalantly as he could, he pretended surprise at seeing his wife beside him.

For the next week he lived in an agony; for, whether by accident or design, he could not find himself alone in the hall for any length of time. At each visit the hair had grown afresh through the crack, and he had to watch it carefully lest his terrible secret should be discovered. He tried to find a receptacle for the body of the murdered woman outside the house, but someone always interrupted him; and once, when he was coming out of the private doorway, he was met by his wife, who began to question him about it, and manifested surprise that she should not have before noticed the key which he now reluctantly showed her. Geoffrey dearly and passionately loved his wife, so that any possibility of her discovering his dread secrets, or even of doubting him, filled him with anguish; and after a couple of days had passed, he could not help coming to the conclusion that, at least, she suspected something.

That very evening she came into the hall after her drive and found him there sitting moodily by the deserted fireplace. She spoke to him directly.

'Geoffrey, I have been spoken to by that fellow Delandre, and he says horrible things. He tells to me that a week ago his sister returned to his house, the wreck and ruin of her former self, with only her golden hair as of old, and announced some fell intention. He asked me where she is—and oh, Geoffrey, she is dead, she is dead! So how can she have returned? Oh! I am in dread, and I know not where to turn!'

For answer, Geoffrey burst into a torrent of blasphemy which made her shudder. He cursed Delandre and his sister and all their kind, and in especial he hurled curse after curse on her golden hair.

'Oh, hush! hush!' she said, and was then silent, for she feared her husband when she saw the evil effect of his humour. Geoffrey in the torrent of his anger stood up and moved away from the hearth; but suddenly stopped as he saw a new look of terror in his wife's eyes. He followed their glance, and then he, too, shuddered—for there on the broken hearth-stone lay a golden streak as the points of the hair rose through the crack.

'Look, look!' she shrieked. 'Is it some ghost of the dead! Come away—come away!' and seizing her husband by the wrist with the frenzy of madness, she pulled him from the room.

That night she was in a raging fever. The doctor of the district attended her at once, and special aid was telegraphed for to London. Geoffrey was in despair, and in his anguish at the danger of his young wife almost forgot his own crime and its consequences. In the evening the doctor had to leave to attend to others; but he left Geoffrey in charge of his wife. His last words were:

'Remember, you must humour her till I come in the morning, or till some other doctor has her case in hand. What you have to dread is another attack of emotion. See that she is kept warm. Nothing more can be done.'

Late in the evening, when the rest of the household had retired, Geoffrey's wife got up from her bed and called to her husband.

'Come!' she said. 'Come to the old hall! I know where the gold comes from! I want to see it grow!'

Geoffrey would fain have stopped her, but he feared for her life or reason on the one hand, and lest in a paroxysm she should shriek out her terrible suspicion, and seeing that it was useless to try to prevent her, wrapped a warm rug around her and went with her to the old hall. When they entered, she turned and shut the door and locked it.

'We want no strangers amongst us three tonight!' she whispered with a wan smile.

'We three! nay we are but two,' said Geoffrey with a shudder; he feared to say more.

'Sit here,' said his wife as she put out the light. 'Sit here by the hearth and watch the gold growing. The silver moonlight is jealous! See it steals along the floor towards the gold—our gold!' Geoffrey looked with growing horror, and saw that during the hours that had passed the golden hair had protruded further through the broken hearth-stone. He tried to hide it by placing his feet over the broken place; and his wife, drawing her chair beside him, leant over and laid her head on his shoulder.

'Now do not stir, dear,' she said; 'let us sit still and watch. We shall find the secret of the growing gold!' He passed his arm round her and sat silent; and as the moonlight stole along the floor she sank to sleep.

He feared to wake her; and so sat silent and miserable as the hours stole away.

Before his horror-struck eyes the golden-hair from the broken stone grew and grew; and as it increased, so his heart got colder and colder, till at last he had not power to stir, and sat with eyes full of terror watching his doom.

In the morning when the London doctor came, neither Geoffrey nor his wife could be found. Search was made in all the rooms, but without avail. As a last resource the great door of the old hall was broken open, and those who entered saw a grim and sorry sight.

There by the deserted hearth Geoffrey Brent and his young wife sat cold and white and dead. Her face was peaceful, and her eyes were closed in sleep; but his face was a sight that made all who saw it shudder, for there was on it a look of unutterable horror. The eyes were open and stared glassily at his feet, which were twined with tresses of golden hair, streaked with grey, which came through the broken hearth-stone.

7

RALPH ADAMS CRAM

In Kropfsberg Keep

To the traveller from Innsbrück to Munich, up the lovely valley of the silver Inn, many castles appear, one after another, each on its beetling cliff or gentle hill—appear and disappear, melting into the dark fir trees that grow so thickly on every side—Laneck, Lichtwer, Ratholtz, Tratzberg, Matzen, Kropfsberg, gathering close around the entrance to the dark and wonderful Zillerthal.

But to us—Tom Rendel and myself—there are two castles only: not the gorgeous and princely Ambras, nor the noble old Tratzberg, with its crowded treasures of solemn and splendid mediævalism; but little Matzen, where eager hospitality forms the new life of a never-dead chivalry, and Kropfsberg, ruined, tottering, blasted by fire and smitten with grievous years—a dead thing, and haunted—full of strange legends, and eloquent of mystery and tragedy.

We were visiting the von C——s at Matzen, and gaining our first wondering knowledge of the courtly, cordial castle life in the Tyrol—of the gentle and delicate hospitality of noble Austrians. Brixleg had ceased to be but a mark on a map, and had become a place of rest and delight, a home for homeless wanderers on the face of Europe, while Schloss Matzen was a synonym for all that was gracious and kindly and beautiful in life. The days moved on in a golden round of riding and driving and shooting: down to Landl and Thiersee for chamois, across the river to the magic Achensee, up the Zillerthal, across the Schmerner Joch, even to the railway station at Steinach. And in the evenings after the late dinners in the upper hall where the sleepy hounds leaned against our chairs looking at us with suppliant eyes, in the evenings when the fire was dying away in the hooded fireplace in

69

the library, stories. Stories, and legends, and fairy tales, while the stiff old portraits changed countenance constantly under the flickering firelight, and the sound of the drifting Inn came softly across the meadows far below.

If ever I tell the story of Schloss Matzen, then will be the time to paint the too inadequate picture of this fair oasis in the desert of travel and tourists and hotels; but just now it is Kropfsberg the Silent that is of greater importance, for it was only in Matzen that the story was told by Fräulein E——, the gold-haired niece of Frau von C——, one hot evening in July, when we were sitting in the great west window of the drawing-room after a long ride up the Stallenthal. All the windows were open to catch the faint wind, and we had sat for a long time watching the Otzethaler Alps turn rose-colour over distant Innsbrück, then deepen to violet as the sun went down and the white mists rose slowly until Lichtwer and Laneck and Kropfsberg rose like craggy islands in a silver sea.

And this is the story as Fräulein E—— told it to us—the Story of Kropfsberg Keep.

A great many years ago, soon after my grandfather died, and Matzen came to us, when I was a little girl, and so young that I remember nothing of the affair except as something dreadful that frightened me very much, two young men who had studied painting with my grandfather came down to Brixleg from Munich, partly to paint, and partly to amuse themselves—'ghost-hunting' as they said, for they were very sensible young men and prided themselves on it, laughing at all kinds of 'superstition', and particularly at that form which believed in ghosts and feared them. They had never seen a real ghost, you know, and they belonged to a certain set of people who believed nothing they had not seen themselves—which always seemed to me *very* conceited. Well, they knew that we had lots of beautiful castles here in the 'lower valley', and they assumed, and rightly, that every castle has at least *one* ghost story connected with it, so they chose this as their hunting ground, only the game they sought was ghosts, not chamois. Their plan was to visit every place that was supposed to be haunted, and to meet every reputed ghost, and prove that it really was no ghost at all.

In Kropfsberg Keep

There was a little inn down in the village then, kept by an old man named Peter Rosskopf, and the two young men made this their head-quarters. The very first night they began to draw from the old innkeeper all that he knew of legends and ghost stories connected with Brixleg and its castles, and as he was a most garrulous old gentleman he filled them with the wildest delight by his stories of the ghosts of the castles about the mouth of the Zillerthal. Of course the old man believed every word he said, and you can imagine his horror and amazement when, after telling his guests the particularly blood-curdling story of Kropfsberg and its haunted keep, the elder of the two boys, whose surname I have forgotten, but whose Christian name was Rupert, calmly said, 'Your story is most satisfactory: we will sleep in Kropfsberg Keep tomorrow night, and you must provide us with all that we may need to make ourselves comfortable.'

The old man nearly fell into the fire. 'What for a blockhead are you?' he cried, with big eyes. 'The keep is haunted by Count Albert's ghost, I tell you!'

'That is why we are going there tomorrow night; we wish to make the acquaintance of Count Albert.'

'But there was a man stayed there once, and in the morning he was dead.'

'Very silly of him; there are two of us, and we carry revolvers.'

'But it's a *ghost*, I tell you,' almost screamed the innkeeper; 'are ghosts afraid of firearms?'

'Whether they are or not, we are *not* afraid of *them*.'

Here the younger boy broke in—he was named Otto von Kleist. I remember the name, for I had a music teacher once by that name. He abused the poor old man shamefully; told him that they were going to spend the night in Kropfsberg in spite of Count Albert and Peter Rosskopf, and that he might as well make the most of it and earn his money with cheerfulness.

In a word, they finally bullied the old fellow into submission, and when the morning came he set about preparing for the suicide, as he considered it, with sighs and mutterings and ominous shakings of the head.

You know the condition of the castle now—nothing but scorched walls and crumbling piles of fallen masonry. Well, at the time I tell you of, the keep was still partially preserved. It was finally burned out only a few years ago by some wicked boys who came over from Jenbach to have a good time. But when the ghost hunters came, though the two lower floors had fallen into the crypt, the third floor remained. The peasants said it *could* not fall, but that it would stay until the Day of Judgment, because it was in the room above that the wicked Count Albert sat watching the flames destroy the great castle and his imprisoned guests, and where he finally hung himself in a suit of armour that had belonged to his mediæval ancestor, the first Count Kropfsberg.

No one dared touch him, and so he hung there for twelve years, and all the time venturesome boys and daring men used to creep up the turret steps and stare awfully through the chinks in the door at that ghostly mass of steel that held within itself the body of a murderer and suicide, slowly returning to the dust from which it was made. Finally it disappeared, none knew whither, and for another dozen years the room stood empty but for the old furniture and the rotting hangings.

So, when the two men climbed the stairway to the haunted room, they found a very different state of things from what exists now. The room was absolutely as it was left the night Count Albert burned the castle, except that all trace of the suspended suit of armour and its ghastly contents had vanished.

No one had dared to cross the threshold, and I suppose that for forty years no living thing had entered that dreadful room.

On one side stood a vast canopied bed of black wood, the damask hangings of which were covered with mould and mildew. All the clothing of the bed was in perfect order, and on it lay a book, open, and face downward. The only other furniture in the room consisted of several old chairs, a carved oak chest, and a big inlaid table covered with books and papers, and on one corner two or three bottles with dark solid sediment at the bottom, and a glass, also dark with the dregs of wine that had been poured out almost half a century before. The tapestry on the walls was green with mould, but hardly torn or otherwise defaced, for although the heavy dust of forty years lay on everything the room had been preserved from further harm. No spider web was to be seen, no trace of nibbling mice, not even a dead moth or fly on the sills of the diamond-paned windows; life seemed to have shunned the room utterly and finally.

The men looked at the room curiously, and, I am sure, not without some feelings of awe and unacknowledged fear; but, whatever they may have felt of instinctive shrinking, they said nothing, and quickly set to work to make the room passably inhabitable. They decided to touch nothing that had not absolutely to be changed, and therefore they made for themselves a bed in one corner with the mattress and linen from the inn. In the great fireplace they piled a lot of wood on the caked ashes of a fire dead for forty years, turned the old chest into a table, and laid out on it all their arrangements for the evening's amusement: food, two or three bottles of wine, pipes and tobacco, and the chess-board that was their inseparable travelling companion.

All this they did themselves: the innkeeper would not even come within the walls of the outer court; he insisted that he had washed his hands of the whole affair, the silly dunderheads might go to their death their own way. *He* would not aid and abet them. One of the stable boys brought the basket of food and the wood and the bed up the winding stone stairs, to be sure, but neither money nor prayers nor threats would bring him within the walls of the accursed place, and he stared fearfully at the hare-brained boys as they worked around the dead old room preparing for the night that was coming so fast.

At length everything was in readiness, and after a final visit to the inn for dinner Rupert and Otto started at sunset for the Keep. Half the village went with them, for Peter Rosskopf had babbled the whole story to an open-mouthed crowd of wondering men and women, and as to an execution the awe-struck crowd followed the two boys dumbly, curious to see if they surely would put their plan into execution. But none went further than the outer doorway of the stairs, for it was already growing twilight. In absolute silence they watched the two foolhardy youths with their lives in their hands enter the terrible Keep, standing like a tower in the midst of the piles of stones that had once formed walls joining it with the mass of the castle beyond. When a moment later a light showed itself in the high windows above, they sighed resignedly and went their ways, to wait stolidly until morning should come and prove the truth of their fears and warnings.

In the meantime the ghost hunters built a huge fire, lighted their many candles, and sat down to await developments. Rupert afterwards told my uncle that they really felt no fear whatever, only a contemptuous curiosity, and they ate their supper with good appetite and an unusual relish. It was a long evening. They played many games of chess, waiting for midnight. Hour passed after hour, and nothing occurred to interrupt the monotony of the evening. Ten, eleven, came and went—it was almost midnight. They piled more wood in the fireplace, lighted new candles, looked to their pistols—and waited. The clocks in the village struck twelve; the sound coming muffled through the high, deep-embrasured windows. Nothing happened, nothing to break the heavy silence; and with a feeling of disappointed relief they looked at each other and acknowledged that they had met another rebuff.

Finally they decided that there was no use in sitting up and boring themselves any longer, they had much better rest; so Otto threw himself down on the mattress, falling almost immediately asleep. Rupert sat a little longer, smoking, and watching the stars creep along behind the shattered glass and the bent leads of the lofty windows; watching the fire fall together, and the strange shadows move mysteriously on the mouldering walls. The iron hook in the oak beam, that crossed the ceiling midway, fascinated him, not with fear, but morbidly. So, it was from that hook that for twelve years, twelve long years of changing summer and winter, the body of Count Albert, murderer and suicide, hung in its strange casing of mediæval steel; moving a little at first, and turning gently while the fire died out on the hearth, while the ruins of the castle grew cold, and horrified peasants sought for the bodies of the score of gay, reckless, wicked guests whom Count Albert had gathered in Kropfsberg for a last debauch, gathered to their terrible and untimely death. What a strange and fiendish idea it was, the young, handsome noble who had ruined himself and his family in the society of the splendid debauchees, gathering them all together, men and women who had known only love and pleasure, for a glorious and awful riot of luxury, and then, when they were all dancing in the great ballroom, locking the doors and burning the whole castle about them, the while he sat in the great keep listening to their screams of agonized fear, watching the fire sweep from wing to wing until the whole mighty mass was one enormous and awful pyre, and then, clothing himself in his great-great-grandfather's armour, hanging himself in the midst of the ruins of what had been a proud and noble castle. So ended a great family, a great house.

But that was forty years ago.

He was growing drowsy; the light flickered and flared in the fireplace; one by one the candles went out; the shadows grew thick in the room. Why did that great iron hook stand out so plainly? why did that dark shadow dance and quiver so mockingly behind it?—why—But he ceased to wonder at anything. He was asleep.

It seemed to him that he woke almost immediately; the fire still burned, though low and fitfully on the hearth. Otto was sleeping, breathing quietly and regularly; the shadows had gathered close around him, thick and murky; with every passing moment the light died in the fireplace; he felt stiff with cold. In the utter silence he heard the clock in the village strike two. He shivered with a sudden and irresistible feeling of fear, and abruptly turned and looked towards the hook in the ceiling.

Yes, It was there. He knew that It would be. It seemed quite natural, he would have been disappointed had he seen nothing; but now he knew that the story was true, knew that he was wrong, and that the dead *do* sometimes return to earth, for there, in the fast-deepening shadow, hung the black mass of wrought steel, turning a little now and then, with the light flickering on the tarnished and rusty metal. He watched it quietly; he hardly felt afraid; it was rather a sentiment of sadness and fatality that filled him, of gloomy forebodings of something unknown, unimaginable. He sat and watched the thing disappear in the gathering dark, his hand on his pistol as it lay by him on the great chest. There was no sound but the regular breathing of the sleeping boy on the mattress.

It had grown absolutely dark; a bat fluttered against the broken glass of the window. He wondered if he was growing mad, for—he hesitated to acknowledge it to himself—he heard music; far, curious music, a strange and luxurious dance, very faint, very vague, but unmistakable.

Like a flash of lightning came a jagged line of fire down the blank wall opposite him, a line that remained, that grew wider, that let a pale cold light into the room, showing him now all its details—the empty fireplace, where a thin smoke rose in a spiral from a bit of charred wood, the mass of the great bed, and, in the very middle, black against the curious brightness, the armoured man, or ghost, or devil, standing, not suspended, beneath the rusty hook. And with the rending of the wall the music grew more distinct, though sounding still very, very far away.

Count Albert raised his mailed hand and beckoned to him; then turned, and stood in the riven wall.

Without a word, Rupert rose and followed him, his pistol in hand. Count Albert passed through the mighty wall and disappeared in the unearthly light. Rupert followed mechanically. He felt the crushing of the mortar beneath his feet, the roughness of the jagged wall where he rested his hand to steady himself.

The keep rose absolutely isolated among the ruins, yet on passing through the wall Rupert found himself in a long, uneven corridor, the floor of which was warped and sagging, while the walls were covered on one side with big faded portraits of an inferior quality, like those in the corridor that connects the Pitti and Uffizzi in Florence. Before him moved the figure of Count Albert—a black silhouette in the ever-increasing light. And always the music grew stronger and stranger, a mad, evil, seductive dance that bewitched even while it disgusted.

In a final blaze of vivid, intolerable light, in a burst of hellish music that might have come from Bedlam, Rupert stepped from the corridor into a vast and curious room where at first he saw nothing, distinguished nothing but a mad, seething whirl of sweeping figures, white, in a white room, under white light, Count Albert standing before him, the only dark object to be seen. As his eyes grew accustomed to the fearful brightness, he knew that he was looking on a dance such as the damned might see in hell, but such as no living man had ever seen before.

Around the long, narrow hall, under the fearful light that came from nowhere, but was omnipresent, swept a rushing stream of unspeakable horrors, dancing insanely, laughing, gibbering hideously; the dead of forty years. White, polished skeletons, bare of flesh and vesture, skeletons clothed in the dreadful rags of dried and rattling sinews, the tags of tattering grave-clothes flaunting behind them. These were the dead of many years ago. Then the dead of more recent times, with yellow bones showing only here and there, the long and insecure hair of their hideous heads writhing in the beating air.

Then green and grey horrors, bloated and shapeless, stained with earth or dripping with spattering water; and here and there white, beautiful things, like chiselled ivory, the dead of yesterday, locked it may be, in the mummy arms of rattling skeletons.

Round and round the cursed room, a swaying, swirling maelstrom of death, while the air grew thick with miasma, the floor foul with shreds of shrouds, and yellow parchment, clattering bones, and wisps of tangled hair.

And in the very midst of this ring of death, a sight not for words nor for thought, a sight to blast forever the mind of the man who looked upon it: a leaping, writhing dance of Count Albert's victims, the score of beautiful women and reckless men who danced to their awful death while the castle burned around them, charred and shapeless now, a living charnel-house of nameless horror.

Count Albert, who had stood silent and gloomy, watching the dance of the damned, turned to Rupert, and for the first time spoke.

'We are ready for you now; dance!'

A prancing horror, dead some dozen years, perhaps, flaunted from the rushing river of the dead, and leered at Rupert with eyeless skull.

'Dance!'

Rupert stood frozen, motionless.

'Dance!'

His hard lips moved. 'Not if the devil came from hell to make me.'

Count Albert swept his vast two-handled sword into the fetid air while the tide of corruption paused in its swirling, and swept down on Rupert with gibbering grins.

The room, and the howling dead, and the black portent before him circled dizzily around, as with a last effort of departing consciousness he drew his pistol and fired full in the face of Count Albert.

Perfect silence, perfect darkness; not a breath, not a sound: the dead stillness of a long-sealed tomb. Rupert lay on his back, stunned, helpless, his pistol clenched in his frozen hand, a smell of powder in the black air. Where was he? Dead? In hell? He reached his hand out cautiously; it fell on dusty boards. Outside, far away, a clock struck three. Had he dreamed? Of course; but how ghastly a dream! With chattering teeth he called softly—

'Otto!'

There was no reply, and none when he called again and again. He staggered weakly to his feet, groping for matches and candles. A panic of abject terror came on him; the matches were gone! He turned towards the fireplace: a single coal glowed in the white ashes. He swept a mass of papers and dusty books from the table, and with trembling hands cowered over the embers, until he succeeded in lighting the dry tinder. Then he piled the old books on the blaze, and looked fearfully around.

No: It was gone—thank God for that; the hook was empty.

But why did Otto sleep so soundly; why did he not awake?

He stepped unsteadily across the room in the flaring light of the burning books, and knelt by the mattress.

So they found him in the morning, when no one came to the inn from Kropfsberg Keep, and the quaking Peter Rosskopf arranged a relief party; found him kneeling beside the mattress where Otto lay, shot in the throat and quite dead.

8

F. MARION CRAWFORD

The Dead Smile

1

Sir Hugh Ockram smiled as he sat by the open window of his study, in the late August afternoon; and just then a curiously yellow cloud obscured the low sun, and the clear summer light turned lurid, as if it had been suddenly poisoned and polluted by the foul vapours of a plague. Sir Hugh's face seemed, at best, to be made of fine parchment drawn skin-tight over a wooden mask, in which two eyes were sunk out of sight, and peered from far within through crevices under the slanting, wrinkled lids, alive and watchful like two toads in their holes, side by side and exactly alike. But as the light changed, then a little yellow glare flashed in each. Nurse Macdonald said once that when Sir Hugh smiled he saw the faces of two women in hell—two dead women he had betrayed. (Nurse Macdonald was a hundred years old.) And the smile widened, stretching the pale lips across the discoloured teeth in an expression of profound self-satisfaction, blended with the most unforgiving hatred and contempt for the human doll. The hideous disease of which he was dying had touched his brain. His son stood beside him, tall, white and delicate as an angel in a primitive picture; and though there was deep distress in his violet eyes as he looked at his father's face, he felt the shadow of that sickening smile stealing across his own lips and parting them and drawing them against his will. And it was like a bad dream, for he tried not to smile and smiled the more. Beside him, strangely like him in her wan, angelic beauty, with the same shadowy golden hair, the same sad violet eyes, the same luminously pale face, Evelyn Warburton rested one hand upon his arm. And as she looked into her uncle's eyes, and could not turn her own away, she knew that the deathly smile was hovering on her own red lips, drawing them tightly across her little teeth, while two bright tears ran down her cheeks to her mouth, and dropped from the upper to the lower lip while she smiled—and the smile was like the shadow of death and the seal of damnation upon her pure, young face.

'Of course,' said Sir Hugh very slowly, and still looking out at the trees, 'if you have made up your mind to be married, I cannot hinder you, and I don't suppose you attach the smallest importance to my consent——'

'Father!' exclaimed Gabriel reproachfully.

'No; I do not deceive myself,' continued the old man, smiling terribly. 'You will marry when I am dead, though there is a very good reason why you had better not—why you had better not,' he repeated very emphatically, and he slowly turned his toad eyes upon the lovers.

'What reason?' asked Evelyn in a frightened voice.

'Never mind the reason, my dear. You will marry just as if it did not exist.' There was a long pause. 'Two gone,' he said, his voice lowering strangely, 'and two more will be four—all together—for ever and ever, burning, burning, burning bright.'

At the last words his head sank slowly back, and the little glare of the toad eyes disappeared under the swollen lids; and the lurid cloud passed from the westering sun, so that the earth was green again and the light pure. Sir Hugh had fallen asleep, as he often did in his last illness, even while speaking.

Gabriel Ockram drew Evelyn away, and from the study they went out into the dim hall, softly closing the door behind them, and each audibly drew breath, as though some sudden danger had been passed. They laid their hands each in the other's, and their strangely like eyes met in a long look, in which love and perfect understanding were darkened by the secret terror of an unknown thing. Their pale faces reflected each other's fear.

'It is his secret,' said Evelyn at last. 'He will never tell us what it is.'

'If he dies with it,' answered Gabriel, 'let it be on his own head!'

'On his head!' echoed the dim hall. It was a strange echo, and some were frightened by it, for they said that if it were a real echo it should repeat everything and not give back a phrase here and there, now speaking, now silent. But Nurse Macdonald said that the great hall would never echo a prayer when an Ockram was to die, though it would give back curses ten for one.

'On his head!' it repeated quite softly, and Evelyn started and looked round.

'It is only the echo,' said Gabriel, leading her away.

They went out into the late afternoon light, and sat upon a stone seat behind the chapel, which was built across the end of the east wing. It was very still, not a breath stirred, and there was no sound near them. Only far off in the park a song-bird was whistling the high prelude to the evening chorus.

'It is very lonely here,' said Evelyn, taking Gabriel's hand nervously, and speaking as if she dreaded to disturb the silence. 'If it were dark, I should be afraid.'

'Of what? Of me?' Gabriel's sad eyes turned to her.

'Oh no! How could I be afraid of you? But of the old Ockrams—they say they are just under our feet here in the north vault outside the chapel, all in their shrouds, with no coffins, as they used to bury them.'

'As they always will—as they will bury my father, and me. They say an Ockram will not lie in a coffin.'

'But it cannot be true—these are fairy tales—ghost stories!' Evelyn nestled nearer to her companion, grasping his hand more tightly, and the sun began to go down.

'Of course. But there is the story of old Sir Vernon, who was beheaded for treason under James II. The family brought his body back from the scaffold in an iron coffin with heavy locks, and they put it in the north vault. But ever afterwards, whenever the vault was opened to bury another of the family, they found the coffin wide open, and the body standing upright against the wall, and the head rolled away in a corner, smiling at it.'

'As Uncle Hugh smiles?' Evelyn shivered.

'Yes, I suppose so,' answered Gabriel, thoughtfully. 'Of course I never saw it, and the vault has not been opened for thirty years—none of us have died since then.'

'And if—if Uncle Hugh dies—shall you——' Evelyn stopped, and her beautiful thin face was quite white.

'Yes. I shall see him laid there too—with his secret, whatever it is.' Gabriel sighed and pressed the girl's little hand.

'I do not like to think of it,' she said unsteadily. 'O Gabriel, what can the secret be? He said we had better not marry—not that he forbade it—but he said it so strangely, and he smiled—ugh!' Her small white teeth chattered with fear, and she looked over her shoulder while drawing still closer to Gabriel. 'And, somehow, I felt it in my own face——'

'So did I,' answered Gabriel in a low, nervous voice. 'Nurse Macdonald——' He stopped abruptly.

'What? What did she say?'

'Oh—nothing. She has told me things—they would frighten you, dear. Come, it is growing chilly.' He rose, but Evelyn held his hand in both of hers, still sitting and looking up into his face.

'But we shall be married, just the same—Gabriel! Say that we shall!'

'Of course, darling—of course. But while my father is so very ill, it is impossible——'

'O Gabriel, Gabriel, dear! I wish we were married now!' cried Evelyn in sudden distress. 'I know that something will prevent it and keep us apart.'

'Nothing shall!'

'Nothing?'

'Nothing human,' said Gabriel Ockram, as she drew him down to her.

And their faces, that were so strangely alike, met and touched—and Gabriel knew that the kiss had a marvellous savour of evil, but on Evelyn's lips it was like the cool breath of a sweet and mortal fear. And neither of them understood, for they were innocent and young. Yet she drew him to her by her lightest touch, as a sensitive plant shivers and waves its thin leaves, and bends and closes softly upon what it wants; and he let himself be drawn to her willingly, as he would if her touch had been deadly and poisonous; for she strangely loved that half voluptuous breath of fear, and he passionately desired the nameless evil something that lurked in her maiden lips.

'It is as if we loved in a strange dream,' she said.

'I fear the waking,' he murmured.

'We shall not wake, dear—when the dream is over it will have already turned into death, so softly that we shall not know it. But until then——'

She paused, and her eyes sought his, and their faces slowly came nearer. It was as if they had thoughts in their red lips that foresaw and foreknew the deep kiss of each other.

'Until then——' she said again, very low, and her mouth was nearer to his.

'Dream—till then,' murmured his breath.

2

Nurse Macdonald was a hundred years old. She used to sleep sitting all bent together in a great old leathern armchair with wings, her feet in a bag footstool lined with sheepskin, and many warm blankets wrapped about her, even in summer. Beside her a little lamp always burned at night by an old silver cup, in which there was something to drink.

Her face was very wrinkled, but the wrinkles were so small and fine and near together that they made shadows instead of lines. Two thin locks of hair, that was turning from white to a smoky yellow again, were drawn over her temples from under her starched white cap. Every now and then she woke, and her eyelids were drawn up in tiny folds like little pink silk curtains, and her queer blue eyes looked straight before her through doors and walls and worlds to a far place beyond. Then she slept again, and her hands lay one upon the other on the edge of the blanket; the thumbs had grown longer than the fingers with age, and the joints shone in the low lamplight like polished crab-apples.

It was nearly one o'clock in the night, and the summer breeze was blowing the ivy branch against the panes of the window with a hushing caress. In the small room beyond, with the door ajar, the girl-maid who took care of Nurse Macdonald was fast asleep. All was very quiet. The old woman breathed regularly, and her indrawn lips trembled each time as the breath went out, and her eyes were shut.

But outside the closed window there was a face, and violet eyes were looking steadily at the ancient sleeper, for it was like the face of Evelyn Warburton, though there were eighty feet from the sill of the window to the foot of the tower. Yet the cheeks were thinner than Evelyn's, and as white as a gleam, and the eyes stared, and the lips were not red with life; they were dead, and painted with new blood.

Slowly Nurse Macdonald's wrinkled eyelids folded themselves back, and she looked straight at the face at the window while one might count ten.

'Is it time?' she asked in her little old, far-away voice.

While she looked the face at the window changed, for the eyes opened wider and wider till the white glared all round the bright violet, and the bloody lips opened over gleaming teeth, and stretched and widened and stretched again, and the shadowy golden hair rose and streamed against the window in the night breeze. And in answer to Nurse Macdonald's question came the sound that freezes the living flesh.

That low-moaning voice that rises suddenly, like the scream of storm, from a moan to a wail, from a wail to a howl, from a howl to the fear-shriek of the tortured dead—he who has heard knows, and he can bear witness that the cry of the banshee is an evil cry to hear alone in the deep night. When it was over and the face was gone, Nurse Macdonald shook a little in her great chair, and still she looked at the black square of the window, but there was nothing more there, nothing but the night, and the whispering ivy branch. She turned her head to the door that was ajar, and there stood the girl in her white gown, her teeth chattering with fright.

'It is time, child,' said Nurse Macdonald. 'I must go to him, for it is the end.'

She rose slowly, leaning her withered hands upon the arms of the chair, and the girl brought her a woollen gown and a great mantle, and her crutch-stick, and made her ready. But very often the girl looked at the window and was unjointed with fear, and often Nurse Macdonald shook her head and said words which the maid could not understand.

'It was like the face of Miss Evelyn,' said the girl at last, trembling.

But the ancient woman looked up sharply and angrily, and her queer blue eyes glared. She held herself by the arm of the great chair with her left hand, and lifted up her crutch-stick to strike the maid with all her might. But she did not.

'You are a good girl,' she said, 'but you are a fool. Pray for wit, child, pray for wit—or else find service in another house than Ockram Hall. Bring the lamp and help me under my left arm.'

The crutch-stick clacked on the wooden floor, and the low heels of the woman's slippers clappered after her in slow triplets, as Nurse Macdonald got toward the door. And down the stairs each step she took was a labour in itself, and by the clacking noise the waking servants knew that she was coming, very long before they saw her.

No one was sleeping now, and there were lights, and whisperings, and pale faces in the corridors near Sir Hugh's bedroom, and now someone went in, and now someone came out, but everyone made way for Nurse Macdonald, who had nursed Sir Hugh's father more than eighty years ago.

The light was soft and clear in the room. There stood Gabriel Ockram by his father's bedside, and there knelt Evelyn Warburton, her hair lying like a golden shadow down her shoulders, and her hands clasped nervously together. And opposite Gabriel, a nurse was trying to make Sir Hugh drink. But he would not, and though his lips were parted, his teeth were set. He was very, very thin and yellow now, and his eyes caught the light sideways and were as yellow coals.

'Do not torment him,' said Nurse Macdonald to the woman who held the cup. 'Let me speak to him, for his hour is come.'

'Let her speak to him,' said Gabriel in a dull voice.

So the ancient woman leaned to the pillow and laid the feather-weight of her withered hand, that was like a brown moth, upon Sir Hugh's yellow fingers, and she spoke to him earnestly, while only Gabriel and Evelyn were left in the room to hear.

'Hugh Ockram,' she said, 'this is the end of your life; and as I saw you born, and saw your father born before you, I am come to see you die. Hugh Ockram, will you tell me the truth?'

The dying man recognized the little faraway voice he had known all his life, and he very slowly turned his yellow face to Nurse Macdonald; but he said nothing. Then she spoke again.

'Hugh Ockram, you will never see the daylight again. Will you tell the truth?'

His toad-like eyes were not yet dull. They fastened themselves on her face.

'What do you want of me?' he asked, and each word struck hollow upon the last. 'I have no secrets. I have lived a good life.'

Nurse Macdonald laughed—a tiny, cracked laugh, that made her old head bob and tremble a little, as if her neck were on a steel spring. But Sir Hugh's eyes grew red, and his pale lips began to twist.

'Let me die in peace,' he said slowly.

But Nurse Macdonald shook her head, and her brown, moth-like hand left his and fluttered to his forehead.

'By the mother that bore you and died of grief for the sins you did, tell me the truth!'

Sir Hugh's lips tightened on his discoloured teeth.

'Not on earth,' he answered slowly.

'By the wife who bore your son and died heart-broken, tell me the truth!'

'Neither to you in life, nor to her in eternal death.'

His lips writhed, as if the words were coals between them, and a great drop of sweat rolled across the parchment of his forehead. Gabriel Ockram bit his hand as he watched his father die. But Nurse Macdonald spoke a third time.

'By the woman whom you betrayed, and who waits for you this night, Hugh Ockram, tell me the truth!'

'It is too late. Let me die in peace.'

The writhing lips began to smile across the set yellow teeth, and the toad eyes glowed like evil jewels in his head.

'There is time,' said the ancient woman. 'Tell me the name of Evelyn Warburton's father. Then I will let you die in peace.'

Evelyn started back, kneeling as she was, and stared at Nurse Macdonald, and then at her uncle.

'The name of Evelyn's father?' he repeated slowly, while the awful smile spread upon his dying face.

The light was growing strangely dim in the great room. As Evelyn looked, Nurse Macdonald's crooked shadow on the wall grew gigantic. Sir Hugh's breath came thick, rattling in his throat, as death crept in like a snake and choked it back. Evelyn prayed aloud, high and clear.

Then something rapped at the window, and she felt her hair rise upon her head in a cool breeze, as she looked around in spite of herself. And when she saw her own white face looking in at the window, and her own eyes staring at her through the glass, wide and fearful, and her own hair streaming against the pane, and her own lips dashed with blood, she rose slowly from the floor and stood rigid for one moment, till she screamed once and fell straight back into Gabriel's arms. But the shriek that answered hers was the fear-shriek of the tormented corpse, out of which the soul cannot pass for shame of deadly sins, though the devils fight in it with corruption, each for their due share.

Sir Hugh Ockram sat upright in his death-bed, and saw and cried aloud:

'Evelyn!' His harsh voice broke and rattled in his chest as he sank down. But still Nurse Macdonald tortured him, for there was a little life left in him still.

'You have seen the mother as she waits for you, Hugh Ockram. Who was this girl Evelyn's father? What was his name?'

For the last time the dreadful smile came upon the twisted lips, very slowly, very surely now, and the toad eyes glared red, and the parchment face glowed a little in the flickering light. For the last time words came.

'They know it in hell.'

Then the glowing eyes went out quickly, the yellow face turned waxen pale, and a great shiver ran through the thin body as Hugh Ockram died.

But in death he still smiled, for he knew his secret and kept it still, on the other side, and he would take it with him, to lie with him for ever in the north vault of the chapel where the Ockrams lie uncoffined in their shrouds—all but one. Though he was dead, he smiled, for he had kept his treasure of evil truth to the end, and there was none left to tell the name he had spoken, but there was all the evil he had not undone left to bear fruit.

As they watched—Nurse Macdonald and Gabriel, who held Evelyn still unconscious in his arms while he looked at the father—they felt the dead smile crawling along their own lips—the ancient crone and the youth with the angel's face. Then they shivered a little, and both looked at Evelyn as she lay with her head on his shoulder, and, though she was very beautiful, the same sickening smile was twisting her young mouth too, and it was like the foreshadowing of a great evil which they could not understand.

But by and by they carried Evelyn out, and she opened her eyes and the smile was gone. From far away in the great house the sound of weeping and crooning came up the stairs and echoed along the dismal corridors, for the women had begun to mourn the dead master, after the Irish fashion, and the hall had echoes of its own all that night, like the far-off wail of the banshee among forest trees.

When the time was come they took Sir Hugh in his winding-sheet on a trestle bier, and bore him to the chapel and through the iron door and down the long descent to the north vault, with tapers, to lay him by his father. And two men went in first to prepare the place, and came back staggering like drunken men, and white, leaving their lights behind them.

But Gabriel Ockram was not afraid, for he knew. And he went in alone and saw that the body of Sir Vernon Ockram was leaning upright against the stone wall, and that its head lay on the ground near by with the face turned up, and the dried leathern lips smiled horribly at the dried-up corpse, while the iron coffin, lined with black velvet, stood open on the floor.

Then Gabriel took the thing in his hands, for it was very light, being quite dried by the air of the vault, and those who peeped in from the door saw him lay it in the coffin again, and it rustled a little, like a bundle of reeds, and sounded hollow as it touched the sides and the bottom. He also placed the head upon the shoulders and shut down the lid, which fell to with a rusty spring that snapped.

After that they laid Sir Hugh beside his father, with the trestle bier on which they had brought him, and they went back to the chapel.

But when they saw one another's faces, master and men, they were all smiling with the dead smile of the corpse they had left in the vault, so that they could not bear to look at one another until it had faded away.

3

Gabriel Ockram became Sir Gabriel, inheriting the baronetcy with the half-ruined fortune left by his father, and still Evelyn Warburton lived at Ockram Hall, in the south room that had been hers ever since she could remember anything. She could not go away, for there were no relatives to whom she could have gone, and, besides, there seemed to be no reason why she should not stay. The world would never trouble itself to care what the Ockrams did on their Irish estates, and it was long since the Ockrams had asked anything of the world.

So Sir Gabriel took his father's place at the dark old table in the dining-room, and Evelyn sat opposite to him, until such time as their mourning should be over, and they might be married at last. And meanwhile their lives went on as before, since Sir Hugh had been a hopeless invalid during the last year of his life, and they had seen him but once a day for the little while, spending most of their time together in a strangely perfect companionship.

But though the late summer saddened into autumn, and autumn darkened into winter, and storm followed storm, and rain poured on rain through the short days and the long nights, yet Ockram Hall seemed less gloomy since Sir Hugh had been laid in the north vault beside his father. And at Christmastide Evelyn decked the great hall with holly and green boughs, and huge fires blazed on every hearth. Then the tenants were all bidden to a New Year's dinner, and they ate and drank well, while Sir Gabriel sat at the head of the table. Evelyn came in when the port wine was brought, and the most respected of the tenants made a speech to propose her health.

It was long, he said, since there had been a Lady Ockram. Sir Gabriel shaded his eyes with his hand and looked down at the table, but a faint colour came into Evelyn's transparent cheeks. But, said the grey-haired farmer, it was longer still since there had been a Lady Ockram so fair as the next was to be, and he gave the health of Evelyn Warburton.

Then the tenants all stood up and shouted for her, and Sir Gabriel stood up likewise, beside Evelyn. And when the men gave the last and loudest cheer of all there was a voice not theirs, above them all, higher, fiercer, louder—a scream not earthly, shrieking for the bride of Ockram Hall. And the holly and the green boughs over the great chimney-piece shook and slowly waved as if a cool breeze were blowing over them. But the men turned very pale, and many of them set down their glasses, but others let them fall upon the floor for fear. And looking into one another's faces, they were all smiling strangely, a dead smile, like dead Sir Hugh's. One cried out words in Irish, and the fear of death was suddenly upon them all, so that they fled in panic, falling over one another like wild beasts in the burning forest, when the thick smoke runs along before the flame; and the tables were overset, and drinking glasses and bottles were broken in heaps, and the dark red wine crawled like blood upon the polished floor.

Sir Gabriel and Evelyn stood alone at the head of the table before the wreck of the feast, not daring to turn to see each other, for each knew that the other smiled. But his right arm held her and his left hand clasped her right as they stared before them; and but for the shadows of her hair one might not have told their two faces apart. They listened long, but the cry came not again, and the dead smile faded from their lips, while each remembered that Sir Hugh Ockram lay in the north vault, smiling in his winding-sheet, in the dark, because he had died with his secret.

So ended the tenants' New Year's dinner. But from that time on Sir Gabriel grew more and more silent, and his face grew even paler and thinner than before. Often without warning and without words, he would rise from his seat, as if something moved him against his will, and he would go out into the rain or the sunshine to the north side of the chapel, and sit on the stone bench, staring at the ground as if he could see through it, and through the vault below, and through the white winding-sheet in the dark, to the dead smile that would not die.

Always when he went out in that way Evelyn came out presently and sat beside him. Once, too, as in summer, their beautiful faces came suddenly near, and their lids drooped, and their red lips were almost joined together. But as their eyes met, they grew wide and wild, so that the white showed in a ring all round the deep violet, and their teeth chattered, and their hands were like hands of corpses, each in the other's, for the terror of what was under their feet, and of what they knew but could not see.

Once, also, Evelyn found Sir Gabriel in the chapel alone, standing before the iron door that led down to the place of death, and in his hand there was the key to the door; but he had not put it into the lock. Evelyn drew him away, shivering, for she had also been driven in waking dreams to see that terrible thing again, and to find out whether it had changed since it had lain there.

'I'm going mad,' said Sir Gabriel, covering his eyes with his hand as he went with her. 'I see it in my sleep, I see it when I am awake—it draws me to it, day and night—and unless I see it I shall die!'

'I know,' answered Evelyn, 'I know. It is as if threads were spun from it, like a spider's, drawing us down to it.' She was silent for a moment, and then she started violently and grasped his arm with a man's strength, and almost screamed the words she spoke. 'But we must not go there!' she cried. 'We must not go!'

Sir Gabriel's eyes were half shut, and he was not moved by the agony of her face.

'I shall die, unless I see it again,' he said, in a quiet voice not like his own. And all that day and that evening he scarcely spoke, thinking of it, always thinking, while Evelyn Warburton quivered from head to foot with a terror she had never known.

She went alone, on a grey winter's morning, to Nurse Macdonald's room in the tower, and sat down beside the great leathern easy-chair, laying her thin white hand upon the withered fingers.

'Nurse,' she said, 'what was it that Uncle Hugh should have told you, that night before he died? It must have been an awful secret—and yet, though you asked him, I feel somehow that you know it, and that you know why he used to smile so dreadfully.'

The old woman's head moved slowly from side to side.

'I only guess—I shall never know,' she answered slowly in her cracked little voice.

'But what do you guess? Who am I? Why did you ask who my father was? You know I am Colonel Warburton's daughter, and my mother was Lady Ockram's sister, so that Gabriel and I are cousins. My father was killed in Afghanistan. What secret can there be?'

'I do not know. I can only guess.'

'Guess what?' asked Evelyn imploringly, and pressing the soft withered hands, as she leaned forward. But Nurse Macdonald's wrinkled lids dropped suddenly over her queer blue eyes, and her lips shook a little with her breath, as if she were asleep.

Evelyn waited. By the fire the Irish maid was knitting fast, and the needles clicked like three or four clocks ticking against each other. And the real clock on the wall solemnly ticked alone, checking off the seconds of the woman who was a hundred years old, and had not many days left. Outside the ivy branch beat the window in the wintry blast, as it had beaten against the glass a hundred years ago.

Then as Evelyn sat there she felt again the waking of a horrible desire—the sickening wish to go down, down to the thing in the north vault, and to open the winding-sheet, and see whether it had changed; and she held Nurse Macdonald's hands as if to keep herself in her place and fight against the appalling attraction of the evil dead.

But the old cat that kept Nurse Macdonald's feet warm, lying always on the bag footstool, got up and stretched itself, and looked up into Evelyn's eyes, while its back arched, and its tail thickened and bristled, and its ugly pink lips drew back in a devilish grin, showing its sharp teeth. Evelyn stared at it, half fascinated by its ugliness. Then the creature suddenly put out one paw with all its claws spread, and spat at the girl, and all at once the grinning cat was like the smiling corpse far down below, so that Evelyn shivered down to her small feet, and covered her face with her free hand, lest Nurse Macdonald should wake and see the dead smile there, for she could feel it.

The old woman had already opened her eyes again, and she touched her cat with the end of her crutch-stick, whereupon its back went down and its tail shrunk, and it sidled back to its place on the bag footstool. But its yellow eyes looked up sideways at Evelyn, between the slits of its lids.

'What is it that you guess, nurse?' asked the young girl again.

'A bad thing—a wicked thing. But I dare not tell you, lest it might not be true, and the very thought should blast your life. For if I guess right, he meant that you should not know, and that you two should marry, and pay for his old sin with your souls.'

'He used to tell us that we ought not to marry——'

'Yes—he told you that, perhaps—but it was as if a man put poisoned meat before a starving beast, and said "do not eat" but never raised his hand to take the meat away. And if he told you that you should not marry, it was because he hoped you would; for of all men living or dead, Hugh Ockram was the falsest man that ever told a cowardly lie, and the cruelest that ever hurt a weak woman, and the worst that ever loved a sin.'

'But Gabriel and I love each other,' said Evelyn very sadly.

Nurse Macdonald's old eyes looked far away, at sights seen long ago, and that rose in the grey winter air amid the mists of an ancient youth.

'If you love, you can die together,' she said, very slowly. 'Why should you live, if it is true? I am a hundred years old. What has life given me? The beginning is fire; the end is a heap of ashes; and between the end and the beginning lies all the pain of the world. Let me sleep, since I cannot die.'

Then the old woman's eyes closed again, and her head sank a little lower upon her breast.

So Evelyn went away and left her asleep, with the cat asleep on the bag footstool; and the young girl tried to forget Nurse Macdonald's words, but she could not, for she heard them over and over again in the wind, and behind her on the stairs. And as she grew sick with fear of the frightful unknown evil to which her soul was bound, she felt a bodily something pressing her, and pushing her, and forcing her on, and from the other side she felt the threads that drew her mysteriously: and when she shut her eyes, she saw in the chapel behind the altar, the low iron door through which she must pass to go to the thing.

And as she lay awake at night, she drew the sheet over her face, lest she should see shadows on the wall beckoning to her; and the sound of her own warm breath made whisperings in her ears, while she held the mattress with her hands, to keep from getting up and going to the chapel. It would have been easier if there had not been a way thither through the library, by a door which was never locked. It would be fearfully easy to take her candle and go softly through the sleeping house. And the key of the vault lay under the altar behind a stone that turned. She knew the little secret. She could go alone and see.

But when she thought of it, she felt her hair rise on her head, and first she shivered so that the bed shook, and then the horror went through her in a cold thrill that was agony again, like myriads of icy needles, boring into her nerves.

4

The old clock in Nurse Macdonald's tower struck midnight. From her room she could hear the creaking chains and weights in their box in the corner of the staircase, and overhead the jarring of the rusty lever that lifted the hammer. She had heard it all her life. It struck eleven strokes clearly, and then came the twelfth, with a dull half stroke, as though the hammer were too weary to go on, and had fallen asleep against the bell.

The old cat got up from the bag footstool and stretched itself, and Nurse Macdonald opened her ancient eyes and looked slowly round the room by the dim light of the night lamp. She touched the cat with her crutch-stick, and it lay down upon her feet. She drank a few drops from her cup and went to sleep again.

But downstairs Sir Gabriel sat straight up as the clock struck, for he had dreamed a fearful dream of horror, and his heart stood still, till he awoke at its stopping, and it beat again furiously with his breath, like a wild thing set free. No Ockram had ever known fear waking, but sometimes it came to Sir Gabriel in his sleep.

He pressed his hands to his temples as he sat up in bed, and his hands were icy cold, but his head was hot. The dream faded far, and in its place there came the master thought that racked his life; with the thought also came the sick twisting of his lips in the dark that would have been a smile. Far off, Evelyn Warburton dreamed that the dead smile was on her mouth, and awoke, starting with a little moan, her face in her hands, shivering.

But Sir Gabriel struck a light and got up and began to walk up and down his great room. It was midnight, and he had barely slept an hour, and in the north of Ireland the winter nights are long.

'I shall go mad,' he said to himself, holding his forehead. He knew that it was true. For weeks and months the possession of the thing had grown upon him like a disease, till he could think of nothing without thinking first of that. And now all at once it outgrew his strength, and he knew that he must be its instrument or lose his mind—that he must do the deed he hated and feared, if he could fear anything, or that something would snap in his brain and divide him from life while he was yet alive. He took the candlestick in his hand, the old-fashioned heavy candlestick that had always been used by the head of the house. He did not think of dressing, but went as he was, in his silk night clothes and his slippers, and he opened the door. Everything was very still in the great old house. He shut the door behind him and walked noiselessly on the carpet through the long corridor. A cool breeze blew over his shoulder and blew the flame of his candle straight out from him. Instinctively he stopped and looked round, but all was still, and the upright flame burned steadily. He walked on, and instantly a strong draught was behind him, almost extinguishing the light. It seemed to blow him on his way, ceasing whenever he turned, coming again when he went on—invisible, icy.

Down the great staircase to the echoing hall he went, seeing nothing but the flaring flame of the candle standing away from him over the guttering wax, while the cold wind blew over his shoulder and through his hair. On he passed through the open door into the library, dark with old books and carved bookcases; on through the door in the shelves, with painted shelves on it, and the imitated backs of books, so that one needed to know where to find it—and it shut itself after him with a soft click. He entered the low-arched passage, and though the door was shut behind him and fitted tightly in its frame, still the cold breeze blew the flame forward as he walked. And he was not afraid; but his face was very pale, and his eyes were wide and bright, looking before him, seeing already in the dark air the picture of the thing beyond. But in the chapel he stood still, his hand on the little turning stone tablet in the back of the stone altar. On the tablet were engraved words: '*Clavis sepulchri Clarissimorum Dominorum De Ockram*'—('the key to the vault of the most illustrious lords of Ockram'). Sir Gabriel paused and listened. He fancied that he heard a sound far off in the great house where all had been so still, but it did not come again. Yet he waited at the last, and looked at the low iron door. Beyond it, down the long descent, lay his father uncoffined, six months dead, corrupt, terrible in his clinging shroud. The strangely preserving air of the vault could not yet have done its work completely. But on the thing's ghastly features, with their half-dried, open eyes, there would still be the frightful smile with which the man had died—the smile that haunted——

As the thought crossed Sir Gabriel's mind, he felt his lips writhing, and he struck his own mouth in wrath with the back of his hand so fiercely that a drop of blood ran down his chin, and another, and more, falling back in the gloom upon the chapel pavement. But still his bruised lips twisted themselves. He turned the tablet by the simple secret. It needed no safer fastening, for had each Ockram been coffined in pure gold, and had the door been open wide, there was not a man in Tyrone brave enough to go down to that place, saving Gabriel Ockram himself, with his angel's face and his thin, white hands, and his sad unflinching eyes. He took the great old key and set it into the lock of the iron door; and the heavy, rattling noise echoed down the descent beyond like footsteps, as if a watcher had stood behind the iron and were running away within, with heavy dead feet. And though he was standing still, the cool wind was from behind him, and blew the flame of the candle against the iron panel. He turned the key.

Sir Gabriel saw that his candle was short. There were new ones on the altar, with long candlesticks, and he lit one, and left his own burning on the floor. As he set it down on the pavement his lip began to bleed again, and another drop fell upon the stones.

He drew the iron door open and pushed it back against the chapel wall, so that it should not shut of itself, while he was within; and the horrible draught of the sepulchre came up out of the depths in his face, foul and dark. He went in, but though the fetid air met him, yet the flame of the tall candle was blown straight from him against the wind while he walked down the easy incline with steady steps, his loose slippers slapping the pavement as he trod.

He shaded the candle with his hand, and his fingers seemed to be made of wax and blood as the light shone through them. And in spite of him the unearthly draught forced the flame forward, till it was blue over the black wick, and it seemed as if it must go out. But he went straight on, with shining eyes.

The downward passage was wide, and he could not always see the walls by the struggling light, but he knew when he was in the place of death by the larger, drearier echo of his steps in the greater space, and by the sensation of a distant blank wall. He stood still, almost enclosing the flame of the candle in the hollow of his hand. He could see a little, for his eyes were growing used to the gloom. Shadowy forms were outlined in the dimness, where the biers of the Ockrams stood crowded together, side by side, each with its straight, shrouded corpse, strangely preserved by the dry air, like the empty shell that the locust sheds in summer. And a few steps before him he saw clearly the dark shape of headless Sir Vernon's iron coffin, and he knew that nearest to it lay the thing he sought.

He was as brave as any of those dead men had been, and they were his fathers, and he knew that sooner or later he should lie there himself, beside Sir Hugh, slowly drying to a parchment shell. But he was still alive, and he closed his eyes a moment, and three great drops stood on his forehead.

Then he looked again, and by the whiteness of the winding-sheet he knew his father's corpse, for all the others were brown with age; and, moreover, the flame of the candle was blown toward it. He made four steps till he reached it, and suddenly the light burned straight and high, shedding a dazzling yellow glare upon the fine linen that was all white, save over the face, and where the joined hands were laid on the breast. And at those places ugly stains had spread, darkened with outlines of the features and of the tight-clasped fingers. There was a frightful stench of drying death.

As Sir Gabriel looked down, something stirred behind him, softly at first, then more noisily, and something fell to the stone floor with a dull thud and rolled up to his feet; he started back, and saw a withered head lying almost face upward on the pavement, grinning at him. He felt the cold sweat standing on his face, and his heart beat painfully.

For the first time in all his life that evil thing which men call fear was getting hold of him, checking his heart-strings as a cruel driver checks a quivering horse, clawing at his backbone with icy hands, lifting his hair with freezing breath, climbing up and gathering in his midriff with leaden weight.

Yet presently he bit his lip and bent down, holding the candle in one hand, to lift the shroud back from the head of the corpse with the other. Slowly he lifted it. Then it clove to the half-dried skin of the face, and his hand shook as if someone had struck him on the elbow, but half in fear and half in anger at himself, he pulled it, so that it came away with a little ripping sound. He caught his breath as he held it, not yet throwing it back, and not yet looking. The horror was working in him, and he felt that old Vernon Ockram was standing up in his iron coffin, headless, yet watching him with the stump of his severed neck.

While he held his breath he felt the dead smile twisting his lips. In sudden wrath at his own misery, he tossed the death-stained linen backward, and looked at last. He ground his teeth lest he should shriek aloud.

There it was, the thing that haunted him, that haunted Evelyn Warburton, that was like a blight on all that came near him.

The dead face was blotched with dark stains, and the thin, grey hair was matted about the discoloured forehead. The sunken lids were half open, and the candlelight gleamed on something foul where the toad eyes had lived.

But yet the dead thing smiled, as it had smiled in life; the ghastly lips were parted and drawn wide and tight upon the wolfish teeth, cursing still, and still defying hell to do its worst—defying, cursing, and always and for ever smiling alone in the dark.

Sir Gabriel opened the winding-sheet where the hands were, and the blackened, withered fingers were closed upon something stained and mottled. Shivering from head to foot, but fighting like a man in agony for his life, he tried to take the package from the dead man's hold. But as he pulled at it the claw-like fingers seemed to close more tightly, and when he pulled harder the shrunken hands and arms rose from the corpse with a horrible look of life following his motion—then as he wrenched the sealed packet loose at last, the hands fell back into their place still folded.

He set down the candle on the edge of the bier to break the seals from the stout paper. And, kneeling on one knee, to get a better light, he read what was within, written long ago in Sir Hugh's queer hand.

He was no longer afraid.

He read how Sir Hugh had written it all down that it might perchance be a witness of evil and of his hatred; how he had loved Evelyn Warburton, his wife's sister; and how his wife had died of a broken heart with his curse upon her, and how Warburton and he had fought side by side in Afghanistan, and Warburton had fallen; but Ockram had brought his comrade's wife back a full year later, and little Evelyn, her child, had been born in Ockram Hall. And next, how he had wearied of the mother, and she had died like her sister with his curse on her. And then, how Evelyn had been brought up as his niece, and how he had trusted that his son Gabriel and his daughter, innocent and unknowing, might love and marry, and the souls of the women he had betrayed might suffer another anguish before eternity was out.

And, last of all, he hoped that some day, when nothing could be undone, the two might find his writing and live on, not daring to tell the truth for their children's sake and the world's word, man and wife.

This he read, kneeling beside the corpse in the north vault, by the light of the altar candle; and when he had read it all, he thanked God aloud that he had found the secret in time. But when he rose to his feet and looked down at the dead face it was changed, and the smile was gone from it for ever, and the jaw had fallen a little, and the tired, dead lips were relaxed. And then there was a breath behind him and close to him, not cold like that which had blown the flame of the candle as he came, but warm and human. He turned suddenly.

There she stood, all in white, with her shadowy golden hair—for she had risen from her bed and had followed him noiselessly, and had found him reading, and had herself read over his shoulder. He started violently when he saw her, for his nerves were unstrung—and then he cried out her name in the still place of death:

'Evelyn!'

'My brother!' she answered, softly and tenderly, putting out both hands to meet his.

9

STEPHEN HALL

By One, By Two, and By Three

1

It was while I was at Cambridge that I first came to know Angus Macbane. We met casually, as undergraduates do, at the breakfast table of a mutual friend, or rather acquaintance, and I remember being struck with the odd, cynical remarks my neighbour threw out at rare intervals, as he watched the argument we had started, about heaven knows what or what not, and were maintaining on either side with the boundless confidence and almost boundless ignorance peculiar to Freshmen. I seem to see him now, leaning back after the meal in a deep armchair, with his host's cat purring her contentment on his knee. He never looked at the semicircle of disputants round the fire, but blew beautiful rings of cigarette-smoke into the air—or gazed with a critical expression, under half-shut lids, at the photographs of actresses forming a galaxy of popular beauty above the mantelpiece. Then he would emit some sentence, sometimes sensible, oftener wildly nonsensical, but always original, unexpected—a stone dropped with a splash and a ripple into the stream of conversation.

I do not think that he showed any very particular power of mind at the breakfast party, or indeed afterwards. What made one notice him was the faint aroma of oddity that seemed to cling to him, and all his ways and doings. He was incalculable, indefinable. This was what made a good many dislike him, and made me, with one or two others, conceive a queer liking for him. I always had a taste, secret or confessed, for those delicate degrees of oddity which require a certain natural bent to appreciate them at all. Extravagance of any kind commands notice, and compels a choice between admiration and contempt; moreover, it generally—and not least at a University—invites imitation. No one ever either admired or despised Macbane, so far as I know, and no one could ever have imitated him. The singularity lay rather in the man himself than in any special habit. For Macbane was not definably different from other young men. He was of medium height, slightly made, but not spare; his face had hardly any colour, and his hair and moustache were light. His eyes were of a tint difficult to define; sometimes they seemed blue, sometimes grey, sometimes greenish, and he had a trick of keeping them half shut, and of looking away from anyone who was with him. This peculiarity is popularly supposed to be the sign of a knave; in his case it was merely a part of the man's general oddity, and did not create any special distrust.

Our acquaintance, thus casually begun, ripened into a strange sort of friendship. Macbane and I saw very little of each other; we did not talk much, nor go for walks and rows together, nor confide to each other our doings and plans, as friends are supposed to do. On rainy afternoons I would stroll round to his rooms and enter, to find him generally seated before the fire, caressing his cat. We did not greet each other; but I generally took up one of the numerous strange and rare books that he contrived to accumulate, though he spent very little money. This I would read, occasionally dropping a remark which he would answer with some cynical, curt sentence, and then both of us relapsed into silence. Tea would be made and drunk, and we sometimes sat thus till dinner-time, or later. Yet though I always felt as if I bored Macbane, I still went to his rooms, and when I did not go for some time he would generally, with an air of extreme lassitude and reluctance, come round to my quarters, there to sit and smoke and turn over my books in much the same way as I did when I visited him.

Angus Macbane never told me anything much about himself or his family; he was one of the most reticent of mortals. All he ever did in that way was to say once in an abrupt manner that some of his ancestors had been executed for witchcraft, and when I vented some of the usual commonplaces on the barbarous ignorance and cruelty of those times, he cut me short by remarking in a tone of profound conviction that he thought his ancestors thoroughly deserved their fate, and that their condemnation was the only oasis of justice in a desert of judicial infamy.

From other sources, however, I discovered that Angus Macbane was an only son, whose parents had both died soon after his birth, leaving nothing behind them but their child. An uncle, a rich Glasgow merchant, had provided in no very lavish way for the boy's education, and was supposed to be intending to leave him a large share of his property. This was all I gathered from those people who made a point of knowing everything about everybody, and there is no lack of them at Universities.

Two striking peculiarities there were about Macbane, which stood out from the general oddity of the man. The first was his fondness for cats, or, to speak more accurately, the fondness of cats for him. He had always one pet cat—generally a black one—in his rooms, and sometimes more, and when he had two, they were invariably jealous of each other. But he seemed to have an irresistible attraction for cats in general. They would come to him uncalled, and show the greatest pleasure when he noticed or caressed them. He did not stroke a cat often, but when he did, it was with a certain delicate and sensitive action of the hand that seemed to delight the animal above everything. So marked was the attraction he exercised that a scientific acquaintance accused him of carrying valerian in his pockets.

The other peculiarity was in his books. He had picked up, in ways only known to himself, a very fine collection of early works on demonology and witchcraft. A more complete account, from all sides, of 'Satan's Invisible World' was seldom accumulated. There were books, pamphlets, and broadsheets in Latin, French, German, English, Italian, and Spanish, and some old family manuscripts relating to the arts or trials of warlocks and witches. There was even an old Arabic manual of sorcery, though this I am sure he could not read. Most of these works were of the sixteenth and seventeenth centuries, since which period, indeed, civilization has ordained a 'close time' for witches, and any treatises on the black art dated after that time Macbane not only did not buy, but as a rule refused to accept as gifts. 'Early in the eighteenth century,' he once remarked, 'men lost their faith in the devil, and they have not as yet recovered it sufficiently to produce any witchcraft worthy of the name.'

And indeed he had the greatest abhorrence and contempt for modern Spiritualism, mesmerism, esoteric Buddhism, etc., and the only occasion during his Cambridge life on which I saw him really lose his temper was when a mild youth, destined to holy orders, called on him and asked him to join a society for investigating ghostly and occult phenomena. He turned on the intruder with something like ferocity, saying that he did not see why people wanted to be wiser than their ancestors, and that the old way of selling oneself to the devil, and getting the price duly paid, was far better, both in its financial and moral aspects, than paying foreign impostors to show the way to his place of business.

'Though what the devil wants at all with such souls as yours,' he added, meditatively, 'is the one point in his character that I have never been able to understand. It is a weakness on his part—I am afraid it is a weakness!'

The incipient curate turned and fled.

A few sayings of this kind, reported and distorted in many little social circles, gave Angus Macbane an evil reputation which he hardly deserved. The College authorities looked askance on him, and some of them, I believe, would have been thankful if his conduct had given them a pretext for 'sending him down', whether for a term or for ever. But no offence or glaring irregularity could be even plausibly alleged against him. He attended the College chapel frequently, and never lost an opportunity of hearing the Athanasian Creed.

'When I hear all those worthy people mumbling their sing-song formulas, without attaching any meaning to them, and chanting forth vague curses into the air,' he once said to me, 'I close my eyes, and can sometimes almost fancy myself on the Brocken, in the midst of the Witches' Sabbath.'

This devout assiduity was only reckoned as one point more against him, for Angus Macbane belonged by birth to the very straitest of Scotch Presbyterians, and evinced no desire to quit them, or to dispute the harshest and most repulsive of the doctrines handed down from his ancestors. Yet to my knowledge he never went near any Presbyterian chapel, but preferred, as his worthy uncle said, 'to bow in the house of Rimmon'.

This uncle, as I gradually divined, was the one being whom my friend regarded with something like hatred. Mr Duncan Macdonald was the brother of Macbane's mother. He was a big, red, sandy man, rich, unmarried, and not unkindly in nature, and an ordinary person with a little tact could have managed him, if not with complete satisfaction, at any rate to no small profit. It is true, the manufacturer was one of those self-made men who think that no man has any business to be otherwise than self-made; but by flattering his pride, he could easily have been induced to support his nephew in ease, and even in luxury and extravagance, if enough show were made for the money. But he was a Philistine of the Philistines, two thirds of his life dominated by gain, and the rest by a rigid sense of duty. Material success and respectability were his two golden calves, and to both of these his nephew's every thought and act did dishonour. Angus Macbane could not have been made a successful man by any process less summary and complete than the creation of a world for his needs alone, and not even this would have given him respectability. He could not live without aid from his uncle, but he accepted from him a mere pittance, which, grudgingly taken, soon came to be as grudgingly given. Yet when he forced himself to compete for scholarships and prizes which would have made him partly independent, he missed them in a way which would have been wilful in any other man. His essays were a byword among examiners for their cynical originality, perverse ability, and instinctive avoidance of the obvious avenues to success. Thus he was constrained to depend on that scanty income of which every coin seemed flung in his face. With his developed misanthropy and contempt for ordinary men, he would at all times have been intolerant of the mere existence of such a man as his uncle, and that he himself should be hopelessly indebted to such a creature for every morsel he ate, for every book he read, was a sheer monstrosity to his mind— or so I should conjecture from what I knew of the two. Angus seldom willingly mentioned his uncle, and when he did so it was with a deadly intensity of contempt in his tone—not his words—such as I never heard before or since.

2

An end comes to all things, and my time at Cambridge, which had passed as swiftly for me as for most men, and left me with the usual abundant third year's crop of unfulfilled purposes, came to its end in due course. Angus Macbane had 'gone down' before I did, with a high second-class degree in mathematics, chiefly gained, as I happened to hear from an examiner, by a very few problems which hardly anyone else solved. A serious quarrel with his uncle followed on this ill-success, but from motives of family duty and respectability Mr Macdonald continued to pay his nephew enough to maintain life. No relation of his, he felt, must come to the workhouse.

For a year or two I lost sight of Macbane, and when I saw him again he was living in lodgings in an obscure street of a London suburb. I had learnt his address from another old college friend, Frank Standish by name, who had kept up relations with Angus. Frank was a complete contrast to Macbane. He was a tall, hearty, handsome, athletic fellow, successful in everything he undertook, and was now making his way as an engineer, and likely to do well. It was this opposition in their natures that had begotten their friendship. I have seen them sitting together at Cambridge, Standish chatting on by the hour, and Macbane watching him in contented silence. As someone remarked, it was like the famous friendship of a racehorse and a cat.

I was myself now an under-master at a large day-school, and my evenings were in general free, so one night I called for Standish at his lodging, and together we trudged off to find Macbane.

Our path led through one of those strange, uncanny wildernesses that lie about the outskirts of every great and growing town. Skeletons of unfinished houses, bristling with scaffolding poles, loomed on us at intervals through the rainy mist. The roads were long heaps of brickbats and loose stones, already varied with blades of coarse grass. The path we followed was seamed across with the ruts of heavy carts that had gone to and from the half-built houses, and we stumbled over posts and through plashy pools, along the ghostly highway, completely deserted now that the workmen were gone, and stretching its miles of raw ruin through the autumn mist. Standish whistled cheerily as he strode on through the desolation, and I was comforted to have him with me. I think I should almost have felt afraid but for his presence.

We crossed the No Man's Land of chaotic brick and mortar, and found ourselves in a street of mean new houses. At No. 21, Wolseley

Road, Standish paused and rang. A slatternly maid-of-all-work answered the bell, and ushered us into the presence of Angus Macbane.

He was sitting by a poor little fire, in a shabby armchair, with his black cat on his knee as usual, and a volume of demonology in his hand, and, save that the room was small, cheaply furnished, and hideously papered, and the occupant looked thinner and wearier, we could have fancied ourselves at Cambridge again. But after the first greetings I soon noticed that Macbane was changed for the worst since I had seen him last. He did not seem at all dissipated, nor had he acquired the air of meanness and shiftiness that marks the needy adventurer, but there was a genuineness, almost a desperation, in his cynical utterances, which they had not had before—a hopelessness of expression and an irritability which I did not like. The misanthropy at which he had played before was now in grim earnest.

He told us a little—very little, and that reluctantly—of his own way of life. He was doing nothing of any moment—a struggling, unknown writer, spasmodically trying to secure some literary foothold, and failing always, whether by the fatality which attended him specially, or by the same chances as befall any author. Added to this misery was the consciousness of his dependence on his uncle, which was bitterer to him, I could see, than ever. He began to talk about Mr Macdonald of his own accord, and that was always a bad sign.

'Do you know,' he said, with a bitter laugh, 'my worthy relative is coming out here before long? He writes me that he is due in London on business in a fortnight or so, and will pay me a visit to see if I am still given over to the same reprobate mind as before, and opposed to what *he* calls my duty. Won't you come and see the fun, you two? I think I know how to aggravate him now, perfectly well. I assure you, at my last interview with him, I made him swear within three minutes—and he an elder!'

'I say, Macbane,' Standish put in, in his good-natured way, 'don't carry that game too far. The old chap is good for a lot if only you don't rub him up the wrong way. If you rile him this time, ten to one he cuts you off with a shilling—and then where will you be?'

'If he only would die!' Macbane went on, not seeming to hear his friend's remonstrance. 'Fellows like that have no sense of fitness. When I saw him last he reminded me of one of those big, fat, coarse speckled spiders that you want to kill, only they make such a mess. I should so like to murder him, if I could do it by deputy.'

He was joking, of course, but there was more earnestness than I liked in his manner. I looked at Standish, and he at me, before I spoke.

'If those are your sentiments,' I said, echoing his light tone, 'we had better come to prevent bloodshed.'

'Yes, do come,' Angus resumed, 'and if you will kindly take off his head outside, I shall be greatly obliged to you. Bring a delightful rusty old axe, Standish, with plenty of notches in the blade. It will be so nice to be like one of those dear Italian despots, and get one's assassination done for one. Though there are better ways than hiring a bravo, even. An ancestor of mine——' and here he stopped suddenly.

'Well, what did your ancestor do?' asked I.

'Oh,' said Macbane coolly, 'he raised a devil of some sort and got scragged by it himself.'

As he spoke these trivial words, there came a faint sound at the door as of something scratching very gently on the panels. I turned to Macbane and asked:—

'Is that your dog, Mac?'

'My dog!' he said, with a shudder. 'Why, I *hate* dogs. I never have one near my room by any chance—except when the landlady sends me up sausages.'

'Perhaps it is another cat come to make friends with you,' suggested Standish. 'There it is again. I will let it in, whatever it is.'

He flung the door open, and the chill air rushed in from the draughty passage and stairs. There was nothing outside or in sight, and he shut the door again with a bang.

'I heard it distinctly,' he said, in the aggrieved tone of one who fancies he has made himself ridiculous. 'What could it have been?'

'Wind, perhaps, or a rat,' said Macbane, lightly. 'There are plenty of rats in the place, and I am glad of it, for it is the only thing that prevents me from expecting the house to fall every moment. When it is going to fall the rats will all run out, and my cat Mephistopheles will run out after them, and I shall run out after Mephistopheles, and the landlady and the first-floor lodgers, and the landlady's cat that eats my tea and sugar, will all be squelched together, to the joy of all good cats and men—eh, Mephisto? Why, what ails the cat?'

For Mephistopheles was standing upon his master's lap, with back arched and tail rigid and bristling, glaring into the darkest corner of the little room, and hissing in a passion of mingled rage and fear. Then, before anyone could stop him, the cat made one leap at the window, with a yell and a great crash of glass, and was gone, leaving us staring at each other.

Angus Macbane spoke first, with a forced laugh.

'There goes my cat,' he said, 'and there goes one-and-nine for broken glass. Cats I may get again, but one-and-ninepence—never. A cat with nine lives, a shilling with nine pence—all lost, all lost!' And he went on laughing in a shrill, hysterical way that I did not at all like. During the pause that followed, Standish looked at his watch.

'It is pretty late now,' he said, 'and I have a lot of working drawings to prepare tomorrow. Goodnight, Macbane. If I come across your cat, I'll remonstrate with him for quitting us so rudely. But no doubt he will come back of himself.'

As Standish said this the rest of the large pane through which the cat had leaped suddenly fell out with a startling crash into the street, making us all wince.

'It was cracked already,' remarked Angus; 'and the glazier does not allow for the pieces. Goodnight, both of you. I fancy I have something to do myself, too.'

I was surprised, and a little hurt, at being thus practically turned out by my friend—for I had expressed no intention of departing, and it was not really very late; but I was not sorry to go now, and have the solace of Standish's cheery company home. A curious, undefined feeling of apprehension was creeping over me, and I wanted to be out in the night air, and shake off my uneasiness by a brisk walk.

We went downstairs, leaving Macbane brooding in his chair. As the landlady saw us out I slipped a half-crown into her hand.

'Mr Macbane's window got broken tonight,' I said. 'Will you have it mended, and not say anything about it to him?'

I knew that he would probably forget the occurrence if not reminded of it. Standish nodded approval, and we went out into the mist.

We walked on in silence till we turned out of the lamp-lit and inhabited part, and then my companion remarked, abruptly:

'That makes one-and-threepence I owe you, Eliot,' and relapsed into silence, not even whistling as he strode along.

We had reached nearly the middle of the long, artificial desert, where a street was some day to be, when Standish stopped and caught me by the arm.

'Eliot, what is that?' he whispered.

We both stood still and listened. From the waste land beyond one of the skeleton houses came a fearful cry, whether of a child or an animal we could not tell—a scream of mere pain and terror, intense and thrilling, neither human nor bestial. Then there was a deep, snarling growl, and the yell died into a choking gurgle, and suddenly fell silent.

'Come on!' Standish gasped, and ran with all his speed in the direction of the sound.

I followed as fast as my shorter legs and wind would take me over the stiff, slimy clay of the waste land, and after a few minutes found him bending over a little dark heap on the ground at the edge of a puddle.

'Have you got a match?' he said.

I nodded—I was too much out of breath to speak—and pulled out my matchbox. I struck a light, screening it with my hand, and we both looked earnestly at the black lump at our feet.

'Bah!' said Standish, as he mopped the perspiration from his face. 'Why, it's only a cat, and it sounded like a baby.'

It was the body of a large black cat, still warm and quivering, but quite dead. The throat was almost entirely severed, and the blood had streamed out, darkly streaking the thick, yellow water of the pool. Of what had killed it there was no sign or sound, only in the soft clay beside the puddle there were marks which seemed those of the poor cat's feet, and other footprints like these, but larger. I pointed them out to Standish.

'I see what it was,' he said, as we trudged laboriously back to the road. 'The cat was out there, and some beast of a dog caught it and killed it—though what cat or dog should be doing there is more than I can say. What teeth the brute must have! Ugh! I hope he's not waiting round to take another bite.'

We got back to the road unbitten, and went on our way in silence, till I said:

'Standish, do you know, that cat was very like Macbane's?'

'Do you know, Eliot,' was his answer, 'that is just what I was going to tell you!'

And not another word did he utter, till I left him at his door and said goodnight.

3

Macbane was never a good correspondent, but he duly informed us of the date of his uncle's expected visit, and when the day came I called for Standish in the evening as before, and we trudged off through another sloppy mist. Standish, good, thoughtful fellow, had brought with him in his overcoat pocket a bottle of very fine old Irish whiskey, which he had long been treasuring up for some festal occasion, but now intended to devote to the mollifying, if possible, of Mr Macdonald.

'Every glass he takes of this,' he solemnly assured me as we went on, 'will be worth a hundred a year to Macbane.'

We did not go by the same dreary road that we had taken before. Frank declared with a shudder that the last cry of that cat was still ringing in his ears, and that he could not stand the ghastly place again. I was rather surprised at his unwonted nervousness, but readily acquiesced in it. So we went a mile or so out of our way, keeping along endless streets of shabby-genteel houses, which were sufficiently hideous, but not appalling, and about nine in the evening we reached Wolseley Road.

I was surprised and almost shocked to notice the change that had passed over Macbane in the few weeks since I had seen him last. He did not seem worse in health—on the contrary, there was at times a nervous alacrity about his movements which I had not remarked before. But his face and expression seemed to have darkened, as it were, and grown evil. His college cynicism had already turned into misanthropy, and now, I thought, it had developed into a positive malevolence. He still was silent and brooding after the first greetings, but he no longer seemed dejected. Altogether a transformation of some kind had come to him, such that I, though not very impressionable, was rather inclined to fear than to pity him.

The conversation, as was natural, turned on the uncle, who might appear at any moment now. Standish and I joined in urging on our friend the necessity of attempting conciliation, of showing some semblance of submission. We had more than once induced him to do so before, though his perverse temper generally made him unable to do more than avert an instant stoppage of the supplies; but tonight he was obstinate, and even spoke as if he were the aggrieved party, and his uncle the one to make advances.

'If the old fool cares to be civil,' he said, fiercely, 'then there's an end of it; and if not, there's an end, too. I am tired of humouring him.'

As he spoke the 'old fool's' heavy tread was heard on the stairs, and in another minute he entered. He was a big, strong, red-faced, coarse-looking fellow, with sandy whiskers and grizzled hair, who nodded awkwardly to us, and gave a surly greeting to his nephew, who sat still in his armchair, looking into the fire with half-shut eyes.

Mr Duncan Macdonald seemed disconcerted by our presence, and I offered to withdraw; but Macbane would not let us.

'You see, uncle,' he remarked, still keeping his eyes averted and using the familiar title solely, I am convinced, because he knew the uncle did not like it, 'these gentlemen know all about our little affairs, and they had better hear your version of matters now than my version afterwards. Besides, one of them is going to be a literary man, and write a tale with Scotch characters in it, and you will be quite a godsend for him, as raw material for a study. If you want to swear at me, pray don't mind him; there is nothing that tells more in literature than a little aboriginal profanity, properly accented.'

This was a bad beginning for an interview, and would have been worse still had Mr Macdonald been able fully to understand his nephew's speech. What he did understand, however, obviously offended him, and he began to address Macbane in no very conciliatory tones, though at first with a forced moderation of language and strained English accent which were evidently the result of the young man's taunt. Then, as Macbane did not answer, but sat still looking into the fire his uncle began to lose temper. His language grew broader and stronger, both as Scotch and as reproach. He addressed us with a sort of rough eloquence on the subject of his nephew's miserable laziness, shiftlessness, effeminacy, pointing at him, and showering down vigorous epithets on him. In the midst of his tirade, as he paused for breath, came a low sound of scratching at the door.

'There's that confounded rat again!' cried Standish, glad of any pretext for interrupting the miserable business. 'Dead, for a ducat, this time.'

He dashed open the door as he spoke, but there was nothing to be seen—only the gaslight in the passage, flickering and flaring in the draught, sent strange shadows flitting across the walls.

Frank came back and sat down, and busied himself in uncorking his bottle of whiskey, and setting the kettle on to boil. I took up a book, so as not to seem to observe a scene which I knew must be so painful and humiliating for Macbane. The uncle again plunged into the stream of his invective, and I kept my eyes on the nephew. I knew that he was really quite as passionate as the elder man, and I was afraid of what he might do if he once lost his self-control; but, though a little shiver passed over him sometimes, he was quite silent, leaning back in the armchair, with his head resting on his right hand, and his left arm hanging listlessly over the side of the chair. Presently he began to move the hands languidly to and fro, with the fingers outstretched, and the palm horizontal and slightly hollowed, keeping it more than a foot from the carpet. It was a curious gesture, but he had many odd tricks of the kind.

At last Mr Macdonald, having spent his store of abuse without any response, began, I fancy, to feel a little ashamed of himself, and became more conciliatory, letting fall some hints as to the terms on which he might even yet receive his prodigal nephew back to favour. The manner of his overtures was far more offensive than their substance, and to one who could make allowance for the man's coarse nature, there was even a trace of a feeling that might be called kindness. But Macbane was always far more sensitive to externals than other men, and his uncle's condescension, I could see, irritated him far more than his anger. He left off moving his hand to and fro and sat up, clutching the arms of his chair. Then, when the older man had done, he cast one deadly look at him, and shook his head as if he would not trust himself to speak.

'Winna ye speak, ye feckless pauper loon!' roared his uncle, with a string of oaths.

Macbane was silent, but that good fellow Standish interposed at what he thought was the right moment.

'Come, Mr Macdonald,' he said, frankly, 'I don't think you should talk like that. After all, Macbane is your own sister's son, and he is not well now, and you must not come down on him too heavily. Let us have a glass of toddy all round now and part friends, and we three will talk it all over, and make matters smooth tomorrow. We can't do any good tonight.'

As he spoke he got out some tumblers from the cupboard and wiped them clean. The Glasgow manufacturer seemed a little mollified. Nobody could help liking Standish or his whiskey, and all might yet have been well if the devil had not seemed to enter suddenly into Angus Macbane. Standish had poured out a generous measure of the fragrant spirit, and was turning to take the kettle off the hob, when Macbane sprang up like a cat, in a white heat of rage, took the tumbler from the table and flung it right into the grate. The glass rang and crashed, and the flame leapt out blue like a tongue of hell-fire, and Angus stood at the table, quivering all over, with his right hand opening and shutting as if feeling for a weapon. Standish caught him by the arm and pulled him back into his chair.

'Are you mad, Mac?' he exclaimed.

Macbane did not seem to hear, but sat glowering at his uncle. As for Mr Duncan Macdonald, he turned purple with anger. The complicated atrocity of the insult—an outrage at once on kinship, hospitality, thrift, and good whiskey—had smitten him dumb for a moment with surprise and rage. He clenched his fist and struck blindly at his nephew, who was fortunately out of reach. Then he spoke in a husky but distinct voice, slowly, as if registering a vow.

'De'il throttle me,' he said, 'if ever you see bawbee of mine again.'

And he took up his hat and umbrella and turned to the door.

'Done with you, in the devil's name!' cried Macbane.

Without another word the uncle flung the door open, and shut it after him with a crash that shook the house. Then we heard him heavily stamping down the stairs and along the passage, till another great bang proclaimed that he had left the house. This last noise seemed to rouse Macbane from a sort of trance. He sprang up again and rushed to the door and threw it open, as if to pursue his uncle. We were going to stop him, for he looked murderous enough, but instead of dashing downstairs he stopped, flung out his hand with a strange gesture, as if

113

he were pointing at something, and muttered a few words that I could not catch. Then he shut the door and came back slowly to his old seat, as pale as a dead man.

In the excitement of the scene we had none of us noticed the time, but now the cheap little clock on the mantelpiece struck twelve, and recalled the fact that two of us were far away from our lodgings. Standish and I looked at each other. We neither of us liked to leave Macbane alone yet. The man's expression as he flung the glass into the fire, still more his look as he pointed down the stairs, was black enough for anything, and if we went now he seemed quite capable of going out and murdering his uncle, or staying and murdering himself. Standish winked at me and went out quietly. In ten minutes he came back and addressed Macbane, who was sunk in one of his reveries again.

'All right, old fellow,' he said, cheerily; 'your landlady tells me her first floor is vacant, and she will put us two up for the night. So cheer up, Mac. It is a bad business, but we will see you through it, never fear. Now let's brew some punch and be jolly tonight at any rate, as we needn't go.'

Macbane woke up again at this, with a sudden feverish gaiety. He eagerly took the steaming tumbler Frank prepared for him, and drained it at a draught—he whose strongest stimulant was coffee. The whiskey did not seem to affect his head, however. More than this, he hunted out a soiled pack of cards from an obscure drawer, and proposed—he who hated all games—that we should play to pass the time. Dummy whist he thought too slow, and I proposed three-handed euchre, generally called 'cut-throat'. The name seemed to amuse our friend vastly. He insisted on learning the game, and we started at once. His spirits were almost uproarious; I had never seen him like this before. Yet his gaiety was very unequal. Sometimes he would cut the wildest jokes till, in spite of our uneasiness about him, we shrieked with laughter, and again he would sink back in his chair, forgetting to play his hand, and seeming as if he listened for some sound. After some time he went to the door and flung it open, declaring that he was 'stifling in this hole of a room'. Then he sat down again to play, but fidgeted about in his chair impatiently. He was studying his cards, which he held up in his left hand, when I happened to look at the other arm hanging down by his chair.

'For goodness' sake!' I exclaimed, 'what have you done to your hand, Macbane?'

He help up his right hand as I spoke, and looked at it. Palm and fingers were dabbled and smeared with watery blood, fresh and wet. For a moment we stared at each other with pale faces.

'I must have cut my hand over that confounded tumbler or something,' said Macbane at last, with an evident effort. 'I will go and wash it off in my bedroom and be back in a moment.'

He slipped out as he spoke, and we heard him washing his hand, muttering to himself all the time.

Then in a few minutes he came back, keeping his hand in his pocket, and resumed the game. But his former high spirits were gone, and another tumbler of punch failed to recall them. He made constant mistakes, played his hand at random, and at last suddenly threw all his cards down on the table, laid his head on them, and burst into a terrible fit of hysterical sobbing.

We did not know what to do with him, but Standish laid him on the hard sofa, and in a little time he seemed better, though greatly shaken, and managed to control himself. He thanked us in a whisper, and told us to go, and he would get to bed alone. We were still rather anxious about him, but there seemed no reason for staying with him now against his will. The natural reaction had followed on all the strain and excitement, and I, for one, was glad that it was no worse. So we left him beginning, in a slow and dazed way, to get to bed, and descended to try and snatch a little sleep in the genteel misery of the first-floor lodgings.

4

We passed a rather disturbed night in our strange quarters. There were rats in the walls, the windows rattled, and altogether there were more queer noises than one generally hears in houses so new. However, we did get to sleep, and did not wake again till the grey, dull, sodden dawn was making ghastly the little strip of sky visible over the grimy roof of the house opposite. We rose and dressed quickly and went up to Macbane's room. I peered in, but he was still sleeping heavily, so we busied ourselves, as quietly as we could, in preparing breakfast, intending, if our friend did not wake, to go off to our own work for the day, leaving a message for him. We purposed, in a rather vague manner, to do something for poor Macbane. Standish hoped to work on the better feelings of his uncle. I had resolved to devote some of my little savings to keeping my friend out of the workhouse.

We were halfway through our scanty and silent meal, when a heavy tread was heard on the stairs, making apparently for the room where we were.

'What luck!' said the sanguine Standish. 'Here's the penitent uncle, come back after the whiskey. Now leave me alone to manage him. There is half the bottle left.'

The steps came up to the door and paused. Then there was a single sharp rap, and in walked—not Mr Macdonald, but a policeman. If Standish and I had been thieves or coiners taken in the act, we could hardly have shown more confusion.

My first thought was that perhaps Macbane had done something wrong, and this suspicion was confirmed by the officer's first words.

'Beg your pardon, gentlemen,' he said, 'but is either of you Mr A. Macbane?'

'No,' said Standish. 'Mr Macbane is asleep in the next room. What do you want with him?'

'I want him to come with me to the station, as soon as convenient, sir,' was the reply.

'What for?' persisted Standish. 'There's nothing wrong, I hope?'

'Nothing wrong about him; leastways, I don't suppose so, sir,' said the man. 'But there's been foul play somewhere. There's been a body found in the road out a mile off, and a card in the pocket with Mr Macbane's name and address on it, and we want him to come and identify the corpse.'

'Do you know the man's name?' I demanded, divining as I asked what the answer would be.

'His linen was marked "Macdonald," sir,' was the cautious reply.

'And how had he been killed?' asked Standish, breathlessly.

'Throat cut from ear to ear,' said the constable, with terrible conciseness.

We looked at each other, and shuddered. Neither of us had any kind feelings for the man thus suddenly cut off. In fact, we had been thoroughly disgusted with his coarse and sordid temper, and had hoped—in jest, it is true—that he might break his neck over the dismal road he had to traverse.

But this sudden, mysterious, hideous murder—for such it must be—struck us with a chill of horror. My first collected thought, I believe, was a feeling of intense thankfulness that we had not left Macbane alone the night before. Now, at any rate, no suspicion could attach to him.

The policeman looked curiously from one to the other of us.

'Perhaps,' he said, at length, 'one of you two gentlemen would know him?'

'If it is the man I suppose,' answered Standish, 'we certainly do know him. Mr Macdonald is Mr Macbane's uncle, and was here last night. We both saw him leave before twelve o'clock, and have not seen him since.'

'Then, sir,' said the policeman, 'perhaps one of you will wake Mr Macbane and bring him along as soon as he can come, and the other will go to the station at once, for there is never any time to lose in these cases.'

I went into Macbane's bedroom, and Standish took up his hat and followed the policeman out. I touched my friend on the arm. He gasped, yawned, then sat up, rubbed his eyes, and stared wildly round him, till his gaze rested on me.

Then the recollection of what had happened seemed to come back on him in a flash, and he laid his head back on the pillow.

'Is that you, Eliot?' he said. 'I have had such a horrible dream. Thank you for waking me. Must I get up now?'

'Yes, you must, Macbane,' I replied, gravely. 'I will tell you why afterwards.'

'Moralities and mysteries!' said he, in his cynical way. 'Well, I shall soon hear if I am a good boy, and don't take long over my dressing. Reach me my trousers, there's a good fellow.'

As I did so I saw that his right hand was again streaked thinly with dried blood, and I could not help an exclamation.

'Ah!' said he, as I called his attention to it. 'That thing has been bleeding again, I see. Well, I can soon wash it off.'

And he sprang up in his nightshirt, and ran to his wash stand.

'Look here!' he cried, as he plunged his hand into the water. 'Shouldn't I make a lovely Lady Macbeth? "Here's the smell of the blood yet. Oh, oh, oh ! All the perfumes of Araby——" How does it go? "Yet who would have thought the old man had so much blood in him?"'

'For goodness' sake, be quiet!' I screamed. 'Your uncle is lying at the police-station with his throat cut ! Be thankful you had nothing to do with killing him!'

Macbane turned faint and sick, and sat down on his bed again; but he bore the news much better than I had thought he would. To be sure, he had no love for his uncle, and could not be expected to sorrow for him but the shock did not seem somehow to affect him greatly, except by a mere physical repulsion at the horrid manner of his uncle's death. He soon got up again, and went on dressing, listening meanwhile as I told him all I knew about the matter, and as soon as he was ready we went out together.

The police-station was soon reached, and we were admitted into a back room, where Mr Macdonald's body lay on a table, covered with a piece of sacking. There was no difficulty in identifying the corpse. The throat was cut, or rather, as it seemed to me, torn almost through with a frightful wound; but the face was uninjured, and still bore an expression of sudden horror and surprise that was very ghastly. We did not care to look on the sight long. When the covering had been replaced the constables told us all they knew. Some workmen, coming to their work at one of the unfinished houses in the new road, had found the body, lying on its back in a pool of clotted blood. There were no marks of a struggle that they noticed. They had put the corpse on a short ladder left in one of the houses, and carried it to the police-station. The nearest surgeon had been called in, and had pronounced that life had been extinct for some hours. A purse and gold watch were found in the pockets. As to the hand or the weapon that had done the deed, neither the surgeon nor the police would offer any suggestion, and we could not help them. Only, as we left the station, the police-sergeant remarked that he thought he had a clue to the murderer.

'Do you hear that, Standish?' said Macbane, in a mocking tone. '*He* thinks he has a clue.'

We walked back to Wolseley Road and left Macbane there, and

then Standish and I trudged off to our work—for work must be done, whoever has died. And all that afternoon and evening, whenever I was within sight or sound of a main street, my eyes were greeted with sensational placards, and my ears deafened with the shouts of newsboys, reiterating the same burden—'Third edition! Awful murder in Craddock Park! A Glasgow merchant murdered!' and over every placard I seemed to see the vision of the dead face, and that gash in the throat.

The inquest was held a few days afterwards, and of course we all attended it. The story of the quarrel with Angus Macbane came out, in its main outlines, from his evidence and ours, and I could tell from the coroner's pointed questions that he suspected our friend. But there was no reasonable doubt that Duncan Macdonald had been killed within an hour after he left the lodging-house, and it was perfectly clear from our evidence and the landlady's that Angus Macbane had been in his room long after this, and practically certain that he had never left the house at all that night.

The medical evidence, when it came, was conclusive. The distinguished surgeon who had made the post-mortem examination gave it as his opinion that the wound in the throat could have been inflicted with no species of weapon with which he was acquainted, and as far as he could venture to form a hypothesis, death had been caused by the bite of some animal armed with exceedingly large and powerful cutting teeth.

This unexpected statement caused quite a sensation in court, and Standish jumped up.

'By Jove! I forgot the cat,' he said to me, and then, advancing to the coroner, he informed him that he had an addition to make to his former statement. He was sworn again, and told the story of the mysterious death of poor Mephistopheles in a straightforward way that evidently impressed the jury. I confirmed his tale in every particular.

There were no more witnesses, and the coroner summed up. He began by stating that all the evidence which could be collected still left this terrible affair in a very mysterious state. So far as he could see, however, there was happily no reason for regarding it as a murder. There had been no robbery of the body, though robbery would have been perfectly easy, and though there might have seemed some *prima facie* grounds for suspecting one person of complicity in the act—here the worthy coroner glanced at Macbane, who smiled slightly—yet it had been proved by reputable witnesses, whose testimony had not been impugned—here Standish blushed, and I think I did too—that the person in question could not possibly have been present on the scene of Mr Macdonald's death at the hour when it took place, and had apparently confined the expression of his ill-will to mere words, which it would be unfair to invest with any special significance—and so on, in the usual moralizing vein of coroners. The medical evidence, he went on to say, pointed to the theory that the death of the deceased was caused by some savage animal, and the further statement of two of the witnesses seemed to indicate that some such ferocious beast, perhaps a dog, was loose in the neighbourhood. It would be for the jury, however, to review all the facts, and return a just and impartial verdict upon the case.

The jury deliberated for some time, and finally determined that the deceased died from the bite of some savage animal, but what animal they were unable to say. A rider to the verdict directed the police to use all possible diligence to track out and destroy so dangerous a beast, and suggested that a reward should be offered for its capture or death. This was done by the local authorities, but with no result, and as weeks went on and no fresh victim fell to the 'ravenous beast or beasts unknown', men ceased to go armed, or to apprehend attacks, and the Craddock Park mystery was forgotten.

Mr Duncan Macdonald had left no will, and though he had torn up a testament providing for his nephew, he had not yet executed his threat of disinheriting him. So Macbane, as the only near relative, came in for the manufacturer's very considerable fortune. He sold out his uncle's share in his business, and his first act almost was to purchase an old, half-ruinous place, called Dullas Tower, which had been, as I gathered from the scanty letter he wrote me about it, the ancestral seat of the Macbanes before the family fell into poverty and ill-repute in the old witchcraft days.

I was prevented by my school duties from seeing Macbane, now that he had gone north, and about this time Standish got a good appointment on an Indian railway in course of construction, and had to sail at once. Thus we three friends were parted for long, and it might be for ever.

I was sorry enough to lose Standish. I think it was rather a relief to see no more of Macbane. He was stranger than ever, now that his sudden prosperity had come upon him—alternately gay and sullen, exalted and depressed, and disquieting enough in either mood. I occasionally sent him a line, and at still rarer intervals received an answer, but on the whole I thought he had dropped out of my life permanently, and I was not sorry to have it so, now that he needed no help. I did not dream of the strange way in which we were once again to be brought together.

5

It was some months after Standish had left for India, and I had already received one letter from him, when I was startled by a brief paragraph among the Indian telegrams in the *Times*. It ran thus:

'I regret to state that Mr F. Standish, the young and talented engineer superintending the construction of the Salampore Junction Railway, has been killed, it is supposed by a tiger.'

This was all—terribly simple, brief and direct, as messages of evil are now. I was greatly shocked and grieved at this sudden death of my old friend, for, though I was not likely to see him again for many years, and college friendships fade sadly when college life is over, yet we had been much together before he left, and my remembrance of him was still warm and affectionate.

As soon as I recovered from the blow of the news, I wrote at once to Lieutenant Johnson, a young officer whom Standish had mentioned as being stationed near his quarters, and as being an acquaintance of his, to ask for some particulars of my friend's death.

The answer was forwarded to me about the end of August. I was not at the time in London, but had been invited by an old friend of my family to stay with him and have some shooting—though this was mere pretence on my part—at his place in Yorkshire. Lieutenant Johnson's letter was sent on from my lodgings to Darton Manor, where I was. It was a good letter, showing in its tone of manly regret how familiar and dear Standish had grown in the short time of intercourse with his new neighbours; but what I turned to most eagerly was of course the account of my poor friend's death. It was brief and rather mysterious.

Standish had gone out for an early walk in the cool of the morning, taking his gun with him, as was his custom. He had walked along the line of the new railway a little distance, and then turned off into the country. As he did not come back at his usual time, two of his servants had gone out to look for him, and found him lying on his back in a path, quite dead. His throat was fearfully torn, but there was no other wound on him. There had been no struggle, and the gun was still loaded. Footprints of some animal were observed in a patch of soft ground near by, but it was not certain whether this was the beast that had killed Standish, for while the footmarks were like those of a small panther, the wound seemed rather as if inflicted by the teeth of a tiger. A large hunting-party had beaten the neighbouring country without finding any dangerous wild animal.

This narrative set me on a very gloomy train of thought. The details of Standish's end were horribly like those of Mr Duncan Macdonald's—the suddenness, the stealth, the mystery, the ferocity of the attack were the same in both cases.

Yet what possible connection could there be between the Craddock Park mystery and the death of an engineer on the Salampore Railway? Still, I could not keep this haunting feeling of some impending doom from shadowing my mind. Four men had met in that little room in Wolseley Road on that memorable night in November. Two of the four had already perished by the same mysterious and horrible death. Was it possible that the same end was reserved for the other two, and, if so, who would be the next victim? It was a wild idea, I felt; but I simply could not get it out of my head, and it made me very gloomy and depressed at the dinner-table that night.

My kindly old host noticed this, and his genial nature could not rest satisfied till all around him were as cheery as himself. So when our tête-à-tête dinner was done—we had been very late in dining that day—he resolved to have up a bottle of a certain very rare old wine, which he kept under special lock and key for great occasions. This precious liquor he was now resolved to devote to clearing away my melancholy.

He would never trust a butler with the key of his cellar, least of all would he let a servant touch this priceless vintage. He was going to fetch the bottle himself, but of course I interposed and insisted on going for him. With a sigh of resignation, he gave me his bunch of cellar keys, carefully instructing me as to their particular uses, and the treasures to which they respectively gave access. Then he dismissed me, and I went down to the cellar.

The cellar of Darton Manor was far older than the house. It was hewn out of the rock on which the hall stood, and was large and lofty. I think that when the old castle, whose walls are still to be traced in the Manor garden, was standing, the vaults beneath must have been the storehouse of the garrison. When the modern house was built two windows were cut up through the rock to give light to the cellars, but the present owner had protected these openings with double gratings, and put an iron-plated door, with a strong and cunning lock, to defend his precious wines.

I took up a candle, lit it, and went down the winding stair that led to the cellar. The vault below was so lofty and so far beneath the floor of the hall, that the staircase, cut in the rock, seemed as if it would never end. I felt like one descending into a sepulchre.

The clash of the keys swinging from my hand was the only sound in the chilly silence, except when noises came, muffled and faint, from the house above. At last I reached the heavy door of the cellar, and with some labour unlocked it and swung it back. Then I drew out the key, as I wanted another on the bunch for releasing the precious bottle I had been sent to fetch.

For a moment I stood in the doorway, holding my light high, and gazing round me into the great cavernous room. I could not see all of it, but the long rows of casks and the racks of bottles were very impressive in their silent array of potential conviviality. Then I glanced up at the windows, whose gratings were now and then made visible by a flicker of summer lightning across the sky, and as I did so I suddenly heard a crash as of glass, far up in the house above. Then, as I still listened, came a faint sound of footfalls rapidly growing louder, as if something was coming down the winding stair with long leaps.

I did not stop to face whatever this might be. I did not pause to think what I should do. In a blind and fortunate impulse of overpowering terror I flung the heavy door to, plunged the key into the lock, and shot the bolt home.

How I managed to do it in the one instant left to me I never could understand. I had found the door hard enough to open before. As I gave the key a last turn, something came against the iron outside with a thud that almost shook the hinges loose. Then there was a moment of quiet, and I, listening behind the door, could catch a quick, hoarse, heavy panting, as of some beast of prey. Then came another great shock, and another, and at every blow the good door creaked and shook, but held firm. Next there was a grating, rending sound, as if teeth and claws were tearing at this last obstacle between my life and its destroyer, and still I stood silent, transfixed with horror, as in a nightmare, expecting to feel the fangs of the unseen Thing close through my throat. How long I stood thus, tasting all the bitterness of death, I cannot tell. It was years in agony; it may have been only minutes of time. To feel that something fiendish, brutal, and merciless was slowly tearing its way to me, and to know nothing of it save that it was death, this was the deadly and overmastering terror. My trance cannot have lasted long. With a start, I awoke to the consciousness that life was still mine, and that a chance of escape yet remained.

The frozen blood again coursed through my veins, and my dead courage revived. I sprang to the nearest large barrel that lay on its side and rolled it close against the door, to keep the panels from giving way. Then I took up an iron bar that I found lying on the floor—perhaps a lever for moving the casks—and stood ready to give one last blow for my life. The sound of tearing ceased; I heard one deep, snarling growl of disappointed rage, and then the quick steps seemed to recede up the stair. I stood there delivered, for a moment.

Only for a moment, however. My candle, which was a mere stump, suddenly flared, flickered, and left me in total darkness, made darker by the little patch of sky seen through the nearer window, across which still ran an occasional flicker of summer lightning.

In trying to strike a light I dropped the matchbox on the rock floor. While I was groping for it I suddenly looked up and saw two eyes.

Two eyes, I say, but they were rather two flames, or two burning coals. For a moment I stood glaring, fascinated at the orbs that glared into mine. Then, as the Thing turned what seemed its head, and the eyes were averted for a moment, I saw, or thought I saw, a dim phosphorescent mass obscuring the faint light of the window. Then the eyes were on me again, and I heard the sound of tearing and wrenching at the outer grating—for there were two, one above the window and one inside. The outer bars were old and rusty, strong enough to resist any common shocks, but not to hold against the unknown might that was rending at them. I heard them creaking, cracking, and then—oh, Heaven!—the whole grating gave way, and I heard it ring as it was hurled aloft and fell far out on the stones.

Next instant the strong glass of the window flew in shivers on the floor, and there were those awful eyes looking into mine now, with only a few bars between us. Then the wrenching began once more at the last barrier. It bent, it shifted. I thought it was giving way, and in a frenzy I rushed forward, whirling the iron bar round my head, and struck with all my force through the grating. Another horrible growl answered the blow, and the bar was seized and dragged from my grasp. It was found next day, deeply indented, on the ground, a hundred yards away.

But now that the prey seemed given over disarmed to its teeth, the devilish fury of the Thing seemed to triumph over the devilish cunning that had directed it. It gave up the persistent assault on the grating, and writhed against the bars in a transport of hissing rage, biting the air, grinding its jaws on the tough iron. And yet—this was the horror of it—I could see nothing distinctly—only a phosphorescent shadow, twisted and tortured with agonies of rage, and turning upon me sometimes those eyes which seemed to redden with the growing frenzy of the Thing, till they were like blood-red lamps.

I think I had lost all fear for my life now. I did not think of danger or resistance; but so mighty was the sheer horror of that bestial rage that I grovelled down in the darkest corner of the vault, and hid my eyes and stopped my ears, and cried to Heaven to deliver me from the presence of the Thing.

Suddenly, as I crouched there, the end came. The noise ceased. I turned and saw that the eyes were gone. I stood up and stretched out my arms, and a cool air blew though the shattered window on my damp forehead. Then every tense fibre of my body seemed to give way, and I fell like one dead on the floor.

I was awakened from my swoon by a thundering at the door, and the sound of voices—human voices once more. I staggered to the door, pushed away the cask, and after long wrenching—for my hands seemed to have lost all strength—got the lock open, and stumbled into the arms of my good host. Above him, on the stairs, were two or three of the men-servants, their pale, frightened faces looking ghastly in the light of the flaring candles.

'My dear boy!' he cried. 'Thank goodness you are alive. We have been so frightened about you.'

I told him faintly that I had fallen in a swoon. I could not yet speak of what I had gone through, and, indeed, it now seemed like a hideous dream.

'Well, do you know', he said, as he took my arm, and helped me up the stair, 'we had such a scare upstairs. Just a few minutes after you had gone, when I was wondering whether you would find the right wine, smash came something right through the dining-room window, and over went the big candlestick, and we were in the dark. And when we got a light again, you never saw such a scared set as we were; but there was nothing to be seen. Did you have a visit, too?'

'Something did come down here,' I managed to articulate. 'But don't ask me about it—not tonight. I want to sleep first.'

'I think we all want that,' he said, briefly, as we reached the lighted hall again, and I, for one, felt as if I had come up from the grave alive.

6

I slept late into the following morning and should have slept later still had I not been aroused about ten o'clock by the butler, who held in his hand a yellow telegram envelope. As soon as I could shake off my drowsiness in part, I tore open the missive and, unfolding the paper, found to my surprise that it was from Macbane. He knew my address, indeed, from a letter that I had sent him; but knowing his ways, I never expected even a note from him, much less a telegram. When I read the message, my surprise was not diminished.

'If safe, and wishing to see me alive,' it ran, 'come at once. If unable, forget me. Nearest station, Kilburgh.'

What could this mean? Could Macbane know anything of my mysterious danger of last night? And if so, was the doom that had missed me impending over him? Or was it merely that he was ill and desponding, and thought himself dying? Turn and twist the message as I could, it puzzled me; but one thing was plain—Macbane was, or thought himself to be, in deadly need of me, his only friend, as far as I knew; and if I did not go, it was possible that he might lose the last chance of any friendly human care in his solitary life. I resolved at once, shaken and weary as I still felt, to start for Dullas Tower.

I rose and dressed hurriedly, and snatched some breakfast alone—for my good old host was too much exhausted by the excitement of the last night to come down yet. While eating, I was studying a railway guide, and discovered that by driving to the nearest station at once I could catch a train that would enable me by devious junction lines to make my way to Kilburgh—a little place in a wild part of a lowland county—by the evening.

While the horse was being put into the dog-cart, I scribbled a note to my host, explaining the reason for my speedy departure, and promising to return as soon as possible, and then I stepped into the cart and was driven off, arriving just in time to catch the train.

My journey was of the exasperatingly tedious character known to all who have ever tried to go any distance by means of crosslines and local lines and junctions. Twice I got some food during my long intervals of waiting at stations, and all the time, whether travelling or resting, I was possessed with a haunting perplexity, a shadowy fear. Through my brain incessantly beat, keeping time to the pulsating roar of the wheels, a text, or something like one—I know not how or why it suggested itself—'One woe is past; behold another woe cometh.' The mysterious peril of the last night seemed already to have happened years ago. The dim terror of the future would be ages in coming, and between them, and in the shadow of both, I was still going on and on, slowly but endlessly—a dream myself, and in a dream.

It was about eight in the evening, I think, when I reached Kilburgh Station; but my watch had stopped, and I could not be sure.

I cast a hasty glance round me, and could just make out the lights of a few houses in the valley below the station, and the dark outlines of hills around, some of them serrated with black pines, and the sky dense with cloud, and with a denser mass of gloom labouring slowly up from the west. There was the weight of a coming storm in the air.

I asked the station-master where Dullas Tower was, and how I was to reach it.

'Dullas Tower?' he said, meditatively, and then, with a sudden flash of comprehension, 'Oh, it's the De'il's Tower ye'll be meaning, sir—Macbane's?'

I nodded acquiescence. This popular corruption of the name seemed ominous, but somehow natural.

'Then ye've a matter of ten miles to go,' he said, deliberately. 'And gin I might offer an opeenion, ye'll do better to tak' Jimmy Brown's bit giggie. The man frae Macbane's tauld him to be ready the morn.'

Guided by the cautious 'opeenion' of the station-master, I found Brown's trap waiting outside the station. He was English, as I could tell by his accent, and this perhaps accounted for the slight tinge of contempt in the worthy official's reference to him and his vehicle. His horse, as far as I could tell by the station lamp, seemed a poor one, but it showed a remarkably vicious temper when I tried to get in, kicking and backing, and seeming possessed by an irrational desire to do me some bodily harm.

'Whoa, then, will ye, ye beast?' called Brown, as he caught hold of the rein and dexterously foiled the brute's instant attempt to bite him. 'You're a harm to others and no good to your owner. You're just like Macbane's muckle cat, that killed two men, and the third was Macbane.'

I had gained my place on the seat at last, but this remark nearly shook me off again.

'What do you mean by that?' I almost screamed at the man.

He turned a puzzled face up to mine, as he climbed into his place and took the reins.

'Oh, I don't know, sir,' he answered, as we rattled off. 'It's just a saying the folks have about here. It's some story about an old warlock Macbane that had the Tower long ago, I believe. Nothing to do with this one, sir—of course not. I got into the way of saying it from hearing it often, that's all.'

I did not answer him, as we drove on between high banks of earth and rock, with now and then a tree nodding threateningly above us. I was faint and tired, and unable to think in a connected manner. The grim old proverb, like the Scriptural or quasi-Scriptural phrase, transformed itself into a dreary refrain, which rang in time to the beat of the horse-hoofs on the dry road: '*Killed* two *men*, and the *third* was

128

Macbane—*killed* two *men*, and the *third* was Macbane.' It seemed a part of me, a pulse in my very brain, till it grew meaningless with incessant repetition.

We drove on westward, toiling up hills, rattling down them, but I hardly saw anything. It was all a part of my dream still, and it seemed natural to me when a black grove of tall trees, and in the midst a denser black mass, with one or two lights twinkling in it, rose up before us, and the driver told me this was the De'il's Tower.

As we came up to it, and I roused myself from my lethargy a little to observe my journey's end, I could see that part of the building seemed ruinous and broken down; the walls ended in a slope bristling with bushes. One grim-looking tower at the corner loomed high above us, apparently uninjured, and half-way up it shone a faint light.

I alighted, paid the driver, who seemed in a hurry to get away, rang, and, when an old woman came to the door, asked if Macbane was at home. She said in reply that he was ill, and could see no one; but when I gave my name she conducted me through a long passage—part of it almost ruinous, part in better repair—to the foot of a winding stair. Here she told me to go up and knock at the first door I came to, and stood at the foot of the stairs with her candle to light me up. When I reached the door, which was some way up, I could hear her hobble away, leaving me in darkness, only relieved by an occasional gleam of lightning through the narrow slits that let in light and air to the staircase.

I knocked gently, and a voice said 'Come in.' I felt along the iron-studded door till I found and turned the handle of the latch. As I entered I saw Macbane sitting back in an old chair, with a shaded lamp on the table beside him, and some books and papers in its circle of light.

The room was small and circular, and was, as I conjectured, half-way up the tower that had given its name to the building. A window, made visible from time to time by the lightning, opened on the outer air, and I noticed with a sort of dull wonder that there seemed to be a set of strong bars defending it—perhaps a relic of old times when the room was a prison; I cannot tell.

My friend did not rise from his chair to greet me. He motioned languidly to a seat near him, and for some minutes I sat and looked at

129

him, and he stared at the door. I noticed a new and alarming change in him since I had seen him last. Then, his look had been almost malevolent, instinct with a positive hatred for men; now all passion, all life, good or bad, seemed extinct in him.

After a long pause, broken by the muffled growls of the nearer thunder, he spoke.

'I hardly thought you would come,' he said, 'but now you are here you had better read this.'

And he pointed to a yellow and torn old manuscript lying on the table. I took up the roll and began to look into it.

It was crabbed and quaint in writing and style, and it would only be perplexing to give its antique phraseology and obsolete Scotch law terms and phrases, even if I remembered them. But the substance of it was plain. It was a record of the trial and condemnation of Alexander Macbane of Dullas Tower for witchcraft, early in the seventeenth century.

After many preliminaries, over which I passed hastily, the narrative came to the confession of the wizard. This was apparently volunteered, and not extorted by any torture; but such cases were by no means rare at that time, I think. The peculiarity of this confession was that it was clear, consistent, rational even—if so wild a tale could be called rational—and did not involve anyone besides the wizard himself. Actual torture was applied, it would seem, to make Alexander Macbane implicate an old crone tried at the same time, but in vain.

'The devil,' he had said, 'was no fool. He had better servants than these poor women.'

Briefly put, the gist of Alexander Macbane's confession was as follows. He admitted that he had, by certain magic processes which he refused to reveal, as their very simplicity might lead others to use them, secured the services of a strange familiar.

This thing owned him as master and did his bidding, though only in one way—it could slay, and nothing more. He had killed by it two men, kinsmen of his, one his enemy and one his friend, who had in fact—a marginal note stated—died in a sudden and strange manner. But that which he had regarded as his servant—the confession went on to say—had become his master, and he a bond slave to its devilish power. It was jealous of all he did; it had cut off any beast for which he showed a fondness, and it had driven him to cast off all his friends, and to give up all friendly feeling for men. One man, whom he loved, he had bidden it slay, or else it would have slain himself.

The Thing needed to have victims pointed out to it at certain intervals, or it turned on its master. Being asked how he knew the intentions of his familiar, the wizard answered that he could not tell how, but he divined its thoughts, even as, he felt sure, it read his. To the enquiry what form his demon assumed, he said that at first it was invisible to him as to others, but could be felt, and that gradually it took visible form as a beast, black and cat-like, with a great mouth.

The judges here asked the reason why Alexander Macbane had turned against his demon; the answer given, in quaint but still pathetic language, was that he had married a woman whom he loved, and had been happy with her for some months, and now he knew that he must choose between her and himself as a sacrifice to his familiar.

In making his confession, he knew that he was devoting himself to death the same night, but he was resolved to do this. Better, he said, was it to die horribly thus, than to live alone with his sin and its punishment.

'And so,' the record concisely ended, 'the said Alexander Macbane, being remanded to his prison, was there found dead the next day, with his throat rent through, and the bars of the window broken. Whereby it was thought that he had said the truth as to himself.'

As I read the last words I dropped the roll, for the lightning glared into my very face, and a moment after a ringing crash of thunder burst over the building as if sky and earth were coming together. Then the roar leaped and rolled through the clouds, and died muttering far away, and through the rush of rain and wind I heard Macbane.

'You understand now,' he said, with that dreadful, hollow sameness in his tone. 'I am glad anyway that you will be left, and not I. I always liked you better than Standish. Perhaps it was a tiger after all that killed him, poor fellow. You are quite safe now. It is coming for me tonight. I thought it would have killed me last night, when I called it back——'

A crash of thunder drowned his last words.

'Macbane !' I cried, finding my power of speech at last, 'it shall not be! Whether it is real or a dream, I do not know; but you shall not die that way. I kept the Thing out; cannot you do it? Never give up hope. Cannot you save yourself?'

Macbane smiled hopelessly.

'Listen,' said he, and held up his hand, and in a pause of the rain I heard, low and distinct, *a scratching on the door*.

'Open it, Eliot,' he said, calmly. 'It must come, and sooner the better. Then go down and wait, for it will not be a pleasant thing to see.'

I sprang to the door, but not to open it. With frenzied speed I locked and double-locked it, and drove the heavy bolts into their sockets. But no rush came against the door, no tearing or grinding of teeth. I could hear nothing—not even a breath, and the stillness was more terrifying than any sound.

'It is no use,' said my friend. 'You could keep yourself safe; you cannot save me. It will have help tonight.'

A gust of wind swept round the tower as he spoke, and mingling in its wail I seemed to hear—or was it but my fancy?—the long, deadly howl of the Thing that I felt was so near us.

For a few moments there was silence. Then, with a crash, the lightning fell close to the tower, and a great pine, shattered by the stroke, rushed down right against the window, and its top crashed into the room, rending away the iron bars like rotten sticks. The wind of the fall extinguished the lamp, but in the darkness and the roar of thunder I could *feel* something pass by me with a mighty leap, and next moment a fainter flash showed me a picture which was but for an instant, but in that instant was branded in on my memory.

Macbane stood upright with arms folded, gazing calmly forward and upward, and before him crouched, as if for a spring, a black mass with blood-red, burning eyes, the same eyes that had glared on me the night before. So much I saw; then, suddenly, the world was one blinding flame, one rending crash around me, and I fell stunned and senseless.

When I lived again, the dawn's grey glimmer was dimly lighting the tower, and outside the blackened and shattered window a bird was singing. As I opened my eyes, my glance fell on something lying in the centre of the room. It was Macbane's body. I crawled to him and looked into the dead face. There was no wound or mark on him, and there even seemed a faint smile on his lips, and near his feet lay a little heap of grey ash.

10

L. A. G. STRONG

The Buckross Ring

I wonder how many people today recall the finding of the Buckross treasure and the excitement it caused. A very few, probably; yet, in those far-off days before the war, it was a newspaper sensation of the first magnitude, and the diagrams of Crippen's progress across the Atlantic were scarcely followed with more care than the daily record of the search, and the progress made in excavating the hoard which had escaped King Hal's commissioners.

It was known that the original clue to the hiding-place lay in a signet ring which had belonged to the last abbot, and the papers published greatly enlarged photographs of this ring, with crosses to mark the tiny secret catch by which it opened. Facsimiles of the folded parchment inside it were published also, with translations, and the portrait of Giddas, who deciphered it, most liberally inset. Scott and I also came in for more than our fair share of publicity. In fact, the public was given every detail of the discovery save one, into which by happy chance it forbore to enquire—namely, the manner in which the ring itself was found.

I say, 'by happy chance', because Scott, Giddas, and myself had decided in any case not to reveal this. As long as a man of science deals in the ascertainable, the public venerate him. Let him once espouse the unknown, the occult, the unknowable—and he is dubbed a madman and a crank, outcast or ridiculed by his fellows: and, what is far worse, any subsequent truth he may discover, in no matter what field of research, is contaminated and suspect because of his name. Therefore, as none of us desired this fate, we rejoiced in the public lack of curiosity on this, the most important point in the story; and remained silent.

Today, however, things are different. Scott is dead, killed, poor fellow, on a minesweeper in the North Sea. Giddas has retired, and lives altogether in Italy now; I have not heard from him for a long time. For myself, I have reached an age when I no longer greatly care if men accept my story or deride it: and they are less likely to deride it now, when the systematic study of the occult is a recognized branch of science and no longer reckoned as a premonitory symptom of lunacy.

It seems good to me, therefore, to set down the story of how the ring was found before all interest in the treasure is completely lost and Buckross itself less than a memory.

One day, then, early in May, in the year nineteen-hundred-and-nine, having come up on business to the city, I made my way into Gatti's for lunch. I spied a table at some distance, and was making my way to it, when a man turned, jumped up, and clapped me on the shoulder.

'Tresilian!' he cried, 'by all that's odd! What brings you here? We've just been talking of you.'

'Scott, my dear man. Why, I thought you were still in Mexico! And Giddas! How are you, my dear Professor? Well, well, this is indeed a fortunate meeting.'

'Come over to our table. It is in a corner, and we can talk.'

As soon as the first greetings and questions were over—for I had not seen my old friends for the better part of four years—Scott leaned over the table towards me and dropped his voice.

'Look here, Tresilian. We have a job on hand that will interest you. You remember that summer we spent together at Abingdon?'

'Very well.'

'Do you remember the story we heard there—the old tale of the Buckross treasure?'

'How the last Abbot was supposed to have buried the treasure to save it from the King's officers, and no one could tell where it had been hidden?'

'That is right. Well—we kept that in mind, Giddas and I; and we have lost no chance, at odd times, of hunting up any information we could find about the old Abbey and the Manor House adjoining it. Giddas dug up something in the Bodleian a good while back; but it was not until I chanced on an even more valuable find, in a little Oxfordshire church, in the cupboard where the old registers were kept, that I became really interested. And now'—he looked quickly from left to right—'I'm hot on the track.'

'No? Tell me.'

Scott leaned back as the waiter flourished the dishes past our heads, and looked at me with a twinkle in his brown eyes. He was dark and bald, though by far the youngest of the three. Giddas all the while rolled little pellets of bread in his fingers, and looked, birdlike, from one to the other of us.

As soon as the waiter had gone, Scott leaned forward again.

'I have found,' he said, 'the journal of one of the monks, Gilbert by name; also a kind of diary written at intervals by a lady who lived at the Manor. The former took ages to read through, for it was written very small in a big book, and contained little enough relevant to our search. The other, which was of more importance, was even more troublesome to read, but Giddas here unravelled it.'

Giddas snorted.

'Yes,' he said, 'and never have I had to decipher such a document. Only Scott's insistence could have made me persevere with it. A pathologist, perhaps—a student of the morbid——'

'Hush, don't spoil the story. Anyway, Tresilian, by putting together what the two writings had to tell us, I believe we're on the track of the treasure.'

Scott spoke quietly, but with a trace of strong excitement. Knowing he would not say thus much without good reason, I became at once deeply interested.

'Tell me all about it,' I begged him.

'A tall order,' said Giddas, attacking a new potato with gusto. 'A tall order. Difficult to know where to begin.'

'Perhaps it will be better if I reconstruct the whole story, to the best of my ability, combining what both documents say; and you, friend Giddas, shall correct me if I go wrong.'

Then Scott pushed away his plate and began.

'I don't exactly know how it was that the Abbey and Manor first became connected; it seems fairly certain that the Abbey was the older of the two. Still, as often in mediæval times, they were inter-related. Whether it was a question of owning adjacent lands, or for purely defensive purposes, we can't be sure; but somehow or other the Abbot had come to be regarded as a kind of Chaplain to the Lord of the Manor. Giddas tells me it is very unlikely that an Abbot would stand in such capacity to a layman; yet the fact remains, that monks from the Abbey used to do secretarial and other work at the Manor, and the Manor folk used to attend services at the Abbey. There were, I believe, monastic orders who discharged secular duties as a means of discipline, or for additional livelihood—is it not so, Giddas?—and that seems to have been the case here. Gilbert, for instance, the monk whose journal has been so valuable to us, acted as librarian, and kept the roll for the Manor; another monk acted as physician, and so forth. Indeed, there seems to have been the greatest freedom of intercourse between both communities. The ladies of the Manor would wander at pleasure in the Abbey gardens, save such parts of them as were reserved for meditation; and the Lady Garda—our diarist—herself records how, when she was a child, the Abbot would take her to help him catch fish from the old stone fish-pond. He was her confessor also, and later on she gave the good man some offence by wishing that another, and younger, ecclesiastic should act in that capacity instead.'

'Very probably,' snapped Giddas, with whom the enforced perusal of the lady's diary seemed to rankle.

'Well,' continued Scott, 'of all the community represented by the Abbey, the Manor, and the village that had grown up around them, we need concern ourselves with only three or four persons. The first of these is the lady, Garda Brent, or as she was simply called, the Lady Garda, who was the author of the diary I mentioned.

'The Lady Garda was the eldest daughter of the house, and she was still a girl when her father died, leaving as his heir a boy of nine. As was only natural, the estates were taken in charge by the Abbey, and administered until the boy should come of age. Possibly it was through some such occurrence in the past that the close association between the Abbey and the Manor first began.

'At the time our story opens, the Lady Garda was a woman of thirty-one, and still unmarried. It is difficult to say why she was so: Gilbert records that she had fair hair, a clear skin, and was pleasant to look on. Maybe the old Abbot's tutelage was not conducive to matrimony, though I cannot think he would have discouraged her from it. Her mother was an invalid, and could do little for her. Perhaps she did not often meet with men of her own class, or perhaps she was one of those good-looking girls who are nevertheless deficient somehow in sex attractiveness. At any rate, the fact is that at thirty-one she was single, and looked like remaining so.

'Well, thirty-one is an unsettled time in a single woman's life, and the Lady Garda appears to have been one of those women to whom marriage is a necessity. Nature, thwarted, took her revenge, and the Lady Garda fell madly in love with a handsome page-boy of fourteen.

'We may read a great deal nowadays about the savage unsatisfied jealous love of an older woman for a boy, but the Lady Garda's diary is a document more convincing than anything I have read. All the pent-up fires in her nature, all the idealism and the morbidity of a passionate imagination, were focused upon an immature boy, little better than a child. Giddas may sniff as he will, but I find a beauty and a pathos, a dignity even, in that diary, and so will you, I think, Tresilian, when you read it. Strong emotion of any kind should never fail to move us, however unhappy its source or morbid its expression, and there is no doubting the strength of Garda's passion for the page-boy Gaston.

'He, for his part, seems to have begun by reverencing her as a goddess. She was fair and moved above him. She was kind, and this won his devotion. For a long time he adored her thus: and when at last he realized that she loved him, he seems to have been equally balanced between terror and worship. One day he kissed her hand.

'Then, poor girl, she made a mistake. She ought to have left him that miracle to ponder on for a while. Instead—she was so transported, I suppose—instead, she caught him up and kissed him passionately on the mouth. He broke from her with a cry, ran away, and she did not see him for a week.

'After that things went more smoothly. He aged rapidly—Lord, how the first knowledge of love ages a boy—and he came back to her. He grew physically, and she, I'm afraid, left nothing undone to centre his love upon her, body and soul. Gaston changed, not altogether for the better. He grew exacting, claiming unconsciously the mastery of sex which she had usurped in declaring her love to him. With a boy's insensitiveness he often hurt her. She could never be sure of him. She had continually to be on the alert, desperately using every device to keep the love that was to her everything upon earth.

'But Gaston was a good lad at heart, and on the whole he was kind to her. Where he failed, it was through youth and want of imagination. He seems, as he grew a little older, to have alternated between periods of feverish devotion, and fits of reticence, shyness, and remorse. After all, such a love-affair was a pretty serious addition to the ordinary complications of adolescence. On the whole, he did well by his lady: and he had no easy time of it, for you may be sure the Abbot soon tumbled to the case, and secret meetings are pretty demoralizing for even the best.

'Now let's leave them for a moment, and come to the other important person in the story—Bibi.'

Scott paused and took a drink.

'Bibi?' I said; 'What a strange name. Who was Bibi?'

'Bibi—well, Gilbert called him "Monstrum"; yet he was only a child. He was presumably six years old when he was found near the Abbey, a child with a small shrunken body, rickety limbs, and a huge head, in which were set little uncanny features and big staring eyes. Some people travelling through the village had abandoned him there. They had stayed a night at the inn, where Bibi had been an object of much terrified curiosity to the village folk, and had left with him the next day. They professed to be his parents, "though," says Gilbert, "how so huge a head can have come through the gate of any woman's body, I cannot tell". However, as his head grew greatly during the eighteen months he was at the Abbey, perhaps it was little above normal size when he was born. Anyhow, for some reason these people abandoned him; and three days later the villagers found him and brought him to the Abbey. He was starving, and his little beaky mouth was green and foul with grass, like a horse's bit.

'The monks took him in, dubiously enough, and fed him with milk. In a few days he recovered, and as there was nowhere else to send him and he was obviously very delicate, they decided in the end to keep him. He was intelligent enough, but spoke little; Bibi was his name, he said, and Bibi they called him.

'It is difficult from the records left of him to say definitely how far his intelligence went. At all events it seems to have been of an unearthly order. He walked slowly, putting one of his weak little feet before the other with care, swaying often beneath the weight of his enormous head, and balancing himself with his hands. His features were of normal size, although old-looking and queer. His eyes, as I have said, were big and staring, and he blinked very seldom, and then rapidly, three or four times. His lips came out almost to a point, and there was a distinct fissure in the lower lip. It was from the forehead upwards that the abnormal growth began, the head suddenly swelling out on either side like a puff-ball, and having scarcely any hair upon it. His skin was almost brown, of a rather parchmentlike texture, smooth on the head, but wrinkled a little on the cheeks and on most of the body. He was pot-bellied also.

'As I said, he spoke little, but his few remarks denoted preternatural intelligence. The monks soon gave up all attempts to instruct him, for he would not attend to them, or, if compelled to do so, would suffer, or feign to suffer, headache. So they contented themselves with baptizing him, and let him roam about as he pleased, and it is not recorded that he was either mischievous or troublesome.

'Loud noises he hated; they hurt his head. For that reason he could not bear to be in the chapel, but would sit outside upon the lawn in summer time, out of the sun, and listen contentedly enough. Once, when a big dog, released from a kennel, barked suddenly near him, he fell in a kind of fit, and was carried away, his face contorted with pain, pressing his hands to his temples and uttering thin little hooting cries.

'After a time the people lost their fear of him, and many treated him with kindness, notably the Lady Garda, for whom alone he showed anything like affection. She would chatter gaily to him, and deck him in all her beads, putting necklace after necklace round his tiny neck. She had to be very careful in putting them on not to touch his head. Gaston, helping her one day, with rather a bad grace, for he was afraid of Bibi, accidentally touched the enormous head with the beads; and it took Garda a long time to console and soothe the child, who distrusted Gaston thereafter.

'In return for her kindness, Bibi would follow her about, waddling carefully after her, and by a strange instinct never losing the trail, however soon she passed from his sight. More than once, while she was with Gaston among the mazy yew hedges and walks, the huge head appeared round a corner a couple of feet from the ground, and gave her a curious shock. Yet she never heeded him, knowing intuitively that he would never attempt to tell what he saw; and so the unblinking eyes of Bibi would stare solemnly upon their endearments.

'There was an even more curious side of him, however. Cats feared and yet were fascinated by him. Several times a crash was heard in the room where he slept, and a monk, rushing to the place, would find an oaken chair or some such heavy object overturned, and Bibi peacefully asleep. Most curious of all, however—I should be inclined to think it a yarn, if it weren't that Gilbert shows no trace in his journal of imaginative gifts—was a performance he went through almost every afternoon. He would disappear into the ante-chapel, and sit down in a rather damp corner furthest from the door. Gilbert, following one day to see where he had gone, found him there, and fearing the cold stones would chill him, tried to persuade him to come back into the sunlight. Bibi refused, so Gilbert went away. As it chanced, he met the Abbot outside and told him of his anxiety; so together they crept in to see what the child was at. He was still sitting there, in exactly the same attitude, making neither sound nor gesture, watching intently a hole in the wall. Presently, to their amazement and horror, there crept from the hole a huge pale toad, which came out a little way and sat before Bibi. For a time they gazed at each other, toad and child; then at last Bibi rose and toddled out, and the toad crept back to its hole.

'This, says Gilbert, happened often. What do you think?—a yarn, eh? Well, it doesn't matter much, either way.

140

'But not long after this, something far more startling occurred. It was towards the close of a spring day, when the long light was beginning to fail and the rooks were going noisily to bed. Bibi had been restless all day, never remaining still, and moving about more quickly than usual. He seemed uneasy in his mind also, and to dislike being left alone, for he kept near whatever monk he could attach himself to, and even stayed for a while close to Gaston, whom he hated. As it grew dusk, he became more and more restless, and was finally seen waddling off in the failing light towards the refectory; but since he was often in there, watching the birds fly in at the windows to pick up crumbs, no one thought anything more of it.

'Suddenly there broke upon the air the most terrible pandemonium, as if in the refectory all hell had been let loose. The monks rushed to the spot, but the great doors were shut and barred. It sounded to the terrified men as if a regiment of fiends were within, flinging the heavy oak benches and tables about, and dashing the ringing flagons on the floor. The doors, the whole building, shook with the concussion. White-faced monks ran for the Abbot, but before bell, book, and candle could be fetched the clamour ceased. The doors were burst open, and, crowding in, they found all the tables and benches piled grotesquely into heaps, and Bibi lying senseless upon the floor.'

'A medium,' I murmured. 'Poltergeist—a low-grade medium. I know of several such cases.'

Scott nodded to me. 'Precisely,' he said. 'I think what astounded the monks more than anything else was that, after all the violence and noise they had heard, none of the furniture had so much as a scratch to show for it.'

'What about Bibi?' I asked.

'At first they thought he was dead; but he still breathed, so they put him to bed and held a consultation. The Abbot wanted to hold a service of exorcism at once, but the monk who served as physician was of opinion that Bibi would die if any further strain were put upon him, and that perhaps the evil spirits had gone out as it was, banging the refectory furniture about in place of rending Bibi. So they put it off for the time.'

'I must tell you, Scott,' interjected Giddas, 'that I am extremely sceptical on the subject of these—er—manifestations.'

141

'I know you are,' replied Scott tolerantly. 'I know you are, my dear Giddas. Yet I think Tresilian here can assure you that, even in our prosaic age, such things can, and do, occur. However, let us get on with the story.

'Late the next day Bibi recovered consciousness, but he was seized with a violent headache and could not lift his head. He remained like this for three days, refusing all nourishment except a little milk which the Lady Garda somehow persuaded him to take. On the fourth day the Abbot decided to hold the service of exorcism, since he considered that some at least of the evil spirits remained and were the cause of Bibi's suffering. So they trooped into the chamber, and there, with bell, book, and candle, the devil was solemnly adjured to leave vexing of Bibi Bighead and come out of him.

'Those who expected terrible convulsions to rack the child did not see their fears realised, for he slept peacefully through the ceremony. It must have been a strange scene—the candles, the robes, the chanted Latin, and the apprehensive eyes fixed upon that monstrous little figure in the bed.

'Maybe the Abbot was right, and the evil spirits did leave Bibi; for although his pain did not go at once, he recovered and was soon about again. But he was shakier than before, and his head began noticeably to grow bigger and bigger. It was as though the skull was thin, almost like elastic, and the fluid—I suppose it was fluid—inside kept distending it more and more. Bibi grew peevish and walked less; his head was becoming too heavy for his wizened neck; and Gilbert has noted in his journal how one day, when Bibi sat in a chair in the great hall, watching a monk at work upon a tapestry, a ray of light coming through one of the windows showed pink through the almost transparent skull.

'It must have been soon after this that the Abbot began to hear disquieting rumours about the King's activities: and one autumn day he received a message from a brother Abbot of Buckland in Devon, which made up his mind for him. It would appear that the King's Commissioners—did you know this, Giddas?—began their search as far away from London as might be, and worked back towards it. I suppose they thought the most distant monasteries the richest, or else imagined that the abbots of far-off places, on being plundered, would conclude that the nearer monasteries had suffered the same fate already, and so would not trouble to give them warning. If so, they were mistaken for once, for his reverence of Buckland sent warning. There was a consultation; and for several days afterwards lanterns were to be seen crossing the fields by the Abbey at night, and maybe the September gales did not altogether drown the occasional clink of spade and mattock.

'The good Abbot did not hide all his treasure. That would have been foolish. Suffice to say that when His Majesty's Commissioners arrived they found the Abbey a deal less rich than they had been led to suppose. I dare say they had their suspicions, but the minutest search revealed no trace of anything more. I am going beyond my story, however; the Commission did not arrive for many months after it was expected.

'As the winter drew on, Bibi rapidly became worse. The last time he sat in the great hall, in his high chair, he turned suddenly a pale yellow colour and his now enormous head rolled to one side. He could no longer support it. Indeed, they thought the weight of it would break his neck, it drooped so hideously, until they undid the strap and got him out of the chair. He was hurried to bed, and it soon became evident that Bibi Bighead had only a few days to live.

'Moved by some impulse—I cannot believe that she felt any real affection for him—the Lady Garda constituted herself his nurse. I think she took a delight in her fearlessness of this little monster, from whom all other women shrank, and was conscious too, perhaps, of a curious bond of intimacy between Bibi and herself. Certainly he would do what she bid him, and at her approach and touch the little whimperings would soon cease. She never appeared to show him any real tenderness, but rallied and mocked him gently, as she had always done when he was up and well. Still the creature seemed perfectly to understand and be content.

'At last he died. Garda herself barely mentions his death. "Bibi is passed this night with great anguish to God" is her only comment. But Gilbert has left a vivid account of the scene, which made a strong impression on him.

'Many of the monks were present, in a wide semicircle about the bed, while Garda herself sat beside it. The only other women present ventured no further than the doorway. From time to time the murmur of a prayer was heard.

143

'Bibi lay upon the bed, his body wriggling, his head perforce still. The horrible thing was that the obvious agony of the child excited not sympathy, but repulsion among the beholders. The good Gilbert takes himself severely to task for this. "I," he says, "who am tender to the worm cut by my unwitting spade, yet had not love enough to pity the torment of this child of God." But there it was: they could not pity him, they only felt sick.

'From time to time Bibi would press his little hands to his temples and utter a little thin scream—"Ee-ee-ee-eee. Ee-ee-ee-eee." Just like that. No human emotion in it; just a detached, unearthly, suffering sound.

'A candle suddenly flared up and went out, frightening them all, for they were on the jump, not knowing what devilment to expect. Yet Bibi's death was unaccompanied by any manifestation. He suddenly screamed and tried to sit up; but the weight of his head held him down, and he died at once. For a time they waited, expecting at any moment to hear the furniture being dashed about, or the very roof taken over their heads; but nothing untoward happened, so by twos and threes they went off to bed. The Lady Garda laid out the body with her own hands, and then went back to the Manor. To do her justice, she had watched over Bibi almost unremittingly, and was always at hand when he grew fractious or was in especial pain.

'Now we come to the most complicated and difficult part of the story, where we have to piece it out with but little to go on. You must remember, Tresilian, that I am all the time at a disadvantage. I am not relating a story prepared for my understanding, with the topography and all incidental matters explained. Instead, I have to reconstruct the whole from a few hasty notes made to refresh the writers' own memories. Even Gilbert takes for granted a knowledge of the Abbey grounds, the country round about, the persons and characters of the monks, et cetera. So if I seem vague at times, you must forgive me.

'Well, it seems that the Abbot had taken Gaston under his wing, and the boy spent much time in the Abbey, and often waited upon the Abbot in person. Whether it was that the boy had taken his fancy, or that he wanted to keep him out of the Lady Garda's way, we cannot be sure; probably the latter. But whatever the reason it did not prevent Gaston and the Lady Garda from having a tiff soon before Bibi died.

Gaston was older now, and I dare say harder to manage. Perhaps he was jealous of her nursing Bibi. Anyway, they had a row, and after a period of distraction for both of them, they met again and were reconciled.

'As I said, Gaston was older. What exactly took place we can only guess, but at any rate Gaston had a fit of scruple after it and decided that they must be betrothed. The Lady hastily explained that this was impossible, but he was firm, and insisted that they should at any rate plight their troth privately to one another. The only drawback was that he had no means of getting a ring.'

'Aha!' said I. 'I see where we're coming to now.'

Scott held up a hand. 'Not too fast,' he smiled, 'we're not there yet. Here—waiter—coffee, please—black?—black?—three black, waiter, and the bill.'

He leaned forward over the table once more.

'Well, Bibi was dead, and nothing happened, so after a while they took courage, and the physician and the village apothecary embalmed him between them. 'Twas a pity, they said, not to preserve such a creature for the admiration of posterity.'

Giddas fidgeted in his chair.

'Oh, I know they didn't put it like that—I'm not quoting. You must allow me a storyteller's licence, Giddas, to—to—modernize the text. Anyhow, embalming didn't seem to suit Bibi. They had put him, for the time, in the little coffin that was made for him first of all, to let him dry, I suppose. This coffin—it was almost heart-shaped, because of his head—lay on a table in a disused room at the Abbey, where furniture was kept, and hunting gear, and the like. Well, that night there were noises, and the coffin levitated——'

'The coffin——?'

'Levitated. Rose in the air and floated about. Several of them saw it, and they were scared out of their wits and shut the door. When they fetched the Abbot and opened the door again, the coffin was back on the table: and the Abbot was inclined to disbelieve them. The next night, however, it happened again; so they took bell, book, and candle, and obediently enough the spirit put Bibi down again. They were much heartened by this exhibition of the power of holiness, and retired to sleep with a good conscience.

'The next evening the Abbot sat peacefully in his chamber after supper, before a fine fire. Gaston came in quietly, and asked him if there were anything he wanted.

'"No, my son," replied the old man; and then, a thought striking him, he called back Gaston, and asked him for his oaken box.

'This was a little box kept beside his bed. When Gaston had brought it him, and retired, the Abbot fumbled for a key that hung from his girdle, opened the box, and took from it a big bunch of keys. Crossing to one of the stone posts by the fireplace, he passed his hand over it. It swung towards him easily, on a hinge, and revealed a strong cupboard, sunk in the stonework of the chimney. A safe, my friends, a mediæval safe!

'From this he took a little leather wallet, swung back the chimney-post, and crossed to the light. Within the wallet lay a large signet ring, apparently of a deep red tarnished gold. He sat down at his writing-table, took a knife from his girdle, whittled a quill to a very delicate point—he was long satisfying himself as to the point—and bent over his work.

'Now we know, my dear Giddas' (for the professor had again exhibited signs of impatience during the narration of these details), 'that the clue to the treasure's whereabouts was contained in the ring. It cannot have been marked on the metal, or the Abbot would not have needed a quill pen. No, the clue must have been written on a piece of parchment and that parchment hidden somehow in the ring. Accordingly, I conjecture that the ring must have been unusually large.

'Well, unless I'm entirely upon a false scent, the Abbot must have finished his task, the addition, I suppose, of some minute detail to the parchment, written very small with his fine pen-point, and must have actually replaced the parchment in the ring, when all of a sudden there broke out the most appalling din. A wave of hideous panic terror shivered through the air; the ink-horn was flung down, a goblet fell from the table with a crash, and from below stairs came a pandemonium as of devils let loose. The Abbot didn't stop to think—he ran.

'For minutes on end it seemed as if the building was beleaguered by the infernal powers. A long oak table in the great hall rose on one leg, swayed, curveted, and hopped sideways, before the eyes of the horrified beholders. A brass bowl of immense size, hanging by a handle from the wall, was unhooked, held in the air for a second or so, and then dropped with an ear-splitting clang. And everywhere was fear, sheer, hair-raising, panic fear.

'How long this lasted no one knows; but suddenly the Abbot's voice was heard on the stair. Strained and clear, it rang out over the tumult.

'"My children, my children!" he called. "Cast out fear. Cast out fear."

'What happened then Gilbert cannot tell us, for he lost consciousness for a brief space, but calm was soon restored and the disturbance ceased. What was more, in that sudden access of courage which the Abbot's words inspired, everyone seems to have felt that the evil was rebuked and overcome, at least for the time.

'They were just breathing thanksgivings for their deliverance, when a sudden remembrance chilled the Abbot. He stopped short in what he was saying, turned and almost ran upstairs.

'It was as he feared. The ring was gone.

'He kept his head, though, did the old Abbot. Very few, of course, knew the real importance of the ring. So in the morning he gave out that his signet ring had gone, and bade a search be made. Folk the more readily joined therein as several objects of value were easily found in places whither the impish power of the night before had flung them. All—save perhaps the Abbot—were convinced that Bibi's devils were the thieves.

'As a matter of fact, Gaston on that same night had given the ring to the Lady Garda.

'If she did not at once realize whose it was, she was not long in doubt, for the loss was speedily made known. She contrived to meet with Gaston among the yews behind the fish-pond, and there scolded him in whispers. Imperiously he put his hand upon her mouth and bade her now declare, was he not indeed a man? And, be damned to it, but he was. It must have taken a deal of cold, determined courage to have gone through all that hell's delight to grab the ring. He had crept back and watched the Abbot through the hangings.

'Indeed, some thought of Gaston came into the Abbot's mind, and he sent for and questioned him, but the boy's story was so natural— how he had run out into the garden in fear of all the clamour—that the old man was satisfied. All the same, he was taking no chances, and night-time vigils were kept near the treasure's hiding-place, so Gilbert tells us, till the advent of the King's men.

'Meantime, however, the search was pursued pretty rigorously, and on the day following a monk came to pray the Lady Garda that she and her wenches would turn out their belongings, in case the powers of evil should have spirited the ring among them. Garda smiled her assent—she had the ring in her bosom—and bade her chamber-woman conduct the monk above stairs and make the search. Somewhat embarrassed, the good man suffered himself to be led off.

'But the Abbot had not done yet. At the conclusion of a day's fruitless hunting, during which every other missing object was found, except one of the handles of a two-handled silver cup, he announced that a solemn service of commination would be held that night to curse the person of the thief, be he human or diabolical. Reminds one of the Jackdaw of Rheims, doesn't it?

'Well, this was more than Garda bargained for. Gaston was shaken too, but not greatly; he had observed that the previous services had taken very little effect upon the evil spirits. Still, he was uneasy, he said, on her account. She reassured him.

'That night, before the service was due to begin, she crept to the room where Bibi lay. Everyone else shunned it like the plague, especially after dark. She herself confesses to more than one qualm of terror. For a few seconds she stood in the doorway, shading her rushlight in her hand from the draught. The flame burnt up again, and she looked for the coffin, half fearing to see it up somewhere in the air; but there it was in its place upon the table.

'Then, catching her breath, she fumbled in her bosom for the ring, crossed over to the coffin and stood the rushlight on the table beside it. Shaken with a nameless repulsion, she forced open Bibi's mouth, rammed the ring hard back into the gullet, and shut the mouth again. She took one quick look to see that the lips were composed as before, then ran off to her room. Then she washed her hands in seven changes of running water, murmuring Paternosters and making the sign of the Cross.

'Well, to cut a long story short, no one was the worse for the commination—not even Gaston. The Lady Garda did not tell him of what she had done. As for the ring, the monks reasoned that a devil who

148

could lift an oaken table several feet could in the nature of things move a mere ring a dozen miles; and so the loss was soon forgotten—except by the Abbot, and those in the know, that is.'

'But what became of Bibi?' I asked.

Scott smiled, rather enigmatically.

'Oh, they were not taking any more risks with him. They packed him out of the way, soon enough.'

I pressed him for more details, but he only smiled and sat back in his seat. 'Well, Professor,' he said, turning to Giddas, 'have I not made good use of the material?'

'You have indeed,' answered the Professor.

'Almost too good in places. I confess I cannot recall some of the details you have mentioned. Yet I own I am amazed at the skill with which you have collated the different accounts into one coherent story.'

'Good,' replied Scott. 'I felt I had to get it all clear in my own mind, before I could be sure where we stood. And that's about as far as we can get. The Lady Garda, after this, seems to have thought the keeping of a journal too risky a business. We hear from Gilbert that not long after the break-up of the monastery, she married a man considerably older than herself, and went to live in an adjoining county. As for the monks, they were scattered far and wide; and the old Abbot did not long survive the dissolution.'

'So you think, then, that the treasure remains where they hid it?' I asked doubtfully.

Scott lifted his shoulders. 'We know the King's men didn't get it,' he said. 'The Abbot died, and you may be sure that the few who were in the secret did not make any attempt to regain it for a considerable period, if at all. The times were too troubled. Besides, what could they have done with it? The Abbey was no more. Unless they smuggled it abroad somehow—which is unlikely, since, even if the digging up were safely accomplished, the conveyance of such a bulky collection must have attracted notice—the only thing they could have done would be to make a gift of it to another branch of their order. Giddas, who has been so good as to investigate for me, can find no evidence of such a gift in any of the available records.'

'But—surely,' I interposed, 'it would be hard to be certain of them all? Would not the gift, in the very nature of things, be made secretly?'

'It is, of course, possible,' replied Scott. 'All the same, I am prepared to bet that the treasure is still where it was left, that the knowledge of it died with those few monks, and that the clue to the hiding-place is where the Lady Garda put it—in Bibi's mouth.'

'Then,' I said jestingly, 'all you have to do is to find Bibi, and the thing is done.'

Scott paused for a moment, and blew out a cloud of smoke.

'I have found Bibi,' he said, carefully inspecting one of his finger-nails.

'What—you have found him? Where is he?'

'In my studio at Kensington.'

I stared at him in amazement.

'Giddas and I were going to open him this afternoon,' he continued, 'and then, luckily, we ran into you; so you will be able to come and help us.'

'I was not aware,' put in Giddas in his precise voice, 'that Scott had unearthed the creature. The first intimation I had was a telegram from him this morning, asking me to meet him here for lunch.'

'I brought the coffin up last night by train,' said Scott, 'left it in the studio, and slept at my club.'

'What! You've had him all this time, and not yet opened him to see if the ring is there?'

He smiled wryly.

'Well, Tresilian, I'm not an unduly superstitious man, I hope, but there are one or two little facts about Bibi—as you've heard—which made me feel I'd like company for the job of opening him. Come, let us be going.'

'He—he—he!' cackled Giddas suddenly, as we fetched our hats and sticks. 'So you slept at the club. He—he—he!'

A few moments later we were in a taxi, speeding westward. There was a feeling in the air of invincible spring. The folk in Piccadilly seemed light of foot and happy, and the Green Park was freshness itself. The gentle air seemed to rebuke our well-fed complacency, and the fantastic business on which we were bound became more and more incredible.

'But tell me, Scott,' I jerked out, as well as the jolting vehicle would let me, 'how did you find Bibi? You told me they had got rid of him. Where was he?'

'In the vault,' he replied. 'I flatter myself I read their minds to a nicety. They wouldn't cast him away altogether—he was a human being, after all, and had been duly baptized into the Church. At the same time they wanted to bottle him up safely.'

'Well?'

'So I explored the vault to see if there was any sign of a chamber, or a hollow, or a corner that had been bricked up. And, sure enough, I found one, with the stones going the opposite way to the wall stones, and smaller. They'd bricked him in.'

'And now he is in your rooms!'

'Yes. I only hope he hasn't kicked up Jack's alive during the night.'

We became silent for a while: indeed, conversation was difficult in this vehicle, to which my old-fashioned tastes still vastly preferred a hansom. Alas, a hansom is a rarity now. I saw one plying in the Strand the other day, and people turned to stare after it.

Still, there can be no denying that the taxi has the advantage if one is in a hurry. Very soon we had passed down Kensington High Street, and a couple of minutes later the cab was paid and we were ascending the wide stairs to Scott's quarters. The latchkey did its work, and almost on tiptoe we crossed the outer room, Scott leading.

'It's all right,' he said in a voice of relief. 'Nothing has happened. I was half expecting to find the whole place upside down.'

He pulled back one of the big roller blinds from the raised skylight, and the afternoon sun streamed into the dusty studio. A couple more, rolled from the big north window, showed us a little square with green grass and budding trees. But we only noted these things mechanically, for our eyes were at once turned elsewhere.

Bibi's little coffin lay upon a table in a corner. It was, as the chronicler had recorded, almost heart shaped. The wood, though scratched and almost colourless with age, seemed in good condition, and the brass-work had gone a dull green.

We pulled the table out into the light, and watched Scott in silence. Quickly he decided upon the line of attack; his deft fingers moved rapidly with chisel and wedge, and in a short space of time he put down his tools and gingerly lifted the lid.

A mass of wrappings confronted us, but these had rotted to the texture of that filmy paper one sees wrapped round oranges; and, as we craned to look, the body of Bibi was suddenly exposed.

What first struck us was that the head was not so very big after all, but it had evidently shrunk, for it was all wrinkled and withered. Indeed, it resembled nothing so much as an enormous medlar. The features were peaked away almost to nothing, but we could see, beneath the stiff lids, that the eyeballs were of great size and that the lips must have had the beaky appearance described. The limbs and trunk were miserably shrunken, except the belly, which was protuberant and hard.

'The coffin's too deep,' whispered Scott. 'We'll have to lift him out.'

He inserted his fingers with great care behind the head, and gradually slid one hand under the shoulders. Not without some repulsion, I worked mine in under the feet.

'Easy does it. He'll quite likely crumble up. Now.'

We lifted him out lightly, but he proved to be much firmer than we had expected. A miserable object was Bibi, with the sun streaming down upon his withered little yellow body, stamped as it somehow was with a look of ineffable age.

Scott was breathing rather hard. 'Now for it,' he said. He picked up a smooth metal paper-knife, took hold of Bibi's head by the back, and gently worked the paper-knife into the shrivelled mouth. The point went easily in, and with a careful movement he prised the lower jaw a little way open, and proceeded to explore the mouth with the blade.

Suddenly his eyes lit up. 'I've touched something hard,' he cried, and in sudden excitement began to dig vigorously. 'Wait a minute—yes, by Jove, I've got it!'

With the point of the knife he worked a dark substance to the lips, and in another moment we were gazing in silence at a large black ring in the palm of his hand.

Giddas moistened his lips with his tongue. 'Well,' he said. 'Well, this is a triumph for you, Scott. Indeed. Well.'

Then something impelled me to look at the body. What, I don't know. There was the ring, the long-lost Buckross ring, so strangely lost, so wonderfully found. Yet suddenly I had to look at the body. Giddas did the same. And seeing us look, Scott abruptly turned his head and looked.

With a quick intake of breath he put down the ring, seized the body and began to cram it back into the coffin. I looked away—again I don't know why. Suddenly Scott burst into a stream of frantic oaths, and I turned to see him, his eyes glaring horribly, his whole face one contorted mask of utter loathing, striving with all his might to force Bibi down. And Bibi was struggling—struggling—I swear to God I saw his little brown legs writhing over the edge of the box.

Then came terror—sickening, soul-killing, panic terror—of a kind I have never known even in the most appalling nightmare: and in a flash I was rising, floating, in the air: we were all three rising, bobbing like corks on a sea of terror, and the furniture with us. My head was level with the skylight, I caught a glimpse of the trees outside; up, thrusting up; and all the while such fear as I pray I may never feel again.

Then, as suddenly as I had risen, something came to my aid. I remembered the old Abbot's words. 'My children, cast out fear. Cast out fear.'

Slowly but firmly there dawned in me a consciousness of myself. I was no longer afraid. Each moment strengthened that inward core of knowledge and control. For the first time in my life, I felt my personality gather itself to a point to resist deadly and unutterable evil. And as the power grew, I grasped it. Shutting my eyes, clenching my hands, I began steadily to exert my will against the force that held us. The pressure was light at first, but grew and grew, until at last my whole consciousness was rigid with the strain. And in my heart I knew that I could do it. I can beat you, I said to myself grimly, I can, I can, I can.

And I was winning. I was coming down. We were all coming down. But the force was strong—stifling—malignant—awful. It beat in my brain, it shrieked in my ears. Then in hatred and loathing and strong clean anger I exerted not only my own will, but the will of the whole world, and my poor body was the focus of such power as nearly burst it asunder. Blackness roared before my senses.

It was over. We were standing on the floor. Giddas collapsed in a heap. Scott staggered over to the coffin, put the lid over it, and then was violently and horribly sick.

There is little more to tell. The rest of the story was made public at the time; how the ring contained the clue, written, as Scott had surmised, upon a tiny folded piece of parchment; how Giddas succeeded in deciphering it; and how, finally, the treasure was located and recovered, not, as one would have expected, in the Abbey grounds, but at a spot measured from St Leonard's Well, almost two miles distant; together with all the incidental and less important details.

All except one, that is. The day after the occurrences above described, three men stood in the stern of a motor-boat near the mouth of the Thames. Between them, on the seat, lay an odd-looking package weighted heavily. The sun sparkled on the morning water as the boat ran out towards the open sea, and little green bubbles danced merrily in her wake.

When they had come far enough, as they judged, the boat slowed down and described a wide curve. One of them rose, and with difficulty raised the package in his arms. Then he lurched forward and dropped it over the side.

All three stared for a few moments at the spot where it had sunk. Scott, straightening himself, broke the silence.

'And that's that,' he observed.

11

BASIL COPPER

The Knocker at the Portico

I discovered the following papers in the form of a diary while going through some old documents. I append them here. They read as follows:

1

I woke again last night after that hideous dream. I sat up in bed in my dark chamber and listened in fearful suspense but there was no sound apart from the faint moan of the wind in the chimney piece. And yet I heard it. I am convinced of that. It was the fifth time I have heard the knocking. And it is getting worse. I intend to leave this record so that those who come after may know my fate, will realize the manner of it and may be thereby warned.

My name is Edward Rayner. I was born, the third son of a third son, in the ancient city of Salzburg, of an English father and a German mother. My father held for some years a position as Professor of Philosophy at the University there and when he accepted a similar post in London, the family followed after a few months. I was privately educated and being much younger than my two brothers grew up a solitary, introspective child, much given to walking through the little-known suburbs and odd corners of the city which still linger in such an ancient metropolis as London.

My family does not much concern this history, apart from establishing the background and circumstances from which I sprang; indeed, my parents were long dead and my brothers and I separated before the events with which this narrative is concerned began. I had followed my father into scholarship but the generous terms of his will

155

and judicious investments allowed me to pursue my own inclinations; I refrained from any paid employment and preferred the retiring, almost monastic life of a scholar and an aesthete to the boisterous debate and what I regarded as the distracting clamour of university life.

I was, then, settled in a large house in St John's Wood, comfortably off, with few but loyal friends and with sufficient funds to enable me to continue the researches dear to my heart. So it came as a considerable surprise to friends and acquaintances alike when I married, at the confirmed bachelor's age of forty-five, a young and beautiful girl of twenty-four. Jane had been my secretary for several years and thus we were necessarily thrown together for long hours of conversation and study.

I had found it convenient, for the work on which I was engaged involved much tedious searching and quotation from the library of five thousand volumes I had assembled, to engage professional help and Jane had been recommended by one of my oldest friends. She settled in and my scholastic life was soon running more smoothly than I had thought possible. Gradually, she began to encroach more on my private time in the evenings. Within a year she was indispensable to my scholarly career; within three years I could not have imagined life without her.

We were married in a quiet ceremony, spent our honeymoon touring the Middle East, and on our return to London resumed a style of placid, uninterrupted happiness which lasted for more than two years. So bringing me to the heart of an affair which has introduced darkness to what was hitherto all sunshine and pleasure, albeit of a somewhat gentle and intellectual sort.

It is difficult to recollect, at this stage in time and under the present distressing circumstances, exactly when it all began. I had been sleeping badly; I was at a crucial phase in my line of investigation and long poring over the crabbed Hebraic texts had wrought me up to a high pitch of tension, which even my wife had been powerless to prevent.

Usually, I followed Jane's sensible advice in all things, but the work on which I was at present engaged, and which had occupied my attention and thoughts for more than four years, could no longer be thrust into the background; my publishers were clamouring for delivery and as the volume had been pre-advertised I had no alternative but to press ahead.

The library in which I worked was a pleasant room and one well suited to my particular vocation; I had all the latest mechanical aids, including the new type of sliding rack so that the selection of the more bulky volumes was a pleasure. But though I used glasses and occasionally a powerful magnifying disc, my eyes were troubling me.

This was no doubt due to the flickering quality of the pressure-lamps I had had installed. These were not yet at a stage of perfection which they might later attain, and long hours of perusing manuscript, coupled with the minute concentration needed for the use of the glass, had made black dots spin in front of my eyes. Every half an hour I was compelled to cease my labours and a turn about the library, followed by a short rest in my chair, eyes closed, brought me once again ready for my sojourn under the lamps.

But it was gruelling, difficult labour of a kind which exacted much from a frame never robust and a constitution perpetually delicate, so that I often felt I was undermining my health on processes of research which might never come to fruition. In fact had it not been for the urgent remonstration of a publisher who had long been a friend and for whom publication augured much, I might well have put the work aside until the following year. Which would have, in my own case, meant quite a different history from the dark byways into which my life has strayed.

The urgency of my work, the irregularity of my hours and the long periods of labour in the library had at first engaged Jane as enthusiastically as myself but as month succeeded month her ardour diminished and she began to excuse herself more and more frequently from the daily sessions. I felt myself growing pale and haggard under the incessant demands of my self-imposed labours but I could not give up a task which had exacted a great deal and which promised to yield so much in distinction and satisfaction when published. So, as Jane absented herself with ever-increasing frequency, I worked later and later into the small hours of the night.

After several months of this, which was the cause of some bickering between us, things reached an impasse; I cannot say I blame Jane. The situation was entirely my own fault; she had grown distant and abstracted. We met only at breakfast, apart from her occasional visits to the library and the supervision of my meals, which I now took almost entirely within its walls. In the meantime she went for long walks and cultivated such friends as we had. It was understood between us that we would, when my researches were concluded, take a long holiday on the Continent together, and in so doing recapture something of the idyllic relationship which had formerly existed between us.

This was the level to which my affairs had been reduced when the name of Dr Spiros first began to be mentioned in the house. He was, I gathered from Jane, a brilliant physician; his surgery was no great walk from our own door. He had attended Jane when she had a minor fall from a horse in the Park; he had diagnosed a simple sprain but after that his presence never seemed to absent itself from the house for long. Summer wore away and autumn succeeded it and still I laboured on. How I sustained myself I know not at this distance in time but despite the immense labours, I managed to take an hour's walk with Jane once a day latterly—this she had at last prevailed upon me to enjoy.

It was on our return from such a walk one evening that I became aware that Dr Spiros had assumed an important place in my own household without my becoming aware of it. He had, I think, far too great an influence on my impressionable young wife, and if my mind had not been above such base suspicions, I might have suspected darker things when I learned that he usually dined alone with Jane most evenings within my own walls. My surprise on learning this was succeeded by consternation when I found him on one occasion within the fastness of my library itself; even my servants knew this was inviolate and the doctor's lame excuse that my housekeeper had showed him in there by mistake left room for the gravest suspicion on my part.

I remained courteous to Spiros but I was now on my guard. I resolved to learn more of his relationship with Jane which seemed to me to have passed beyond that of a mere physician-patient basis. Dr Spiros was, I should have said, about five and thirty years of age; broad, black-browed and strong in feature with square white teeth which were perpetually smiling beneath his thick black moustache. He was much addicted to perfume or pomades and the aroma of these had a habit of lying subtly in odd corners about the house so that one was always conscious of his presence, even when his physical self was absent from my walls. This was then, the somewhat curious circumstance of my life, when the events I am about to relate crystallized and first assumed menacing shape on the tranquil horizon of my existence.

2

It was, I think, a cold, blustery evening in November when the first manifestation forced itself to my attention. The icy rain had been tapping with obtrusive fingers at the smeared panels all day long and I had heaped the fire in the library with small coal and turned up the brilliance of the lamps in order to keep the dreary night at bay.

The first volume of my work was about to appear from the press; the second and third were in proof form. I was now engaged upon the last, following which I looked forward to the cultivation of my wife's friendship and the resumption of that intimacy which my protracted labours had interrupted. I had just got up on to the stool before my work table when the knocking began. It seemed to emanate from the inner recesses of my brain. A great hammering thunder that commenced as a slight reverberation and then finally shook and tottered the very foundations of the house.

The noise was such that I ran from the library and to the balustrade that ran round the landings commanding the main staircase and hall of the house. The door set under the great portico of the building must have given way under the knocking, but I saw it was still secure. Moreover, to my amazement I saw one of my own staff pass it without a second glance on her way across the hall.

I stood with the massive echoes ringing through my ears before running down the stairs, three at a time. I wrestled with the bronze bolt on the oak-panelled door and flung it back. Nothing but the night wind and the tapping of the rain against my face. The entrance was empty, the brass lantern with its flickering candle, swaying uneasily in the wind.

I slammed the door with a hollow thunder behind me and made my way back up the stairs. In the passage outside the library stood my wife; she looked at me strangely. I said nothing but returned to my place at the desk and bolted the door after me. I was not disturbed again that evening. I have a great fear over something but I know not what. I went to bed early but did not sleep. It was the beginning of many such nights.

3

Dr Spiros is coming to assume a quite disproportionate part in my life of late. Twice more have I seen him in the last few days within my own house, on both occasions unannounced and uninvited by me. I really must speak to Jane about this some time. It was almost as if he had assumed proprietorship of my establishment; there are times when I feel like a stranger in my own household. And yet the man has a kindly face; on the last instance of our meeting I had an impulse to consult him on the subject of the knocking.

He smiled encouragingly as we passed on the stairs. But then something in his eyes hardened my heart against him and I brushed by somewhat discourteously. I do not know what to make of the man but I fear a straight encounter with Jane upon the subject. I badly need a friend and some disinterested advice, though it seems I cannot get this, even within my own family. There is a dark labyrinth in which I wander during the waking hours; I fear sleep also for that is when the knocking is certain to manifest itself.

But I must not run ahead. The second time I heard the knocking was an even more shattering experience than the first. It affected my nerves; I think this must inevitably be so, for curious occurrences at night, when one is hovering halfway between sleep and waking, undressed and abed, are inevitably more disturbing than when we have our wits about us during the blessed day. My dread of these long winter evenings dates definitely from this second occasion. And, like the long progression of a nightmare that has no end, I accelerate silently and inevitably into a situation which leads to the incident of the door.

The next time I heard the knocking was at night; it was so late I should rather call it morning. I had worked on in the library until well past one a.m. and it must have been nearer two when I finally sought my bed. I slept for what seemed a long time but may have been in reality but an hour or so. I was suddenly awake, it appeared, without being conscious of any transitional stage between the sleeping and the state of awareness.

It was quite dark in the chamber, the fire having died to a faint glow by which I could make out various objects in the room. I lay drenched in sweat for perhaps a minute, or longer, terror struggling with reason in my heart. The echo of some gigantic hammering was still within me, but I knew that the echo was merely the reflection of an outward tumult that had its creation in the physical world. The lurid silence was at length broken by a tremendous fusillade of blows with the knocker of the great door in the portico of the house. The tumult was again so great that it seemed as if the whole household must be thrown into uproar; I expected lights, running footsteps, startled cries.

But there was nothing; only the darkness and for the second time the echoes of the knocker's terrifying tattoo dying away against the bruised silence. I lay with my heart thumping and it was like a physical shock when that terrible summons again sounded through the corridors of the darkened house. Somehow, trembling, sick and terrified I found myself at the head of the stairs; I approached a window in an angle of a wing, which commanded a view of the porch. There was nothing but the shadows of the trees in the wild moonlight which fell across the porch door.

Fortunately, I was not called upon to undergo any further ordeal that night; I continued, with ebbing will-power, to watch the empty porch, but the knocking was not renewed. It was just possible that the unknown visitor had covered the space between the door and the street corner before I had approached the window. Cold, in turmoil and half worn-out with the shadowy terrors of that sudden awakening, I was again back at my bedside. I crept between the sheets a badly frightened man and slept fitfully till the friendly light of morning allowed me the comfort of a deeper sleep.

I spent the next few days in a fever of hesitation between work and sleep until it seemed as though the night had blended into the day.

I had no nocturnal disturbances until the fourth evening; Jane had been absent from the house during the earlier part of the afternoon and I had been so immersed in my researches that the tray my house-keeper brought up remained untasted on my study desk. Rain had been spitting fitfully against the opaque panes of the window glass for some hours. Towards nine o'clock I had become aware that I had not eaten for a long time and had emptied a flask of cold coffee and fin-ished the dry toast under the cover, all that now remained fit to digest.

It must have been about ten o'clock when the knocking came. It seemed to split my head asunder. I clung to my desk, my nerves shrieking, my body wet with perspiration until that massive thunder had temporarily subsided. Once more the drama was repeated. I again rushed to the window to see nothing in the porch. But to my horror the hollow thunder recommenced, even though the evidence of my eyes told me that no knocker was within the porch. Dropping the volume I had been perusing, I ran, eyes staring and with clothing awry, to the ground floor. I flung wide the door; there was only shadow within the porch; that, a tendril of vine that tapped dismally against the wall and the ceaseless spitting of the rain.

Just then a serving woman of my household appeared, startled, in the hall behind me.

I seized her by the arm. 'Did you not hear it?' I said in an agitated voice. To my anger the girl shrank away from me with a whimpering cry.

'Fool!' I shrieked and ran from her, leaving her to close the great door. Spiros is concerned in this in some way and I am convinced Jane is helping him. I feel so helpless and yet I am master in my own house-hold; albeit a master without power. Even the servants are turning against me. My housekeeper has a strange face when she brings in my trays, for Jane will not now even perform that simple duty for me.

The knocking was not heard again that night, thank God, though I slept but fitfully. I hear much whispering in the house and Spiros seems to spend a great deal of time here so I am resolved to be on my guard. I cannot catch them at the knocking; they are too clever for that. But I can spy on them in other ways when they think I am in the library; yes, that is what I will do.

What I must do if I am to solve this hideous curse which is hanging over me. How dark the house seems these winter days; even my researches, which were once so dear to me, have lost their savour. My eyes too, trouble me inordinately; I must consult an oculist, or blindness may ensue. Strange, how my mind is at this moment dominated by the absence of light; darkness, absolute and imbued with terror, reigns supreme.

4

Later. I have heard the knocking twice again, each time more demoniacal than the last. As before, there was nothing in the porch. I have been quite ill. I would not have Spiros near my bedside but consulted my own man, Dr Fossey. Though I fear they have conspired together. Jane has not been to see me after the first time. She said my condition had upset her so powerfully that she could not bear to come again, at least for the time being. I suspect otherwise. She and Dr Spiros have been drawing ever closer during these past weeks. I distrust most medical men, but he particularly, though he smiles amiably enough. But all these grimaces and airs and blandness with the patient do not for one moment deceive a person as shrewd as myself.

I feigned unconsciousness the last time Fossey called. He went away after a while. I took the opportunity of slipping from my bedchamber—Jane now sleeps apart, on the excuse of my illness—and putting on a robe descended to the lower floor of the house. I could hear muffled voices from the dining room. The door was ajar. Looking in I saw Spiros hand Fossey some strange, greenish-hued capsules. I see what he is at. What a mercy I came down.

Fossey tried to introduce Spiros' poison among my medicaments tonight. He handed me the deadly capsule together with a draught of water. On pretence of swallowing it I managed to drop it to the floor on the far side of the bed, where it rolled into a dark corner. Fossey seemed satisfied. I am better now and up and about again, working in my library. Spiros seemed puzzled the next time I encountered him in the corridor, as well he might. But for my shrewdness I should now be lying in the churchyard with its crooked headstones, which can be seen from the tallest attic of the house. If only I could talk to Jane, but she will not see me unless accompanied by a third person, usually Spiros or my housekeeper. And that will not do at all.

Thank God the knocking has not been heard for some time. I must take comfort from that. In my weakened condition it might have incalculable effects upon my general health. In the meantime I have resumed my studies, am even struggling on with the fourth volume of my sadly interrupted work. Thanks to the improved cones on the pressure lamps, which have just been delivered, my eyes are holding out. I could not bear it if eternal darkness should descend.

This was the situation which obtained for several weeks more; Jane remained aloof; the consultations with Spiros and Fossey continuing; the servants discreetly neutral; while I strove, under terrible conditions to bring my great work to a close. January of a new year came in thick with snow; I could not forbear contrasting my present straits with the happy New Year rituals Jane and I had been wont to share in earlier days. February followed with bleak winds and heavy rain. But my work was progressing well and it wanted but two or three pages more to round off the labour of more than half a lifetime.

But at the same moment my health, which had been robust by my standards, began to worsen again. My eyesight too, troubled me and my peace of mind was tortured by Spiros' sly machinations. Twice had I caught him walking in the street with Jane; on another occasion I saw them one evening descending from a cab. I followed along the crooked alleys until I saw them go into the lantern-lit entrance of the Medical Institute. This situation seems to plunge me deeper into even darker subterranean passages of unfathomable depth.

5

The crisis has come. I am no longer my own master. I think that I have had more to bear than almost any wretch on earth. Tonight I finished my immense labours, wrote finis to the script with a triumphant flourish of my pen and flung the thing down. I even executed a little dance around the shadowy library, whose silence was broken only by the lonely hissing of the lamps. I sought the small liquor cabinet I keep in there, and poured myself a glass of port for a solitary toast.

I had no sooner lowered the glass than a splintering crash made the whole building shudder; the amber liquid splashed in carmine rivulets across my manuscript as I staggered to my feet, my hands clasped over my ears to keep out the insane cacophony of those mighty thunder claps. I groaned aloud as the unseen knocker dispensed his mad tattoo; the crashing and pounding were enough to rend the door asunder and the echoes fled shrieking into every corner of the house.

I tottered from the library as the alarmed figure of my housekeeper crossed the hall below me. I descended the curving staircase in frenzy. We reached the door almost together.

'What is it, woman?' I shouted, convinced that she knew something of this fearsome mystery which was slowly draining life itself from me. My wild and haggard eyes must have startled the woman because she fell back against the door as though she would prevent me from opening it.

'Mrs Rayner is leaving, sir,' she said.

'Leaving!' I shouted. 'What means this?'

I pushed past her as a cab-wheel grated at the curb. Outside, through the porch window I could see Jane and Dr Spiros, entering a barouche in the windy night. The glimmer of light from a nearby gas-lamp fell square upon Jane's face so that I could not be mistaken.

'Let me pass, woman,' I told the housekeeper. She stood foursquare against the door.

'It is better this way, sir,' she said, with a white face. I was in a passion of rage by this time.

'Woman, you shall let me pass,' I shrieked. There was a rack of Oriental curios inside the hall. Almost without realizing it I found a Malay kris in my hand; I passed it not once but several times through her body, my hand seemingly without volition of its own. Horrified, I saw Mrs Carfax hang there as though crucified, before sliding to the floor in bloody death. I opened the door and fled into the wild night.

I could hear the scraping of the barouche's wheels on the cobbles ahead of me. I followed, cutting through small alleys and courts. I knew this portion of the city intimately and by this method could be sure of keeping abreast of them. I still carried the knife, I know not why. Presently, I was in a deserted part of the metropolis, which was unknown to me; I could still hear the cab's progress but was obliged to keep it in sight, for fear of losing my way.

Presently it stopped in front of a fine, Georgian building with a large porch, lit by a brass lantern from above. Spiros, for I could now see clearly that it was he, paid off the cab and he and Jane entered the house. I waited until the barouche had disappeared. The street was quite empty and deserted. With a mad cry I rushed across to the house, from which light now shone brightly and seized the iron knocker.

As it crashed against the door, the same terrible thunder I had heard so many times, rushed upon me, seeming to mingle with the frenzied tattoo of which I was myself the author. I reeled in agony, clinging to the knocker. The knocking rose to a horrendous crescendo which seemed to penetrate and split my brain. A moment longer and the door was flung wide. I saw first the horrified face of a manservant, with Spiros and Jane behind him.

I screamed and sprang forward with the knife. 'Wifestealer!' I shouted and lunged at Spiros' throat. He was too quick and strong for me. He and the manservant attempted to pinion me. A terrible, silent struggle now began.

Jane was at my side, white and distraught. 'Edward,' she pleaded. 'Dr Spiros is only trying to help you as am I.'

'Fools,' I shrieked. 'I am fully awake for the first time. It is he, THE KNOCKER, who is responsible!'

For I had looked beyond my struggling adversaries. It was indeed a dreadful sight. A tall, emaciated stranger, with parchment face, stubbled beard and the white hair of an old man. Pale yellow eyes proclaimed the madman. Then I reeled, my senses tottering, as the two men bore me down. Another servant produced a strait-jacket.

As I went backwards a fearful mosaic formed before my eyes. I saw the knife in the madman's hand, still smeared with blood, and the sign in wrought iron over the porch: SPIROS ASYLUM FOR THE INSANE.

The truth was borne in upon me as my senses collapsed. For the back of the hall was a brightly illuminated mirror and this pitiful madman reflected in the glare, with writhing features and foaming jaws was beyond all mortal help. THE KNOCKER AT THE PORTICO WAS MYSELF!

6

The manuscript had a note attached to it in another hand. It said that the Patient 642 had spent three and thirty years in the asylum and had died there at the age of seventy-eight.

I put back the papers in the box and sat in thought. My name is also Edward Rayner. I am the third son of a third son. The writer of the narrative was my great-grandfather. I heard the knocking for the first time tonight.

12

GERALD DURRELL

The Entrance

My friends Paul and Marjorie Glenham are both failed artists or, perhaps, to put it more charitably, they are both unsuccessful. But they enjoy their failure more than most successful artists enjoy their success. This is what makes them such good company and is one of the reasons that I always go and stay with them when I am in France. Their rambling farmhouse in Provence was always in a state of chaos, with sacks of potatoes, piles of dried herbs, plates of garlic and forests of dried maize jostling with piles of half-finished watercolours and oil-paintings of the most hideous sort, perpetrated by Marjorie, and strange, Neanderthal sculpture which was Paul's handiwork. Throughout this market-like mess prowled cats of every shade and marking and a river of dogs from an Irish wolfhound the size of a pony to an old English bulldog which made noises like Stephenson's *Rocket*. Around the walls in ornate cages were housed Marjorie's collection of Roller canaries, who sang with undiminished vigour regardless of the hour, thus making speech difficult. It was a warm, friendly, cacophonous atmosphere and I loved it.

When I arrived in the early evening I had had a long drive and was tired, a condition that Paul set about remedying with a hot brandy and lemon of Herculean proportions. I was glad to have got there for, during the last half hour, a summer storm had moved ponderously over the landscape like a great black cloak and thunder reverberated among the crags, like a million rocks cascading down a wooden staircase. I had only just reached the safety of the warm, noisy kitchen, redolent with the mouth-watering smells of Marjorie's cooking, when the rain started in torrents. The noise of it on the tile roof combined with the massive thunderclaps that made even the solid stone farmhouse shudder, aroused the competitive spirit in the canaries and they all burst into song simultaneously. It was the noisiest storm I had ever encountered.

'Another noggin, dear boy?' enquired Paul, hopefully.

'No, no!' shouted Marjorie above the bubbling songs of the birds and the roar of the rain, 'the food's ready and it will spoil if you keep it waiting. Have some wine. Come and sit down, Gerry dear.'

'Wine, wine, that's the thing. I've got something special for you, dear boy,' said Paul and he went off into the cellar to reappear a moment later with his arms full of bottles, which he placed reverently on the table near me. 'A special Gigondas I have discovered,' he said. 'Brontosaurus blood I do assure you, my dear fellow, pure prehistoric monster juice. It will go well with the truffles and the guinea-fowl Marjorie's run up.'

He uncorked a bottle and splashed the deep red wine into a generously large goblet. He was right. The wine slid into your mouth like red velvet and then, when it reached the back of your tongue, exploded like a firework display into your brain cells.

'Good, eh?' said Paul, watching my expression. 'I found it in a small *cave* near Carpentras. It was a blistering hot day and the *cave* was so nice and cool that I sat and drank two bottles of it before I realized what I was doing. It's a seducing wine, all right. Of course when I got out in the sun again the damn stuff hit me like a sledgehammer. Marjorie had to drive.'

'I was so ashamed,' said Marjorie, placing in front of me a black truffle the size of a peach encased in a fragile, feather-light overcoat of crisp brown pastry. 'He paid for the wine and then bowed to the *Patron* and fell flat on his face. The *Patron* and his sons had to lift him into the car. It was disgusting.'

'Nonsense,' said Paul, 'the *Patron* was enchanted. It gave his wine the accolade it needed.'

'That's what you think,' said Marjorie. 'Now start, Gerry, before it gets cold.'

I cut into the globe of golden pastry in front of me and released the scent of the truffle, like the delicious aroma of a damp autumn wood, a million leafy, earthy smells rolled up into one. With the Gigondas as

Gerald Durrell

an accompaniment this promised to be a meal for the Gods. We fell silent as we attacked our truffles and listened to the rain on the roof, the roar of thunder and the almost apoplectic singing of the canaries. The bulldog, who had, for no apparent reason, fallen suddenly and deeply in love with me, sat by my chair watching me fixedly with his protuberant brown eyes, panting gently and wheezing.

'Magnificent, Marjorie,' I said as the last fragment of pastry dissolved like a snowflake on my tongue. 'I don't know why you and Paul don't set up a restaurant: with your cooking and Paul's choice of wines you'd be one of the three-star Michelin jobs in next to no time.'

'Thank you, dear,' said Marjorie, sipping her wine, 'but I prefer to cook for a small audience of gourmets rather than a large audience of gourmands.'

'She's right, there's no gainsaying it,' agreed Paul, splashing wine into our glasses with gay abandon. A sudden prolonged roar of thunder directly overhead precluded speech for a long minute and was so fierce and sustained that even the canaries fell silent, intimidated by the sound. When it had finished Marjorie waved her fork at her spouse.

'You mustn't forget to give Gerry your thingummy,' she said.

'Thingummy?' asked Paul, blankly. 'What thingummy?'

'You *know*,' said Marjorie, impatiently, 'your thingummy . . . your manuscript . . . it's just the right sort of night for him to read it.'

'Oh, the manuscript . . . yes,' said Paul, enthusiastically. 'The *very* night for him to read it.'

'I refuse,' I protested. 'Your paintings and sculptures are bad enough. I'm damned if I'll read your literary efforts as well.'

'Heathen,' said Marjorie, good-naturedly. 'Anyway, it's not Paul's, it's someone else's.'

'I don't think he *deserves* to read it after those disparaging remarks about my art,' said Paul. 'It's too good for him.'

'What is it?' I asked.

'It's a very curious manuscript I picked up . . .' Paul began, when Marjorie interrupted.

'Don't tell him about it, let him read it,' she said. 'I might say it gave *me* nightmares.'

While Marjorie was serving helpings of guinea-fowl wrapped in an almost tangible aroma of herbs and garlic, Paul went over to the

170

corner of the kitchen where a tottering mound of books, like some ruined castle, lay between two sacks of potatoes and a large barrel of wine. He rummaged around for a bit and then emerged triumphantly with a fat red notebook, very much the worse for wear, and came and put it on the table.

'There!' he said with satisfaction. 'The moment I'd read it I thought of you. I got it among a load of books I bought from the library of old Doctor Lepître, who used to be prison doctor down in Marseilles. I don't know whether it's a hoax or what.'

I opened the book and on the inside of the cover found a bookplate in black, three cypress trees and a sundial under which was written, in Gothic script '*Ex Libras Lepître*'. I flipped over the pages and saw that the manuscript was in longhand, some of the most beautiful and elegant copperplate handwriting I had ever seen, the ink now faded to a rusty brown.

'I wish I had waited until daylight to read it,' said Marjorie with a shudder.

'What is it? A ghost story?' I asked curiously.

'No,' said Paul uncertainly, 'at least, not exactly. Old Lepître is dead, unfortunately, so I couldn't find out about it. It's a very curious story. But the moment I read it I thought of you, knowing your interest in the occult and things that go bump in the night. Read it and tell me what you think. You can have the manuscript if you want it. It might amuse you, anyway.'

'I would hardly call it amusing,' said Marjorie, 'anything but amusing. I think it's horrid.'

Some hours later, full of good food and wine, I took the giant golden oil lamp, carefully trimmed, and in its gentle daffodil-yellow light I made my way upstairs to the guest room and a feather bed the size of a barn door. The bulldog had followed me upstairs and sat wheezing, watching me undress and climb into bed. He now lay by the bed looking at me soulfully. The storm continued unabated and the rumble of thunder was almost continuous, while the dazzling flashes of lightning lit up the whole room at intervals. I adjusted the wick of the lamp, moved it closer to me, picked up the red notebook and settled myself back against the pillows to read. The manuscript began without preamble.

March 16th 1901. Marseilles.

I have all night lying ahead of me and, as I know I cannot sleep—
in spite of my resolve—I thought I would try to write down in detail
the thing that has just happened to me. I am afraid that setting it down
like this will not make it any the more believable, but it will pass the
time until dawn comes and with it my release.

Firstly I must explain a little about myself and my relationship with
Gideon de Teildras Villeray so that the reader (if there ever is one) will
understand how I came to be in the depths of France in mid-winter. I
am an antiquarian bookseller and can say, in all modesty, that I am at
the top of my profession. Or perhaps it would be more accurate to say
that I *was* at the top of my profession. I was even once described by
one of my fellow booksellers—I hope more in a spirit of levity than of
jealousy—as a 'literary truffle hound', a description which I suppose,
in its amusing way, does describe me.

A hundred or more libraries have passed through my hands, and I
have been responsible for a number of important finds; the original
Gottenstein manuscript, for example; the rare 'Conrad' illustrated
Bible, said by some to be as beautiful as the *Book of Kells*; the five new
poems by Blake that I unearthed at an unpromising country house
sale in the Midlands; and many lesser but none-the-less satisfying dis-
coveries, such as the signed first edition of *Alice in Wonderland* that I
found in a trunk full of rag books and toys in the nursery of a vicarage
in Shropshire and a presentation copy of *Sonnets from the Portuguese*,
signed and with a six-line verse written on the flyleaf by both Robert
and Elizabeth Browning.

To be able to unearth such things in unlikely places is rather like
water divining, either you are born with the gift or not; it is not something you can acquire, though most certainly, with practice, you are
able to sharpen your perceptions and make your eye keener. In my
spare time I also catalogue some of the smaller and more important
libraries, as I get enormous pleasure out of simply *being* with books.
To me the quietness of a library, the smell and the feel of the books, is
like the taste and texture of food to a gourmet. It may sound fanciful,
but I can stand in a library and hear the myriad voices around me as
though I was standing in the middle of a vast choir, a choir of knowledge and beauty.

Naturally, because of my work, it was at Sotheby's that I first met Gideon. I had unearthed in a house in Sussex a small but quite interesting collection of first editions and, being curious to know what they would fetch, had attended the sale myself. As the bidding was in progress I got the uncomfortable feeling that I was being watched. I glanced around but could see no one whose attention was not upon the auctioneer. Yet, as the sale proceeded I got more and more uncomfortable. Perhaps this is too strong a word, but I became convinced that I was the object of an intense scrutiny.

At last the crowd in the saleroom moved slightly and I saw who it was. He was a man of medium height with a handsome but somewhat plump face, piercing and very large dark eyes and smoky-black, curly hair, worn rather long. He was dressed in a well-cut dark overcoat with an astrakhan collar, and in his elegantly gloved hands he carried the sales catalogue and a wide-brimmed dark velour hat. His glittering, gypsy-like eyes were fixed on me intently, but when he saw me looking at him the fierceness of his gaze faded, and he gave me a faint smile and a tiny nod of his head, as if to acknowledge that he had been caught out staring at me in such a vulgar fashion. He turned then, shouldered his way through the people that surrounded him and was soon lost to my sight.

I don't know why but the intense scrutiny of this stranger disconcerted me, to such an extent that I did not follow the rest of the sale with any degree of attention, except to note that the items I had put up fetched more than I had anticipated. The bidding over, I made my way through the crush and out into the street.

It was a dank, raw day in February, with that unpleasant smoky smell in the air that augurs fog and makes the back of your throat raw. As it looked unpleasantly as though it might drizzle I hailed a cab. I have one of those tall, narrow houses in Smith Street, just off the King's Road. It was bequeathed to me by my mother and does me very well. It is not in a fashionable part of Town, but the house is quite big enough for a bachelor like myself and his books, for I have, over the years, collected a small but extremely fine library on the various subjects that interest me: Indian art, particularly miniatures; some of the early Natural Histories; a small but rather rare collection of books on the occult; a number of volumes on plants and great gardens, and a good collection of first editions of contemporary novelists. My home is simply furnished but comfortable; although I am not rich, I have sufficient for my needs and I keep a good table and very reasonable wine cellar.

As I paid off the cab and mounted the steps to my front door I saw that, as I had predicted, the fog was starting to descend upon the city. Already it was difficult to see the end of the street. It was obviously going to turn out to be a real peasouper and I was glad to be home. My housekeeper, Mrs Manning, had a bright and cheerful fire burning in my small drawing-room and, next to my favourite chair, she had, as usual, laid out my slippers (for who can relax without slippers?) and on a small table all the accoutrements for a warming punch. I took off my coat and hat, slipped off my shoes and put on my slippers.

Presently Mrs Manning appeared from the kitchen below and asked me, in view of the weather, if I would mind if she went home since it seemed as if the fog was getting thicker. She had left me some soup, a steak and kidney pie and an apple tart, all of which only needed heating. I said that this would do splendidly, since on many occasions I had looked after myself in this way.

'There was a gentleman come to see you a bit earlier,' said Mrs Manning.

'A gentleman? What was his name?' I asked, astonished that anyone should call on such an evening.

'He wouldn't give no name, sir,' she replied, 'but said he'd call again.'

I thought that, in all probability, it had something to do with a library I was cataloguing, and thought no more about it. Presently Mrs Manning reappeared, dressed for the street. I let her out of the front door and bolted it securely behind her, before returning to my drink and the warm fire. My cat Neptune appeared from my study upstairs, where his comfortable basket was, gave a faint mieouw of greeting and jumped gracefully on to my lap where, after paddling with his forepaws for a short while, he settled down to dream and doze, purring like a great tortoiseshell hive of bees. Lulled by the fire, the punch and the loud purrs of Neptune, I dropped off to sleep.

I must have slept heavily for I awoke with a start and was unable to recall what it was that had awakened me. On my lap Neptune rose, stretched and yawned as if he knew he was going to be disturbed. I listened but the house was silent. I had just decided that it must have been the rustling scrunch of coals shifting in the grate when there came an imperious knocking at the front door. I made my way there, repairing, as I went, the damage that sleep had perpetrated on my neat appearance, straightening my collar and tie and smoothing down my hair which is unruly at the best of times.

I lit the light in the hall, unbolted the front door and threw it open. Shreds of mist swirled in, and there standing on the top step was the curious, gypsy-like man that I had seen watching me so intently at Sotheby's. Now he was dressed in a well-cut evening suit and was wearing an opera cloak lined with red silk. On his head was a top hat whose shining appearance was blurred by the tiny drops of moisture deposited on it by the fog which moved, like an unhealthy yellow backdrop, behind him. In one gloved hand he held a slender ebony cane with a beautifully worked gold top and he swung this gently between his fingers like a pendulum. When he saw that it was I who had opened the door and not a butler or some skivvy, he straightened up and removed his hat.

'Good evening,' he said, giving me a most charming smile that showed fine, white, even teeth. His voice had a peculiar husky, lilting, musical quality that was most attractive, an effect enhanced by his slight but noticeable French intonation.

'Good evening,' I said, puzzled as to what this stranger could possibly want of me.

'Am I addressing Mr Letting . . . Mr Peter Letting?'

'Yes. I am Peter Letting.'

He smiled again, removed his glove and held out a well-manicured hand on which a large blood opal gleamed in a gold ring.

'I am more delighted than I can say at this opportunity of meeting you, sir,' he said, as he shook my hand, 'and I must first of all apologize for disturbing you at such a time, on such a night.'

He drew his cloak around him slightly and glanced at the damp, yellow fog that swirled behind him. Noting this I felt it incumbent upon me to ask him to step inside and state his business, for I felt it would hardly be good manners to keep him standing on the step in such unpleasant weather. He entered the hall, and when I had turned from

Gerald Durrell

closing and bolting the front door, I found that he had divested himself of his hat, stick, and cloak, and was standing there, rubbing his hands together looking at me expectantly.

'Come into the drawing-room, Mr . . .' I paused on a note of interrogation.

A curious, childlike look of chagrin passed across his face, and he looked at me contritely.

'My dear sir,' he said, 'my dear Mr Letting. How excessively remiss of me. You will be thinking me totally lacking in social graces, forcing my way into your home on such a night and then not even bothering to introduce myself. I do apologize. I am Gideon de Teildras Villeray.'

'I am pleased to meet you,' I said politely, though in truth I must confess that, in spite of his obvious charm, I was slightly uneasy, for I could not see what a Frenchman of his undoubted aristocratic lineage would want of an antiquarian bookseller such as myself. 'Perhaps,' I continued, 'you would care to come in and partake of a little refreshment . . . some wine perhaps, or maybe since the night is so chilly, a little brandy?'

'You are very kind and very forgiving,' he said with a slight bow, still smiling his beguiling smile. 'A glass of wine would be most welcome, I do assure you.'

I showed him into my drawing-room and he walked to the fire and held his hands out to the blaze, clenching and unclenching his white fingers so that the opal in his ring fluttered like a spot of blood against his white skin. I selected an excellent bottle of Margaux and transported it carefully up to the drawing-room with two of my best crystal glasses. My visitor had left the fire and was standing by my bookshelves, a volume in his hands. He glanced up as I entered and held up the book.

'What a superb copy of Eliphas Levi,' he said enthusiastically, 'and what a lovely collection of *grimoires* you have got. I did not know you were interested in the occult.'

'Not really,' I said, uncorking the wine. 'After all, no sane man would believe in witches and warlocks and sabbaths and spells and all that tarradiddle. No, I merely collect them as interesting books which are of value and in many cases, because of their contents, exceedingly amusing.'

176

'Amusing?' he said, coming forward to accept the glass of wine I held out to him. 'How do you mean, amusing?'

'Well, don't you find amusing the thought of grown men mumbling all those silly spells and standing about for hours in the middle of the night expecting Satan to appear? I confess I find it very amusing indeed.'

'I do not,' he said, and then, as if he feared that he had been too abrupt and perhaps rude, he smiled and raised his glass. 'Your very good health, Mr Letting.'

We drank. He rolled the wine round his mouth and then raised his eyebrows.

'May I compliment you on your cellar,' he said. 'This is an excellent Margaux.'

'Thank you,' I said, flattered, I must confess, that this aristocratic Frenchman should approve my choice in wine. 'Won't you have a chair and perhaps explain to me how I may be of service to you.'

He seated himself elegantly in a chair by the fire, sipped his wine and stared at me thoughtfully for a moment. When his face was in repose you noticed the size and blackness and lustre of his eyes. They seem to probe you, almost as if they could read your very thoughts. The impression they gave made me uncomfortable, to say the least. But then he smiled and immediately the eyes flashed with mischief, good humour and an overwhelming charm.

'I'm afraid that my unexpected arrival so late at night . . . and on such a night . . . must lend an air of mystery to what is, I'm afraid, a very ordinary request that I have to make of you. Simply, it is that I should like you to catalogue a library for me, a comparatively small collection of books, not above twelve hundred I surmise, which was left to me by my aunt when she died last year. As I say, it is only a small collection of books and I have done no more than give it a cursory glance. However, I believe it to contain some quite rare and valuable things and I feel it necessary to have it properly catalogued, a precau- tion my aunt never took, poor dear. She was a woman with a mind of cotton wool and never, I dare swear, opened a book from the start of her life until the end of it. She led an existence untrammelled and unruffled by the slightest breeze of culture. She had inherited the books from her father and from the day they came into her possession she never paid them the slightest regard. They are a muddled and confused mess, and I would be grateful if you would lend me your expertise in sorting them out. The reason that I have invaded your house at such an hour is force of circumstances, for I must go back to France tomorrow morning very early, and this was my only chance of seeing you. I do hope you can spare the time to do this for me?'

'I shall be happy to be of what assistance I can,' I said, for I must admit that the idea of a trip to France was a pleasant thought, 'but I am curious to know why you have picked on me when there are so many people in Paris who could do the job just as well, if not better.'

'I think you do yourself an injustice,' said my visitor. 'You must be aware of the excellent reputation you enjoy. I asked a number of people for their advice and when I found that they all spontaneously advised me to ask you, then I was sure that, if you agreed to do the work, I would be getting the very best, my dear Mr Letting.'

I confess I flushed with pleasure, since I had no reason to doubt the man's sincerity. It was pleasant to know that my colleagues thought so highly of me.

'When would you wish me to commence?' I asked.

He spread his hands and gave an expressive shrug.

'I'm in no hurry,' he said. 'Naturally I would have to fall in with your plans. But I was wondering if, say, you could start some time in the spring? The Loire valley is particularly beautiful then and there is no reason why you should not enjoy the countryside as well as catalogue books.'

'The spring would suit me admirably,' I said, pouring out some more wine. 'Would April be all right?'

'Excellent,' he said. 'I would think that the job would take you a month or so, but from my point of view please stay as long as it is necessary. I have a good cellar and a good chef, so I can minister to the wants of the flesh at any rate.'

I fetched my diary and we settled on April the fourteenth as being a suitable date for both of us. My visitor rose to go.

'Just one other thing,' he said as he swirled his cloak around his shoulders. 'I would be the first to admit that I have a difficult name both to remember and to pronounce. Therefore, if you would not consider it presumptuous of me, I would like you to call me Gideon and may I call you Peter?'

'Of course,' I said immediately and with some relief, for the name de Teildras Villeray was not one that slid easily off the tongue.

He shook my hand warmly, once again apologized for disturbing me, promised he would write with full details of how to reach him in France and then strode off confidently into the swirling yellow fog and was soon lost to view.

I returned to my warm and comfortable drawing-room and finished the bottle of wine while musing on my strange visitor. The more I thought about it the more curious the whole incident became. For example, why had Gideon not approached me when he first saw me at Sotheby's? He said that he was in no hurry to have his library catalogued and yet felt it imperative that he should see me, late at night, as if the matter was of great urgency. Surely he could have written to me? Or did he perhaps think that the force of his personality would make me accept a commission that I might otherwise refuse?

I was in two minds about the man himself. As I said, when his face was in repose his eyes were so fiercely brooding and penetrating that they made me uneasy and filled almost with a sense of repugnance. But then when he smiled and his eyes filled with laughter and he talked with that husky, musical voice, I had been charmed in spite of myself. He was, I decided, a very curious character, and I determined that I would try to find out more about him before I went over to France. Having made this resolution, I made my way down to the kitchen, preceded by a now hungry Neptune, and cooked myself a late supper.

A few days later I ran into my old friend Edward Mallenger at a sale. During the course of it I asked him casually if he knew of Gideon. He gave me a very penetrating look from over the top of his glasses.

'Gideon de Teildras Villeray?' he asked. 'D'you mean the Count . . . the nephew of the old Marquis de Teildras Villeray?'

'He didn't tell me he was a Count, but I suppose it must be the same one,' I said. 'Do you know anything about him?'

'When the sale is over we'll go and have a drink and I'll tell you,' said Edward. 'They are a very odd family . . . at least, the old Marquis is distinctly odd.'

The sale over we repaired to the local pub and over a drink Edward told me what he knew of Gideon. It appeared that, many years previously, the Marquis de Teildras Villeray had asked my friend to go to France (just as Gideon had done with me) to catalogue and value his extensive library. Edward had accepted the commission and had set off for the Marquis's place in the Gorge du Tarn.

'Do you know that area of France?' Edward asked.

'I have never been to France at all,' I confessed.

'Well, it's a desolate area. The house is in a wild and remote district right in the Gorge itself. It's a rugged country, with huge cliffs and deep gloomy gorges, waterfalls and rushing torrents, not unlike the Gustave Doré drawings for Dante's Inferno, you know.'

Edward paused to sip his drink thoughtfully, and then occupied himself with lighting a cigar. When it was drawing to his satisfaction, he went on. 'In the house, apart from the family retainers of which there only seemed to be three (a small number for such a large establishment) was the uncle and his nephew whom, I take it, was your visitor of the other night. The uncle was—well, not to put too fine a point on it, a most unpleasant old man. He must have been about eighty-five, I suppose, with a really evil, leering face, and an oily manner that he obviously thought was charming. The boy was about fourteen with huge dark eyes in a pale face. He was an intelligent lad, old for his age, but the thing that worried me was that he seemed to be suffering from intense fear, a fear, I felt, of his uncle.

'The first night I arrived, after we had had dinner, which was, to my mind meagre and badly cooked fare for France, I went to bed early, for I was fatigued after my journey. The old man and the boy stayed up. As luck would have it the dining-room was directly below my bedroom, and so, although I could not hear clearly all that passed between them I could hear enough to discern that the old man was doing his best to persuade his nephew into some course of action that the boy found repugnant, for he was vehement in his refusal. The argument went on for some time, the uncle's voice getting louder and louder and more angry. Suddenly, I heard the scrape of a chair as the boy stood and shouted, positively shouted, my dear Peter—in French at his uncle: "No, no, I will not be devoured so that you may live . . . I hate you." I heard it quite clearly and I thought it an astonishing thing for a young boy to say. Then I heard the door of the dining-salon open and bang shut, the boy's footsteps running up stairs and, eventually, the banging of what I assumed was his bedroom door.

'After a short while I heard the uncle get up from the table and start to come upstairs. There was no mistaking his footfall, for one of his feet was twisted and misshapen and so he walked slowly with a pronounced limp, dragging his left foot. He came slowly up the stairs, and I do assure you, my dear Peter, there was positive evil in this slow, shuffling approach that really made my hair stand on end. I heard him go to the boy's bedroom door, open it and enter. He called the boy's name two or three times, softly and cajolingly, but with indescribable menace. Then he said one sentence which I could not catch. After this he closed the boy's door and for some moments I could hear him dragging and shuffling down the long corridor to his own quarters.

'I opened my door and from the boy's room I could hear muffled weeping, as though the poor child had his head under the bedclothes. It went on for a long time, and I was very worried. I wanted to go and comfort the lad, but I felt it might embarrass him, and in any case it was really none of my business. But I did not like the situation at all. The whole atmosphere, my dear Peter, was charged with something unpleasant.

'I am not a superstitious man, as you well know, but I lay awake for a long time and wondered if I could stay in the atmosphere of that house for the two or three weeks it would take me to finish the job which I had agreed to do. Fortunately, fate gave me the chance I needed: the very next day I received a telegram to say that my sister had fallen gravely ill and so, quite legitimately, I could ask de Teildras Villeray to release me from my contract. He was, of course, most reluctant to do so, but he eventually agreed with ill-grace.

'While I was waiting for the dog cart to arrive to take me to the station, I had a quick look round some of his library. Since it was really extensive it spread all over the house, but the bulk of it was housed in what he referred to as the Long Gallery, a very handsome, long room, that would not have disgraced one of our aristocratic country houses. It was hung with giant mirrors between the bookcases, in fact, the whole house was full of mirrors. I can never remember being in a house with so many before.

'He certainly had a rare and valuable collection of books, particularly on one of your pet subjects, Peter, the occult. I noticed, in my hurried browse, among other things, some most interesting Hebrew

181

manuscripts on witchcraft, as well as an original of Matthew Hopkins's *Discovery of Witches* and a truly beautiful copy of Dee's *De Mirabilius Naturae*. But then the dog cart arrived and, making my farewells, I left.

'I can tell you, my dear boy, I was never so glad in my life to be quit of a house. I truly believe the old man to have been evil and would not be surprised to learn that he practised witchcraft and was trying to involve that nice young lad in his foul affairs. However, I have no proof of this, you understand, so that is why I would not wish to repeat it. I should imagine that the uncle is now dead, or, if not, he must be in his nineties. As to the boy, I later heard from friends in Paris that there were rumours that his private life was not all that it should be, some talk of his attachment to certain women, you know, but this was all circumstantial, and in any case, as you know dear boy, foreigners have a different set of morals to an Englishman. It is one of the many things that sets us apart from the rest of the world, thank God.'

I had listened with great interest to Edward's account, and I resolved to ask Gideon about his uncle if I got the chance.

I prepared myself for my trip to France with, I must admit, pleasurable anticipation, and on April the fourteenth I embarked on the train to Dover and thence, uneventfully (even to *mal de mer*), to Calais. I spent the night in Paris, sampling the delights of French food and wine, and the following day I embarked once more on the train. Eventually I arrived at the bustling station at Tours. Gideon was there to meet me as he had promised he would. He seemed in great spirits and greeted me as if I was an old and valued friend, which, I confess, flattered me. I thanked him for coming to meet me, but he waved my thanks away.

'It's nothing, my dear Peter,' he said. 'I have nothing to do except eat, drink, and grow fat. A visit from someone like you is a rare pleasure.'

Outside the station we entered a handsome brougham drawn by two beautiful bay horses and we set off at a spanking pace through the most delicious countryside, all green and gold and shimmering in the sunlight.

We drove for an hour along roads that got progressively narrower and narrower, until we were travelling along between high banks emblazoned with flowers of every sort, while overhead, the branches of the trees on each side of the road entwined, covered with the delicate green leaves of spring. Occasionally there would be a gap in the trees and high banks and I would see the silver gleam of the Loire between the trees. I realized that we were driving parallel to the great river. Once we passed the massive stone gateposts and wrought-iron gates that guarded the drive up to an immense and very beautiful château in gleaming pinky-yellow stone. Gideon saw me looking at it, perhaps with an expression of wonder, for it did look like something out of a fairy tale. He smiled.

'I hope, my dear Peter, that you do not expect to find me living in a monster like that? If so, you will be doomed to disappointment. I am afraid that my château is a miniature one, but big enough for my needs.'

I protested that I did not care if he lived in a cow shed: for me the experience of being in France for the first time and seeing all these new sights and with the prospect of a fascinating job at the end of it, was more than sufficient.

It was not until evening, when the mauve tree shadows were stretched long across the green meadows, that we came to Gideon's establishment, the Château St Claire. The gateposts were surmounted by two large, delicately carved owls in a pale honey-coloured stone, and I saw that the same motif had been carried out most skilfully in the wrought-iron gates that hung from the pillars.

As soon as we entered the grounds I was struck by the contrast to the countryside we had been passing through, which had been exuberant and unkempt, alive with wild flowers and meadows, shaggy with long rich grass. Here the drive was lined with giant oak and chestnut trees, each the circumference of a small room, gnarled and ancient, with bark as thick as an elephant's hide. How many hundred years these trees had guarded the entrance to the Château St Claire, I could not imagine, but many of them must have been well-grown when Shakespeare was a young man. The green sward under them was as smooth as baize on a billiard table, and responsible for this, were several herds of spotted fallow deer, grazing peacefully in the setting sun's rays. The bucks, with their fine twisted antlers, threw up their heads and gazed at us without fear as we clopped past them and down the avenue.

Beyond the green sward I could see a line of gigantic poplars and, gleaming between them, the Loire. Then the drive turned away from the river and the château came into sight. It was, as Gideon had said, small but perfect, as a miniature is perfect. In the evening sun its pale straw-coloured walls glowed and the light gave a soft and delicate patina to the blueish slate of the roofs of the main house and its two turrets.

It was surrounded by a wide veranda of great flagstone, hemmed in by a wide balustrade on which were perched above thirty peacocks, their magnificent tails trailing down towards the well-kept lawn. Around the balustrade, the flower beds, beautifully kept, were ablaze with flowers in a hundred different colours that seemed to merge with the tails of the peacocks that trailed amongst them. It was a breathtaking sight. The carriage pulled up by the wide steps, the butler threw open the door of the brougham, and Gideon dismounted, took off his hat and swept me a low bow, grinning mischievously.

'Welcome to the Château St Claire,' he said.

Thus for me began an enchanted three weeks, for it was more of a holiday than work. The miniature, but impeccably kept and furnished château was a joy to live in. The tiny park that meandered along the river bank was also beautifully kept, for every tree looked as if it were freshly groomed, the emerald lawns combed each morning, and the peacocks, trailing their glittering tails amongst the massive trees, as if they had just left the careful hands of Fabergé. Combine this with a fine cellar and a kitchen ruled over by a red balloon of a chef whose deft hands would conjure up the most delicate and aromatic of meals, and you had a close approach to an earthly paradise.

The morning would be spent sorting and cataloguing the books (and a most interesting collection it was) and then in the afternoon Gideon would insist that we went swimming or else for a ride round the park, for he possessed a small stable of very nice horses. In the evenings, after dinner, we would sit on the still sun-warmed terrace and talk, our conversation made warm and friendly by the wine we had consumed and the excellent meal we had eaten.

Gideon was an excellent host, a brilliant raconteur and this, together with his extraordinary gift for mimicry, made him a most entertaining companion. I shall never know now, of course, whether he deliberately exerted all his charm in order to ensnare me. I like to think not; that he quite genuinely liked me and my company. Not that I suppose it matters now. But certainly, as day followed day, I grew fonder and fonder of Gideon.

I am a solitary creature by nature, and I have only a very small circle of friends—close friends—whom I see perhaps once or twice a year, preferring, for the most part, my own company. However, my time spent at the château with Gideon had an extraordinary effect upon me. It began to dawn upon me that I had perhaps made myself into too much of a recluse. It was also borne upon me most forcibly that all my friends were of a different age group, much older than I was. Gideon, if I could count him as a friend (and by this time I certainly did), was the only friend I had who was, roughly speaking, my own age. Under his influence I began to expand. As he said to me one night, a slim cigar crushed between his strong white teeth, squinting at me past the blue smoke, 'the trouble with you, Peter, is that you are in danger of becoming a young fogey'. I laughed, of course, but on reflection I knew he was right. I also knew that when the time came for me to leave the château I would miss his volatile company a great deal, probably more than I cared to admit, even to myself.

In all our talks Gideon discussed his extensive family with a sort of ironic affection, telling me anecdotes to illustrate their stupidity or their eccentricity, never maliciously but rather with a sort of detached good humour. However, the curious thing was that he never once mentioned his uncle, the Marquis, until one evening. We were sitting out on the terrace, watching the white owls that lived in the hollow oaks along the drive doing their first hunting swoops across the green sward in front of us. I had been telling him of a book which I knew was to be put up for sale in the autumn and which I thought could be purchased for some two thousand pounds. It was an important work and I felt he should have it in his library as it complemented the other works he had on the subject. Did he want me to bid for him? He flipped his cigar butt over the balustrade into the flower bed where it lay gleaming like a monstrous red glow worm, and chuckled softly.

'Two thousand pounds?' he said. 'My dear Peter, I am not rich enough to indulge my hobby to that extent, unfortunately. If my uncle were to die now it would be a different story.'

'Your uncle?' I queried cautiously. 'I did not know you had any uncles.'

'Only one, thank God,' said Gideon, 'but unfortunately he holds the purse strings of the family fortunes and the old swine appears to be indestructible. He is ninety-one and when I last saw him, a year or two back, he did not look a day over fifty. However, in spite of all his efforts I do not believe him to be immortal and so one day the devil will gather him to his bosom. On that happy day I will inherit a very large sum of money and a library that will make even you, my dear Peter, envious. Until that day comes I cannot go around spending two thousand pounds on a book. But waiting for dead men's shoes is a tedious occupation, and my uncle is an unsavoury topic of conversation, so let's have some more wine and talk of something pleasant.'

'If he is unsavoury, then he is in contrast to the rest of your relatives you have told me about,' I said lightly, hoping that he would give me further information about his infamous uncle.

Gideon was silent for a moment.

'Yes, a great contrast,' he said, 'but as every village must have its idiot, so every family must have its black sheep or its madman.'

'Oh, come now, Gideon,' I protested. 'Surely that's a bit too harsh a criticism?'

'You think so?' he asked and in the half light I could see that his face was shining with sweat. 'You think I am being harsh to my dear relative? But then you have not had the pleasure of meeting him, have you?'

'No,' I said, worried by the savage bitterness in his voice and wishing that I had let the subject drop since it seemed to disturb him so much.

'When my mother died I had to go and live with my dear uncle for several years until I inherited the modest amount of money my father left me in trust and I could be free of him. For ten years I lived in purgatory with that corrupt old swine. For ten years not a day or a night passed without my being terrified out of my soul. There are no words to describe how evil he is, and there are no lengths to which he will not go to achieve his ends. If Satan prowls the earth in the guise of a man then he surely inhabits the filthy skin of my uncle.'

He got up abruptly and went into the house. I was puzzled and alarmed at the vehemence with which he had spoken. I did not know whether to follow him or not, but presently he returned carrying the brandy decanter and two glasses. He sat down and poured us both a generous amount of the spirit.

'I must apologize, my dear Peter, for all my histrionics, for inflicting you with melodrama that would be more in keeping in the *Grande Guignol* than on this terrace,' he said, handing me my drink. 'Talking of my old swine of an uncle has that effect on me, I'm afraid. At one time I lived in fear because I thought he had captured my soul . . . you know the stupid ideas children get? It was many years before I grew out of that. But it still, as you can see, upsets me to talk of him, so let's drink and talk of other things, eh?'

I agreed wholeheartedly, and we talked pleasantly for a couple of hours or so. But that night was the only time I saw Gideon go to bed the worse for liquor. I felt most guilty since I felt it was due to my insistence that he talk about his uncle who had made such a deep, lasting and unpleasant impression on his mind.

Over the next four years I grew to know Gideon well. He came to stay with me whenever he was in England and I paid several delightful visits to the Château St Claire. Then for a period of six months I heard nothing from him. I could only presume that he had been overcome by what he called his 'travel disease' and had gone off to Egypt or the Far East or even America on one of his periodic jaunts. However, this coincided with a time when I was, myself, extremely busy and so I had little time to ponder on the whereabouts of Gideon. Then, one evening, I returned home to Smith Street dead tired after a long journey from Aberdeen and I found awaiting me a telegram from Gideon.

Arriving London Monday thirty can I stay stop Uncle put to death I inherit library would you catalogue value move stop explain all when we meet regards Gideon.

I was amused that Gideon, who prided himself on his impeccable English, should have written 'put to death' instead of 'died' until he arrived and I discovered that this is exactly what had happened to his uncle, or, at least, what appeared to have happened. Gideon arrived quite late on the Monday evening and as soon as I looked at him I could see that he had been undergoing some harrowing experience.

Surely, I thought to myself, it could not be the death of his uncle that was affecting him so. If anything I would have thought he would have been glad. But my friend had lost weight, his handsome face was gaunt and white and he had dark circles under his eyes that seemed suddenly to have lost all their sparkle and lustre. When I poured him out a glass of his favourite wine he took it with a hand that trembled slightly and tossed it back in one gulp as if it had been mere water.

'You look tired, Gideon,' I said. 'You must have a few glasses of wine and then I suggest an early dinner and bed. We can discuss all there is to be discussed in the morning.'

'Dear old Peter,' he said, giving me a shadow of his normally effervescent smile. 'Please don't act like an English nanny, and take that worried look off your face. I am not sickening for anything. It's just that I have had rather a hard time these last few weeks and I'm suffering from reaction. However, it's all over now, thank God. I'll tell you all about it over dinner, but before then I would be grateful if I could have a bath, my dear chap.'

'Of course,' I said immediately, and went to ask Mrs Manning to draw a bath for my friend, and to take his baggage up to the guest room.

He went upstairs to bathe and change, and very shortly I followed him. Both my bedroom and the guest room had their own bathrooms, for there was sufficient room on that floor to allow this little luxury. I was just about to start undressing in order to start my own ablutions when I was startled by a loud moaning cry, almost a strangled scream, followed by a crash of breaking glass which appeared to emanate from Gideon's bathroom. I hastened across the narrow landing and tapped on his door.

'Gideon?' I called. 'Gideon, are you all right . . . can I come in?'

There was no reply and so, greatly agitated, I entered the room. I found my friend in his bathroom, bent over the basin and holding on to it for support, his face the ghastly white of cheese, sweat streaming down it. The big mirror over the basin had been shattered and the fragments, together with a broken bottle of what looked like hair shampoo, littered the basin and the floor around.

'He did it . . . he did it . . . he did it . . .' muttered Gideon to himself, swaying, clutching hold of the basin. He seemed oblivious of my presence. I seized him by the arm and helped him into the bedroom where I made him lie down on the bed and called down the stairs for Mrs Manning to bring up some brandy and look sharp about it.

When I went back into the room Gideon was looking a little better, but he was lying there with his eyes closed, taking deep, shuddering breaths like a man who has just run a gruelling race. When he heard me approach the bed he opened his eyes and gave me a ghastly smile.

'My dear Peter,' he said, 'I do apologize . . . so stupid of me . . . I suddenly felt faint . . . I think it must be the journey and lack of food, plus your excellent wine . . . I fear I fell forward with that bottle in my hand and shattered your beautiful mirror . . . I'm so sorry . . . of course I will replace it.'

I told him, quite brusquely, not to be so silly and, when Mrs Manning came panting up the stairs with the brandy, I forced him to take some in spite of his protests. While he was drinking it, Mrs Manning cleaned up the mess in the bathroom.

'Ah. That's better,' said Gideon at last. 'I feel quite revived now. All I want is a nice relaxing bath and I shall be a new man.'

I felt that he ought to have his food in bed, but he would not hear of it, and when he descended to the dining-room half an hour later I must say he did look better and much more relaxed. He laughed and joked with Mrs Manning as she served us and complimented her lavishly on her cooking, swearing that he would get rid of his own chef, kidnap Mrs Manning and take her to his château in France to cook for him. Mrs Manning was enchanted by him, as indeed she always was, but I could see that it cost him some effort to be so charming and jovial. When at last we had finished the pudding and cheese and Mrs Manning put the decanter of port on the table and saying goodnight, left us, Gideon accepted a cigar. Having lit it he leant back in his chair and smiled at me through the smoke.

'Now, Peter,' he began, 'I can tell you something of what's been happening.'

'I am most anxious to know what it is that has brought you to this low ebb, my friend,' I said seriously.

He felt in his pocket and produced from it a large iron key with heavy teeth and an ornate butt. He threw it on the table where it fell with a heavy thud.

'This was one of the causes of the trouble,' he said, staring at it moodily. 'The key to life and death, as you might say.'

'I don't understand you,' I said, puzzled.

'Because of this key I was nearly arrested for murder,' said Gideon, with a smile.

'Murder? You?' I exclaimed, aghast. 'But how can that possibly be?'

Gideon took a sip at his glass of port and settled himself back in his chair.

'About two months ago I got a letter from my uncle asking me to go to see him. This I did, with considerable reluctance as you may imagine for you know what my opinion of him was. Well, to cut a long story short, there were certain things he wanted me to do . . . er . . . family matters . . . which I refused to do. He flew into a rage and we quarrelled furiously. I am afraid that I left him in no doubt as to what I thought of him and the servants heard us quarrel. I left his house and continued on my way to Marseilles to catch a boat for Morocco where I was going for a tour. Two days later my uncle was murdered.'

'So that's why you put "uncle put to death" in your telegram,' I said. 'I wondered.'

'He *had* been put to death, and in the most mysterious circumstances,' said Gideon. 'He was found in an empty attic at the top of the house which contained nothing but a large broken mirror. He was a hideous mess, his clothes torn off him, his throat and body savaged as if by a mad dog. There was blood everywhere. I had to identify the body. It was not a pleasant task, for his face had been so badly mauled that it was almost unrecognizable.' He paused and took another sip of port. Presently he went on. 'But the curious thing about all this was that the attic was locked, *locked on the inside* with that key.'

'But how could that be?' I asked, bewildered. 'How did his assailant leave the room?'

'That's exactly what the police wanted to know,' said Gideon dryly. 'As you know the French police are very efficient but lacking in imagination. Their logic worked something like this: I was the one that stood to gain by my uncle's death because I inherit the family fortune and his library and several farms dotted about all over France. So, as I was the one that stood to gain, *enfin*, I must be the one who committed murder.'

'But that's ridiculous,' I broke in indignantly.

'Not to a policeman,' said Gideon, 'especially when they heard that at my last meeting with my uncle we had quarrelled bitterly and one of the things that the servants heard me saying to him was that I wished he would drop dead and thus leave the world a cleaner place.'

'But in the heat of a quarrel one is liable to say anything,' I protested. 'Everyone knows that . . . And how did they suggest you killed your uncle and then left the room locked on the inside?'

'Oh, it was possible, quite possible,' said Gideon. 'With a pair of long-nosed, very slender pliers, it could have been done, but it would undoubtedly have left marks on the end of the key, and as you can see it's unmarked. The real problem was that at first I had no alibi. I had gone down to Marseilles and, as I had cut my visit to my uncle short, I was too early for my ship. I booked into a small hotel and enjoyed myself for those few days in exploring the port. I knew no one there so, naturally, there was no one to vouch for my movements. As you can imagine, it took time to assemble all the porters, maids, *maîtres d'hôtel*, restaurant owners, hotel managers and so on, and through their testimony prove to the police that I was, in fact, in Marseilles and minding my own business when my uncle was killed. It has taken me the last six weeks to do it, and it has been extremely exhausting.'

'Why didn't you telegraph me?' I asked. 'I could have come and at least kept you company.'

'You are very kind, Peter, but I did not want to embroil my friends in such a sordid mess. Besides, I knew that if all went well and the police released me (which they eventually did after much protest) I should want your help on something appertaining to this.'

'Anything I can do,' I said. 'You know you have only to ask, my dear fellow.'

'Well, as I told you I spent my youth under my uncle's care, and after that experience I grew to loathe his house and everything about it. Now, with this latest thing, I really feel I cannot set foot in the place again. I am not exaggerating but I seriously think that if I were to go there and stay I should become seriously ill.'

'I agree,' I said firmly. 'On no account must you even contemplate such a step.'

'Well, the furniture and the house I can of course get valued and sold by a Paris firm: that is simple. But the most valuable thing in the house is the library. This is where you come in, Peter. Would you be willing to go down and catalogue and value the books for me. Then I can arrange for them to be stored until I can build an extension to my library to house them?'

'Of course I will,' I said. 'With the greatest of pleasure. You just tell me when you want me to come.'

'I shall not be with you, you'll be quite alone,' Gideon warned.

'I am a solitary creature, as I have told you,' I laughed, 'and as long as I have a supply of books to amuse me I shall get along splendidly, don't worry.'

'I would like it done as soon as possible,' said Gideon, 'so that I may get rid of the house. How soon could you come down?'

I consulted my diary and found that, fortunately, I was coming up to a rather slack period.

'How about the end of next week?' I asked and Gideon's face lit up.

'So soon?' he said delightedly. 'That would be splendid! I could meet you at the station at Fontaine next Friday. Would that be all right?'

'Perfectly all right,' I said, 'and I will soon have the books sorted out for you. Now, another glass of port and then you must away to bed.'

'My dear Peter, what a loss you are to Harley Street,' joked Gideon, but he took my advice.

Twice during the night I awakened, thinking that I heard him cry out but, after listening for a while all was quiet and I concluded that it was just my imagination. The following morning he left for France and I started making my preparations to follow him, packing sufficient things for a prolonged stay at his late uncle's house.

The whole of Europe was in the grip of an icy winter and it was certainly not the weather to travel in. Indeed no one but Gideon could have got me to leave home in such weather. Crossing the Channel was a nightmare and I felt so sick on arrival in Paris that I could not do more than swallow a little broth and go straight to bed. The following day it was icy cold, with a bitter wind, grey skies and driving veils of rain that stung your face. Eventually I reached the station and boarded the train for what seemed an interminable journey, during which I had to change and wait at more and more inhospitable stations, until

I was so numbed with cold I could hardly think straight. All the rivers wore a rim of lacy ice along their shores, and the ponds and lakes turned blank, frozen eyes to the steel grey sky.

At length, the local train I had changed to dragged itself, grimy and puffing, into the station of Fontaine. I disembarked and made my way with my luggage to the tiny booking office and minute waiting-room. Here, to my relief I found that there was an old-fashioned, pot-bellied stove stuffed with chestnut roots and glowing almost red hot. I piled my luggage in the corner and spent some time thawing myself out, for the heating on the train had been minimal. There was no sign of Gideon. Presently, warmed by the fire and a nip of brandy, I had taken from my travelling flask, I began to feel better. Half an hour passed and I began to worry about Gideon's absence. I went out on to the platform and discovered that the grey sky seemed to have moved closer to the earth and a few snowflakes were starting to fall, huge lacy ones the size of a half crown, that augured a snowstorm of considerable dimensions in the not too distant future. I was just wondering if I should try walking to the village when I heard the clop of hooves and made out a dog cart coming along the road driven by Gideon muffled up in a glossy fur coat and wearing an astrakhan hat.

'I'm so very sorry, Peter, for keeping you waiting like this,' he said, wringing my hand, 'but we seem to have one catastrophe after another. Come, let me help you with your bags and I will tell you all about it as we drive.'

We collected my baggage, bundled it into the dog cart and then I climbed up on to the box alongside Gideon and covered myself thankfully with the thick fur rug he had brought. He turned the horse, cracked his whip and we went, bowling down the snowflakes which were now falling quite fast. The wind whipped our faces and made our eyes water, but still Gideon kept the horse at a fast trot.

'I am anxious to get there before the snowstorm really starts,' he said, 'that is why I am going at this uncivilized pace. Once these snowstorms start up here they can be very severe. One can get snowed in for days at a time.'

'It is certainly becoming a grim winter,' I said.

'The worst we've had here for fifty years,' said Gideon.

We came to the village and Gideon was silent as he guided his horse through the narrow, deserted streets, already white with settling snow. Occasionally a dog would run out of an alley and run barking alongside us for a way, but otherwise there was no sign of life. The village could have been deserted for all evidence to the contrary.

'I am afraid that once again, my dear Peter, I shall have to trespass upon your good nature,' said Gideon, smiling at me, his hat and his eyebrows white with snow. 'Sooner or later my demands on our friendship will exhaust your patience.'

'Nonsense,' I said, 'just tell me what the problem is.'

'Well,' said Gideon, 'I was to leave you in the charge of François and his wife, who were my uncle's servants. Unfortunately, when I went to the house this morning I found that François's wife Marie, had slipped on the icy front steps and had fallen some thirty feet on to the rocks and broken her legs. They are, I'm afraid, splintered very badly, and I don't hold out much hope for them being saved.'

'Poor woman, how dreadful,' I exclaimed.

'Yes,' Gideon continued. 'Of course François was nearly frantic when I got there, and so there was nothing for it but to drive them both to the hospital in Milau which took me over two hours, hence my being so late meeting you.'

'That doesn't matter at all,' I said. 'Of course you had to drive them to the hospital.'

'Yes, but it created another problem as well,' said Gideon. 'You see, none of the villagers liked my uncle, and François and Marie were the only couple who would work for him. With both of them in Milau, there is no one to look after you, at least for two or three days until François comes back.'

'My dear chap, don't let that worry you,' I laughed. 'I am quite used to fending for myself, I do assure you. If I have food and wine and a fire I will be very well found I promise you.'

'Oh, you'll have all that,' said Gideon. 'The larder is well stocked, and down in the game room there is a haunch of venison, half a wild boar, some pheasants and partridge and a few brace of wild duck. There is wine aplenty, since my uncle kept quite a good cellar, and the cellar is full of chestnut roots and pine logs, so you will be warm. You will also have for company the animals.'

'Animals, what animals?' I asked, curious.

'A small dog called Agrippa,' said Gideon, laughing, 'a very large and idiotic cat called Clair de Lune, or Clair for short, a whole cage of canaries and various finches and an extremely old parrot called Octavius.'

'A positive menagerie,' I exclaimed. 'It's a good thing that I like animals.'

'Seriously, Peter,' asked Gideon, giving me one of his very penetrating looks, 'are you sure you will be all right? It seems a terrible imposition to me.'

'Nonsense,' I said heartily, 'what are friends for?'

The snow was coming down with a vengeance and we could only see a yard or two beyond the horse's ears, so dense were the whirling clouds of huge flakes. We had now entered one of the many tributary gorges that led into the Gorge du Tarn proper. On our left the brown and black cliffs, dappled with patches of snow on sundry crevices and ledges, loomed over us, in places actually overhanging the narrow road. On our right the ground dropped away, almost sheer, five or six hundred feet into the gorge below where, through the wind-blown curtains of snow, one could catch occasional glimpses of the green river, its tumbled rocks snow-wigged, their edges crusted with ice. The road was rough, snow and water worn, and in places covered with a sheet of ice which made the horse slip and stumble and slowed our progress. Once a small avalanche of snow slid down the cliff face with a hissing sound and thumped on to the road in front of us, making the horse shy so badly that Gideon had to fight to keep control. For several hair-raising minutes I feared that we, the dog cart and the terrified horse might slide over the edge of the gorge and plunge down into the river below. But eventually Gideon got it under control and we crawled along our way.

Eventually the gorge widened a little and presently we rounded a corner and there before us was the strange bulk of Gideon's uncle's house. It was an extraordinary edifice and I feel I should describe it in some detail. To begin with the whole thing was perched on top of a massive rock that protruded from the river far below so that it formed what could only be described as an island, shaped not unlike an isosceles triangle, with the house on top. It was connected to the road by a massive and very old stone bridge. The tall outside walls of the house fell sheer down to the rocks and river below, but as you crossed the bridge and drove under a huge arch, guarded by thick oak doors, you found that the house was built round a large centre courtyard, cobblestoned and with a pond with a fountain in the middle. This depicted a dolphin held up by cherubs, the whole thing polished with ice, and with icicles hanging from it.

All the many windows that looked down into the court were shuttered with a fringe of huge icicles hanging from every cornice. Between the windows were monstrous gargoyles depicting various forms of animal life, known and unknown to science, each one seeming more malign than the last and their appearance not improved by the ice and snow that blurred their outlines so that they seemed to be peering at you from snowy ambush. As Gideon drew the horse to a standstill by the steps that led to the front door we could hear the barking of the dog inside. My friend opened the front door with a large, rusty key and immediately the dog tumbled out, barking vociferously and wagging its tail with pleasure. The large black and white cat was more circumspect and did not deign to come out into the snow, but merely stood, arching its back and mewing in the doorway. Gideon helped me carry my bags into the large marble hall where a handsome staircase led to the upper floors of the house. All the pictures, mirrors, and furniture were covered with dust sheets.

'I am sorry about the covers,' said Gideon. It seemed to me that, as soon as he had entered the house, he had become nervous and ill at ease. 'I meant to remove them all this morning and make it more habitable for you, but what with one thing and another I did not manage it.'

'Don't worry,' I said, making a fuss of the dog and cat, who were both vying for my attention. 'I shan't be inhabiting all the house, so I will just remove the sheets in those parts that I shall use.'

'Yes, yes,' said Gideon, running his hands through his hair in a nervous fashion. 'Your bed is made up ... the bedroom is the second door on the left as you reach the top of the stairs. Now, come with me and I'll show you the kitchen and cellar.'

He led me across the hall to a door that was hidden under the main staircase. Opening this he made his way down broad stone steps that spiralled their way down into the gloom. Presently we reached a passageway that led to a gigantic stoneflagged kitchen and, adjoining it, cavernous cellars and a capacious larder, cold as a glacier, with the carcases of game, chicken, duck, legs of lamb and saddles of beef hanging from hooks or lying on the marble shelves that ran around the walls. In the kitchen was a great range, each fire carefully laid, and on the huge table in the centre had been arranged various commodities that Gideon thought I might need, rice, lentils as black as soot, potatoes, carrots, and other vegetables in large baskets, pottery jars of butter and conserves, and a pile of freshly baked loaves. On the opposite side of the kitchen to the cellars and larder lay the wine store, approached through a heavy door, bolted and padlocked. Obviously Gideon's uncle had not trusted his staff when it came to alcoholic beverages. The cellar was small, but I saw at a glance it contained some excellent vintages.

'Do not stint yourself, Peter,' said Gideon. 'There are some really quite nice wines in there and they will be some small compensation for staying in the gloomy place alone.'

'You want me to spend my time in an inebriated state?' I laughed. 'I would never get the books valued. But don't worry Gideon, I shall be quite all right. I have food and wine enough for an army, plenty of fuel for the fire, a dog and a cat and birds to bear me company and a large and interesting library. What more could any man want?'

'The books, by the way, are mainly in the Long Gallery, on the south side of the house. I won't show it to you . . . it's easy enough to find, and I really must be on my way,' said Gideon, leading the way up into the hall once more. He delved into his pocket and produced a huge bunch of ancient keys. 'The keys of the kingdom,' he said with a faint smile. 'I don't think anything is locked, but if it is, please open it. I will tell François that he is to come back here and look after you as soon as his wife is out of danger, and I, myself, will return in about four weeks' time. By then you should have finished your task.'

'Easily,' I said. 'In fact, if I get it done before then I will send you a telegram.'

'Seriously, Peter,' he said, taking my hand, 'I am really most deeply in your debt for what you are doing. I shall not forget it.'

'Rubbish, my friend,' I said. 'It gives me great pleasure to be of service to you.'

I stood in the doorway of the house, the dog panting by my side, the cat arching itself around my legs and purring loudly, and watched Gideon get back into the dog cart, wrap the rug around himself and then flick the horses with the reins. As they broke into a trot and he steered them towards the entrance to the courtyard he raised his whip in salute. He disappeared through the archway and soon the sound of the hoof beats were muffled by the snow and faded altogether. Picking up the warm, silky body of the cat and whistling to the dog, which had chased the dog cart to the archway, barking exuberantly, I went back into the house and bolted the front door behind me.

The first thing to do was to explore the house and ascertain where the various books were that I had come to work with, and thus to make up my mind which rooms I needed to open. On a table in the hall I had spotted a large six-branched silver candelabra loaded with candles and with a box of matches lying beside it. I decided to use this in my exploration since it would relieve me of the tedium of having to open and close innumerable shutters. Lighting the candles and accompanied by the eager, bustling dog, whose nails rattled on the bare floors like castanets, I started off.

The whole of the ground floor consisted of three very large rooms and one smaller one, which comprised the drawing-room, the dining-room, a study and then this smaller salon. Strangely enough, this room—which I called the blue salon since it was decorated in various shades of blue and gold—was the only one that was locked, and it took me some time to find the right key for it. This salon formed one end of the house and so it was a long, narrow, shoe-box shape, with large windows at each end.

The door by which one entered was mid-way down one of the longer walls and hanging on the wall opposite was one of the biggest mirrors I have ever seen. It must have been fully nine feet high, stretching from floor level almost to the ceiling and some thirty-five feet in length. The mirror itself was slightly tarnished, which gave it a pleasant blueish tinge, like the waters of a shallow lake, but it still reflected clearly and accurately. The whole was encompassed in a wide and very ornate gold frame, carved to depict various nymphs and satyrs, unicorns, griffons, and other fabulous beasts. The frame in itself was a work of art. By seating oneself in one of the comfortable chairs that stood one on each side of the fireplace one could see the whole room reflected in this remarkable mirror and, although the room was somewhat narrow, this gave one a great sense of space.

Owing to the size, the convenience and—I must admit—the novelty of the room, I decided to make it my living-room, and in a very short space of time I had the dust covers off the furniture and a roaring blaze of chestnut roots in the hearth. Then I moved in the cage of finches and canaries and placed them at one end of the room together with Octavius the parrot, who seemed pleased by the change for he shuffled his feathers, cocked his head on one side and whistled a few bars of the Marseillaise. The dog and cat immediately stretched themselves out in front of the blaze and fell into a contented sleep. Thus, deserted by my companions, I took my candelabra and continued my investigation of the house alone.

The next floor I found comprised mainly of bed- and bathrooms, but a whole wing of the house (which formed the hollow square in which the courtyard lay) was one enormous room, the Long Gallery as Gideon had called it. Down one side of this long, wide room there were very tall windows, and opposite each window was a mirror, similar to the one downstairs, but long and narrow. Between these mirrors stood the bookcases of polished oak and piled on the shelves haphazardly were a myriad of books, some on their sides, some upside down in total confusion. Even a cursory glance was enough to tell me that the library was so muddled that it would take me some considerable time to sort the books into subjects before I could even start to catalogue and value them.

Leaving the Long Gallery shrouded in dust sheets and with the shutters still closed, I went one floor higher. Here there were only attics. In one of them I came upon the gilt frame of a mirror and I shivered, for I presumed that this was the attic in which Gideon's uncle had been found dead. The mirror frame was identical with the one in the blue salon, but on a much smaller scale. Here, again were the satyrs, the unicorns, the griffons and hippogryphs, but in addition was a small area at the top of the frame, carved like a medallion, in which were inscribed the words: *I am your servant. Feed and liberate me. I am you.* It did not seem to make sense. I closed the attic door and, chiding myself for being a coward, locked it securely and in consequence felt much better.

When I made my way downstairs to the blue salon I was greeted with rapture by both dog and cat, as if I had been away on a journey of many days. I realized that they were hungry. Simultaneously I realized that I was hungry too, for the excitement of arriving at the house and exploring it had made me forget to prepare myself any luncheon and it was now past six o'clock in the evening. Accompanied by the eager animals, I made my way down to the kitchen to cook some food for us all. For the dog I stewed some scraps of mutton, and a little chicken for the cat, combined with some boiled rice and potatoes, they were delighted with this menu. For myself I grilled a large steak with an assortment of vegetables and chose from the cellar an excellent bottle of red wine.

When this was ready I carried it up to the blue salon and, pulling my chair up to the fire, made myself comfortable and fell to hungrily. Presently the dog and the cat, replete with food, joined me and spread themselves out in front of the fire. I got up and closed the door once they were settled, for there was a cold draught from the big hall which, with its marble floor, was now as cold as an ice-chest. Finishing my food I lay back contentedly in my chair sipping my wine and watching the blue flames run to and fro over the chestnut roots in the fire. I was relaxed and happy and the wine, rich and heavy, was having a soporific effect upon me. I slept for perhaps an hour. Suddenly, I was fully awake with every nerve tingling, as if someone had shouted my name. I listened, but the only sounds were the soft breathing of the sleeping dog and the contented purr of the cat curled up on the chair opposite me. It was so silent that I could hear the faint bubble and crackle of the chestnut roots in the fire. Feeling sure I must have imagined a sound and yet unaccountably uneasy for no discernible reason, I threw another log on the fire and settled myself back in the chair to doze.

It was then that I glanced across at the mirror opposite me and noticed that, in the reflection, the door to the salon that I had carefully closed was now ajar. Surprised, I twisted round in my chair and looked at the real door, only to find it was securely closed as I had left it. I looked again into the mirror and made sure my eyes—aided by the wine—were not playing me tricks, but sure enough, in the reflection the door appeared to be slightly ajar.

I was sitting there looking at it and wondering what trick of light and reflection could produce the effect of an open door when the door responsible for the reflection was securely closed, when I noticed something that made me sit up, astonished and uneasy. *The door in the reflection was being pushed open still further*. I looked at the real door again and saw that it was still firmly shut. Yet its reflection in the mirror was opening, slowly millimetre by millimetre. I sat there watching it, the hair on the nape of my neck stirring. Suddenly, round the edge of the door, on the carpet, there appeared something that at first glance I thought was some sort of caterpillar. It was long, wrinkled and yellowish-white in colour, and at one end it had a long blackened horn. It humped itself up and scrabbled at the surface of the carpet with its horn in a way that I had seen no caterpillar behave. Then, slowly, it retreated behind the door.

I found that I was sweating. I glanced once more at the real door to assure myself that it was closed because I did not fancy having that caterpillar or whatever it was crawling about the room with me. The door was still shut. I took a draught of wine to steady my nerves, and was annoyed to see that my hand was shaking. I, who had never believed in ghosts, or hauntings, or magic spells or any of that claptrap, here I was imagining things in a mirror and convincing myself to such an extent they were real, that I was actually afraid.

It was ridiculous, I told myself as I drank the wine. There was some perfectly rational explanation for the whole thing. I sat forward in my chair and gazed at the reflection in the mirror with great intentness. For a long time nothing happened and then the door in the mirror swung open a fraction and the caterpillar appeared again. This time it was joined by another and then, after a pause, yet another.

Suddenly my blood ran cold for I realized what it was. They were not caterpillars but attenuated yellow fingers with long twisted black nails tipping each one like gigantic misshapen rose thorns. The moment I realized this the whole hand came into view, feeling its way feebly along the carpet. The hand was a mere skeleton covered with the pale yellow, parchment-like skin through which the knuckles and joints showed like walnuts. It felt around on the carpet in a blind, groping sort of way, the hand moving from a bony wrist, like the tentacles of some strange sea anemone from the deep sea, one that has

201

become pallid through living in perpetual dark. Then slowly it was withdrawn behind the door. I shuddered for I wondered what sort of body was attached to that horrible hand. I waited for perhaps quarter of an hour, dreading what might suddenly appear from behind the mirror door, but nothing happened.

After a while I became restive. I was still attempting to convince myself that the whole thing was an hallucination brought on by the wine and the heat of the fire without success. For there was the door of the blue salon carefully closed against the draught and the door in the mirror still ajar with apparently something lurking behind it. I wanted to walk over to the mirror and examine it, but did not have the courage. Instead I thought of a plan which, I felt, would show me whether I was imagining things or not. I woke Agrippa the dog and, crumpling up a sheet of the newspaper I had been reading into a ball, threw it down the room so that it landed just by the closed door. In the mirror it lay near the door that was ajar.

Agrippa, more to please me than anything else, for he was very sleepy, bounded after it. Gripping the arms of my chair I watched his reflection in the mirror as he ran towards the door. He reached the ball of newspaper and paused to pick it up. Then something so hideous happened that I could scarcely believe my eyes. The mirror door was pushed open still further and the hand and a long white bony arm shot out. It grabbed the dog in the mirror by the scruff of its neck and pulled it speedily, kicking and struggling, behind the door.

Agrippa had now come back to me, having retrieved the newspaper, but I took no notice of him for my gaze was fixed on the reflection in the mirror. After a few minutes the hand suddenly reappeared. Was it my imagination or did it now seem stronger? At any event, it curved itself round the woodwork of the door and drew it completely shut, leaving on the white paint a series of bloody fingerprints that made me feel sick. The real Agrippa was nosing my leg, the newspaper in his mouth, seeking my approval, while behind the mirror door, God knows what fate had overtaken his reflection.

To say that I was shaken means nothing. I could scarcely believe the evidence of my senses. I sat staring at the mirror for a long time, but nothing further happened. Eventually, and with my skin prickling with fear, I got up and examined the mirror and the door into the salon. Both bore a perfectly ordinary appearance. I wanted very much to open the door to the salon and see if the reflection in the mirror opened as well but, if I must tell the truth, I was too frightened of disturbing whatever it was that lurked behind the mirror door.

I glanced up at the top of the mirror and saw for the first time that it bore the same inscription as the one I had found in the attic: *I am your servant. Feed and liberate me. I am you.* Did this mean the creature behind the door, I wondered? *Feed and liberate me*, was that what I had done by letting the dog go near the door? Was the creature now feasting upon the dog it had caught in the mirror? I shuddered at the thought. I determined that the only thing to do was to get a good night's rest, for I was tired and overwrought. In the morning, I assured myself, I would hit upon a ready explanation for all this mumbo-jumbo.

Picking up the cat and calling the dog (for, if the truth be known, I needed the company of the animals) I left the blue salon. As I was closing the door I was frozen into immobility as I heard a cracked, harsh voice bid me '*Bonne nuit*' in wheedling tones. It was a moment or so before I realized it was Octavius the parrot, and went limp with relief.

Clair the cat drowsed peacefully in my arms, but Agrippa needed some encouraging to accompany me upstairs, for it was obvious that he had never been allowed above the ground floor before. At length, with reluctance that soon turned to excitement at the novelty, he followed me upstairs. The fire in the bedroom had died down, but the atmosphere was still warm. I made my toilet and, without further ado, climbed into bed, with Agrippa lying one side of me and Clair the other. I received much comfort from the feel of their warm bodies but, in addition, I am not ashamed to say that I left the candles burning and the door to the room securely locked.

The following morning when I awoke I was immediately conscious of the silence. Throwing open the shutters I gazed out at a world muffled in snow. It must have been snowing steadily all night, and great drifts had piled up on the rock faces, on the bare trees, along the river bank and piled in a great cushion some seven feet deep along the crest of the bridge that joined the house to the mainland. Every window-sill and every projection of the eaves was a fearsome armoury of icicles, and the window-sills were varnished with a thin layer of ice. The sky was dark grey and lowering so that I could see we were in for yet more snow.

Even if I had wanted to leave the house the roads were already impassable; with another snowfall I would be completely cut off from the outside world. I must say that, thinking back on my experiences of the previous night, this fact made me feel somewhat uneasy. But I chided myself and by the time I had finished dressing I had managed to convince myself that my experience in the blue salon was due to a surfeit of good wine and an over-excited imagination.

Thus comforting myself I went downstairs, picked up Clair in my arms, called Agrippa to heel and, steeling myself, threw open the door of the blue salon and entered. It was as I had left it, the dirty plates and wine bottle near my chair, the chestnut roots in the fire burnt to a delicate grey ash that stirred slightly at the sudden draught from the open door. But it was the only thing in the room that stirred. Everything was in order. Everything was normal. I heaved a sigh of relief. It was not until I was halfway down the room that I glanced at the mirror. I stopped as suddenly as if I had walked into a brick wall and my blood froze, for I could not believe what I was seeing.

Reflected in the mirror was myself, with the cat in my arms, but *there was no dog at my heels, although Agrippa was nosing at my ankles*.

For several seconds I stood there thunderstruck unable to believe the evidence of my own senses, gazing first at the dog at my feet and then at the mirror with no reflection of the animal. I, the cat and the rest of the room were reflected with perfect clarity, but there was no reflection of Agrippa. I dropped the cat on the floor (and she remained reflected by the mirror) and picked up Agrippa in my arms. In the mirror I appeared to be carrying an imaginary object in my arms. Hastily I picked up the cat and so, with Clair under one arm and an invisible dog under the other, I left the blue salon and securely locked the door behind me.

Down in the kitchen I was ashamed to find that my hands were shaking. I gave the animals some milk (and the way Agrippa dealt with his left no doubt he was a flesh and blood animal) and made myself some breakfast. As I fried eggs and some heavily smoked ham, my mind was busy with what I had seen in the blue salon. Unless I was mad—and I had never felt saner in my life—I was forced to admit that I had really experienced what I had seen, incredible though it seemed and indeed still seems to me. Although I was terrified at whatever it was that lurked behind the door in the mirror, I was also filled with an overwhelming curiosity, a desire to see whatever creature it was that possessed that gaunt and tallow hand, yellow and emaciated arm.

I determined that very evening I would attempt to lure the creature out so that I could examine it. I was filled with horror at what I intended to do, but my curiosity was stronger than my fear. I spent the day cataloguing the books in the study and, when darkness fell, once again lit the fire in the salon, cooked myself some supper, carried it and a bottle of wine upstairs, and settled myself by the hearth. This time, however, I had taken the precaution of arming myself with a stout ebony cane. This gave me a certain confidence though what use a cane was going to be against a looking-glass adversary, heaven only knew. As it turned out, arming myself with the stick was the worst thing I could have done and nearly cost me my life.

I ate my food, my eyes fixed on the mirror, the two animals lying asleep at my feet as they had done the night before. I finished my meal and still there was no change to the mirror image of the door. I sat back sipping my wine and watching. After an hour or so the fire was burning low. I got up to put some logs on it, and had just settled myself back in my chair when I saw the handle of the mirror door start to turn very slowly. Millimetre by millimetre, the door was pushed open a foot or so. It was incredible that the opening of a door should be charged with such menace, but the slow furtive way it swung across the carpet was indescribably evil.

Then the hand appeared, again moving very slowly, humping its way across the carpet until the wrist and part of the yellowish forearm was in view. It paused for a moment, lying flaccid on the carpet, then, in a sickening sort of way, started to grope around, as if the creature in control of the hand was blind.

Now it seemed to me was the moment to put my carefully thought-out plan into operation. I had deliberately starved Clair so that she would be hungry; now I woke her up and waved under her nose a piece of meat which I had brought up from the kitchen for this purpose. Her eyes widened and she let out a loud mew of excitement. I waved the meat under her nose until she was frantic to get the morsel and then I threw it down the room so that it landed on the carpet near the firmly closed door of the salon. In the mirror I could see that it had landed near, but not too near the reflection of the hand which was still groping about blindly.

Uttering a loud wail of hunger, Clair sped down the room after it. I had hoped that the cat would be so far away from the door that it would tempt the creature out into the open, but I soon realized that I had thrown the meat too close to the door. As Clair's reflection stopped and the cat bent down to take the meat in her mouth, the hand ceased its blind groping. Shooting out with incredible speed, it seized Clair by the tail and dragged the cat, struggling and twisting, behind the door. As before, after a moment the hand reappeared, curved round the door and slowly drew it shut, leaving bloody finger-prints on the woodwork.

I think what made the whole thing doubly horrible was the con-trast between the speed and ferocity with which the hand grabbed its prey, and the slow, furtive way it opened and closed the door. Clair now returned with the meat in her mouth to eat it in comfort by the fire and, like Agrippa, seemed none the worse for now having no reflection. Although I waited up until after midnight the hand did not appear again. I took the animals and went to bed, determined that on the morrow I would work out a plan that would force the thing behind the door to show itself.

By evening on the following day I had finished my preliminary sort-ing and listing of the books on the ground floor of the house. The next step was to move upstairs to where the bulk of the library was housed in the Long Gallery. I felt somewhat tired that day and so, towards five o'clock, decided to take a turn outside to get some fresh air into my lungs. Alas for my hopes! It had been snowing steadily since my arrival and now the glistening drifts were so high I could not walk through them. The only way out of the central courtyard and across the bridge would have been to dig a path, and this would have been through snow lying in a great crusty blanket some six feet deep. Some of the icicles hanging from the guttering, the window ledges, and the gargoyles were four or five feet long and as thick as my arm.

The animals would not accompany me, but I tried walking a few steps into this spacious white world, as silent and as cold as the bottom of a well. The snow squeaked protestingly, like mice, beneath my shoes and I sank in over my knees and soon had to struggle back to the house. The snow was still falling in flakes as big as dandelion clocks, thickening the white pie-crusts on the roof ridges and gables. There was that complete silence that snow brings, no sound, no bird song, no whine of wind, just an almost tangible silence, as though the living world had been gagged with a crisp white scarf.

Rubbing my frozen hands I hastened inside, closed the front door and hastened down to the kitchen to prepare my evening meal. While this was cooking I lit the fire in the blue salon once more, and when the food was ready carried it up there as had become my habit, the animals accompanying me. Once again I armed myself with my stout stick and this gave me a small measure of comfort. I ate my food and drank my wine, watching the mirror, but the hand did not put in an appearance. Where was it, I wondered. Did it stalk about and explore a reflection of the house that lay behind the door, a reflection I could not see? Or did it only exist when it became a reflection in the mirror that I looked at? Musing on this I dozed, warmed by the fire, and presently slept deeply, which I had not meant to do. I must have slept for about an hour when I was suddenly shocked awake by the sound of a voice, a thin cracked voice, singing shrilly:

> *'Auprès de ma blonde, auprès de ma blonde,*
> *Qu'il fait bon dormir . . .'*

This was followed by a grating peal of hysterical laughter.

Half asleep as I was, it was a moment before I realized that the singing and laughter came from Octavius. The shock of suddenly hearing a human voice like that was considerable, and my heart was racing. I glanced down the room and saw that the cages containing the canaries and Octavius were still as I had placed them. Then I glanced in the mirror and sat transfixed in my chair. I suffered a revulsion and terror that surpassed anything that I had felt up until then. My wish had been granted and the thing from behind the door had appeared. As I watched it, how fervently I wished to God that I had left well alone, that I had locked the blue salon after the first night and never revisited it.

The creature—I must call it that, for it seemed scarcely human—was small and hump-backed and clad in what I could only believe was a shroud, a yellowish linen garment spotted with gobbets of dirt and mould, torn in places where the fabric had worn thin, pulled over the thing's head and twisted round, like a scarf. At that moment, all that was visible of its face was a tattered fringe of faded orange hair on a heavily lined forehead and two large, pale-yellow eyes that glared with the fierce, impersonal arrogance of a goat. Below them the shroud was twisted round and held in place by one of the thing's pale, black-nailed hands.

It was standing behind the big cage that had contained the canaries. The cage was now twisted and wrenched and disembowelled like a horse in a bull ring, and covered with a cloud of yellow feathers that stuck to the bloodstains on the bars. I noticed that there were a few yellow feathers between the fingers of the creature's hand. As I watched, it moved from the remains of the canary cage to the next table where the parrot cage had been placed. It moved slowly and limped heavily, appearing more to drag one foot after the other than anything else. It reached the cage, in which the reflection of Octavius was weaving from side to side on his perch.

The real bird in the room with me was still singing and cackling with laughter periodically. In the mirror the creature studied the parrot in its cage with its ferocious yellow eyes. Then, suddenly, the thing's hand shot out and the fingers entwined themselves in the bars of the cage and wrenched and twisted them apart.

While both hands were thus occupied the piece of shroud that had been covering the face fell away and revealed the most disgusting face I have ever seen. Most of the features below the eyes appeared to have been eaten away, either by decay or some disease akin to leprosy. Where the nose should have been there were just two black holes with tattered rims. The whole of one cheek was missing and so the upper and lower jaw, with mildewed gums and decaying teeth, were displayed. Trickles of saliva flooded out from the mouth and dripped down into the folds of the shroud. What was left of the lips were serrated with fine wrinkles, so that they looked as though they had been stitched together and the cotton pulled tight.

What made the whole thing even worse, as a macabre spectacle, was that on one of the creature's disgusting fingers it wore a large gold ring in which an opal flashed like flame as its hands moved, twisting the metal of the cage. This refinement on such a corpse-like apparition only served to enhance its repulsive appearance.

Presently it had twisted the wires enough so that there was room for it to put its hands inside the cage. The parrot was still bobbing and weaving on his perch, and the real Octavius was still singing and laughing. The creature grabbed the parrot in the reflection and it flapped and struggled in its hands, while Octavius continued to sing. It dragged the bird from the broken cage, lifted it to its obscene mouth and cracked the parrot's skull as it would a nut. Then, with enjoyment, it started to suck the brains from the shattered skull, feathers and fragments of brain and skull mixing with the saliva that fell from the thing's mouth on to the shroud.

I was filled with such revulsion and yet such rage at the creature's actions that I grasped my stick and leapt to my feet, trembling with anger. I approached the mirror and as I did so, and my reflection appeared, I realized that (in the mirror) I was approaching the thing from behind. I moved forward until, in the reflection, I was close to it and then I raised my stick.

Suddenly the creature's eyes appeared to blaze in its disintegrating face. It stopped its revolting feast and dropped the corpse of the parrot to the ground, at the same time whirling round to face my reflection with such speed that I was taken aback and stood there, staring at it, my stick raised. The creature did not hesitate for a second, but dived forward and fastened its lean and powerful hands round my throat in the reflection.

This sudden attack made my reflection stagger backwards and it dropped the stick. The creature and my reflection fell to the floor behind the table and I could see them both thrashing about together. Horrified I dropped my stick and, running to the mirror, beat futilely against the glass. Presently all movement ceased behind the table. I could not see what was happening but, convinced the creature was dealing with my reflection as it had done with the dog and the cat, I continued to beat upon the mirror's surface.

Presently, from behind the table, the creature rose up unsteadily, panting. It had its back to me. It remained like that for a moment or two; then it bent down and, seizing my reflection body, dragged it slowly through the door. As it did so I could see that the body had had its throat torn out.

Presently the creature reappeared, licking its lips in an anticipatory sort of way. Then it picked up the ebony stick and once more disappeared. It was gone some ten minutes and when it came back it was—to my horror and anger—feasting upon a severed hand, as a man might eat the wing of a chicken. Forgetting all fear I beat on the mirror again. Slowly, as if trying to decide where the noise was coming from, it turned round, its eyes flashing terribly, its face covered with blood that could only be mine.

It saw me and its eyes widened with a ferocious, knowing expression that turned me cold. Slowly it started to approach the mirror, and as it did so I stopped my futile hammering on the glass and backed away, appalled by the menace in the thing's goat-like eyes. Slowly it moved forward, its fierce eyes fixed on me as if stalking me. When it was close to the mirror it put out its hands and touched the glass, *leaving bloody fingerprints and yellow and grey feathers stuck to the glass*. It felt the surface of the mirror delicately as one would test the fragility of ice on a pond, and then bunched its appalling hands into knobbly fists and beat a sudden furious tattoo on the glass like a startling rattle of drums in the silent room. It unbunched its hands and felt the glass again.

The creature stood for a moment watching me, as if it were musing. It was obvious that it could see me and I could only conclude that, although I possessed no reflection on my side of the mirror, I must be visible as a reflection in the mirror that formed part of the looking-glass world that this creature inhabited. Suddenly, as if coming to a decision, it turned and limped off across the room. To my alarm, it disappeared through the door, only to reappear a moment later carrying in its hands the ebony stick that my reflection had been carrying. Terrified, I realized that if I could hear the creature beating on the glass with its hands it must be in some way *solid*. This meant that if it attacked the mirror with the stick the chances were that the glass would shatter and that the creature could then, in some way, get through to me.

As it limped down the room I made up my mind. Neither I nor the animals were going to stay in the blue salon any longer. I ran to where the cat and the dog lay asleep in front of the fire and gathered them up in my arms, then ran down the room and threw them unceremoniously into the hall. As I turned and hurried towards the bird cages the creature reached the mirror, whirled the stick around its head and brought it crashing down. I saw that part of the mirror whiten and star in the way that ice on a pond does when struck with a stone.

I did not wait. I seized the two cages, fled down the room with them, threw them into the hall and followed them. As I grabbed the door and was pulling it shut there came another crash. I saw a large portion of the mirror tinkle down on to the floor and, sticking through the mirror protruding into the blue salon, was the emaciated, twisted arm of the creature brandishing the ebony cane. I did not wait to see more, but slammed the door shut, turned the key in the lock and leant against the solid wood, the sweat running down my face, my heart hammering.

I collected my wits after a moment and made my way down to the kitchen where I poured myself out a stiff brandy. My hand was trembling so much that I could hardly hold the glass. Desperately I marshalled my wits and tried to think. It seemed to me that the mirror, when broken, acted as an *entrance* for the creature into my world. I did not know whether it was just this particular mirror or all mirrors, nor did I know whether—if I broke any mirror that might act as an entrance for the thing—I would be preventing it or aiding it.

I was shaking with fear but I knew that I would have to do something, for it was obvious that the creature would hunt me through the house. I went into the cellar, found myself a short, broad-bladed axe and then, picking up the candelabra, made my way upstairs. The door to the blue salon was securely locked. I steeled myself and went into the study next door where there was, I knew, a medium-sized mirror hanging on the wall. I approached it, the candelabra held high, my axe ready.

It was a curious sensation to stand in front of a mirror and not see yourself. I stood thus for a moment and then started with fright, for there appeared in the mirror, where my reflection should have been, the ghastly face of the creature glaring at me with a mad, lustful look in its eyes. I knew that this was the moment that I would have to test my theory, but even so I hesitated for a second before I smashed the axe head against the glass, saw it splinter and heard the pieces crash to the floor.

I stepped back after I had dealt the blow and stood with my weapon raised, ready to do battle should the creature try to get at me through the mirror, but with the disappearance of the glass it was as if the creature had disappeared as well. I knew my idea was correct: if the mirror was broken from my side it ceased to be an entrance. To save myself, I had to destroy every mirror in the house and do it quickly, before the creature got to them and broke through. Picking up the candelabra, I moved swiftly to the dining-salon where there was a large mirror and reached it just as the creature did. Luckily, I dealt the glass a shivering blow before the thing could break it with the cane that it still carried.

Moving as quickly as I could without quenching the candles I made my way up to the first floor. Here I moved swiftly from bedroom to bedroom, bathroom to bathroom, wreaking havoc. Fear must have lent my feet wings since I arrived at all these mirrors before the creature did and managed to break them without seeing a sign of my adversary. All that was left was the Long Gallery with its ten or so huge mirrors hanging between the tall bookcases. I made my way there as rapidly as I could, walking, for some stupid reason, on tip-toe. When I reached the door I was overcome with terror lest the creature should have reached there before me and broken through and was, even now, waiting for me in the darkness. I put my ear to the door but could hear nothing. Taking a deep breath I threw open the door holding the candelabra high.

Ahead of me lay the Long Gallery in soft velvety darkness as anonymous as a mole's burrow. I stepped inside the door and the candle flames rocked and twisted on the ends of the candles, flapping the shadows like black funeral pennants on the floor and walls. I walked a little way into the room, peering at the far end of the gallery which was too far away to be illuminated by my candles, but it seemed to me that all the mirrors were intact. Hastily I placed the candelabra on a table and turned to the long row of mirrors. At that moment a sudden loud crash and tinkle sent my heart into my mouth. It was a moment or so before I realized, with sick relief, that it was not the sound of a breaking mirror I had heard but the noise of a great icicle that had broken loose from one of the windows and fallen, with a sound like breaking glass, into the courtyard below.

I knew that I had to act swiftly before that shuffling, limping monstrosity reached the Long Gallery and broke through. Taking a grip upon the axe I hurried from mirror to mirror, creating wreckage that a gang of schoolboys would have relished. Again and again I would smash the head of the axe into the smooth surface like a man clearing ice from a lake, and the surface would star and whiten and then slip, the pieces chiming musically as they fell, to crash on the ground. The noise, in that silence, was extraordinarily loud.

I reached the last mirror but one. As my axe head splintered it the one next door cracked and broke and the ebony stick, held in the awful hand, came through. Dropping the axe in my fright I turned and fled, pausing only to snatch up the candelabra. As I slammed the door shut and locked it I caught a glimpse of something white struggling to disentangle itself from the furthest mirror in the Gallery.

I leant against the door, shaking with fright, my heart hammering, listening. Dimly, through the locked door, I could hear faint sounds of tinkling glass; then there was silence. I strained my ears but could hear nothing. Then, against my back, I felt the handle of the door being slowly turned. Cold with fear, I leapt away and, fascinated, watched the handle move round until the creature realized that the door was locked. There came such an appalling scream of frustrated rage, shrill, raw and indescribably evil and menacing that I almost dropped the candelabra in my fright.

I leant against the wall, shaking, wiping the sweat from my face but limp with relief. All the mirrors in the house were broken and the only two rooms that thing had access to were securely locked. For the first time in twenty-four hours I felt safe. Inside the Long Gallery the creature was snuffling round the door like a pig in a trough. Then it gave another blood-curdling scream of frustrated rage and there was silence. I listened for a few minutes but could hear nothing so, taking up my candelabra, started to make my way downstairs.

I paused frequently to listen. I moved slowly so that the tiny scraping noises of my sleeve against my coat would not distract my hearing. I held my breath. All I could hear was my heart, hammering against my ribs like a desperate hand, and the faint rustle and flap of the candle flames as they danced to my movement. Slowly, every sense alert, I made my way down to the lower floor of that gaunt, cold, empty house.

I paused to listen at the bend in the staircase that led down into the hall, and stood so still that even the candle flames stood upright, like a little grove of orange cypress trees. I could hear nothing. I let my breath out slowly in a sigh of relief, rounded the corner and saw the one thing I had forgotten, the tall pier-glass that hung at the foot of the stairs.

In my horror I nearly dropped the candelabra. I gripped it more firmly in my sweating hands. The mirror hung there, innocently on the wall, reflecting nothing more alarming than the flight of steps I was about to descend. All was quiet. I prayed that the thing was still upstairs snuffling around in the wreckage of a dozen broken mirrors. Slowly I started to descend the stairs. Half-way down, I stopped suddenly paralysed with fear, for reflected in the top of the mirror, descending as I was towards the hall, appeared the bare, misshapen feet of the creature.

I felt panic-stricken and did not know what to do. I knew that I should break the mirror before the creature had descended to the level where it could see me, but to do this I would have to throw the candelabra at the mirror to shatter it and this would leave me in the dark. And supposing I missed? To be trapped on the stairs, in the dark, by that monstrous thing was more than I could stand. I hesitated, and hesitated too long, for with surprising speed, the limping creature descended the stairs, using the stick in one hand to support it while the other ghastly hand clasped the banister rail, the opal ring glinting as it moved. Its head and decaying face came into view and it glared through the mirror at me and snarled. Still I could do nothing. I stood rooted to the spot, holding the candles high, unable to move.

It seemed to me more important that I should have light so that I could see what the thing was doing, than that I should use the candelabra to break the mirror. The creature drew back its emaciated arm, lifted the stick high and brought it down. There was a splintering crash, the mirror splinters became opaque, and through the falling glass the creature's arm appeared. More glass fell, until it was all on the floor and the frame was clear. The creature, snuffling and whining eagerly, like a dog that had been shown a plate of food, stepped through the mirror and, its feet scrunching and squeaking, trod on the broken glass. Its blazing eyes fixed upon me, it opened its mouth and uttered a shrill, gargling cry of triumph, the saliva flowed out of the decomposing ruins of its cheeks. I could hear its teeth squeak together as it ground them.

It was such a fearful sight that I was panicked into making a move. Praying that my aim would be sure I raised the heavy candelabra and hurled it down at the creature. For a moment it seemed as though the candelabra hung in mid-air, the flames still on the candles, the creature standing in the wreckage of the mirror, glaring up at me; then the heavy ornate weapon struck it. As the candles went out I heard the soggy thud and the grunt that the creature gave, followed by the sound of the candelabra hitting the marble floor and of a body falling. Then there was darkness and complete silence.

I could not move. I was shaking with fear and at any minute expected to feel those hideous white hands fasten around my throat or round my ankles. Nothing happened. How many minutes I stood there I do not know. At length I heard a faint, gurgling sigh and then there was silence again. I waited, immobile in the darkness and still nothing happened. Taking courage I felt in my pocket for the matches. My hands were shaking so much that I could hardly strike one, but at length I succeeded. The feeble light it threw was not enough for me to discern anything except that the creature lay huddled below the mirror, a hunched heap that looked very dark in the flickering light. It was either unconscious or dead, I thought, and then cursed as the match burnt my hand and I dropped it. I lit another and made my way cautiously down the stairs. Again the match went out before I reached the bottom and I was forced to pause and light another one. I bent over the thing, holding out the match and then recoiled with sudden horror at what I saw.

Lying with his head in a pool of blood was Gideon.

I stared down at his face in the flickering light of the match, my senses reeling. He was dressed as I had last seen him. His astrakhan hat had fallen from his head, and the blood had gushed from his temple where the candelabra had hit him. I felt for his heart-beat and his pulse, but he was dead. His eyes, now lacking the fire of his personality, gazed blankly up at me. I re-lit the candles and then sat on the stairs and tried to work it out. I am still trying to work it out today.

I will spare my readers the details of my subsequent arrest and my trial. All those who read newspapers will remember my humiliation; how they would not believe (particularly as they found the strangled and half-eaten corpses of the dog, the cat, and the birds) that after the creature had appeared we had merely become the reflections in its mirror. If I was baffled to find an explanation you may imagine how the police treated the whole affair. The newspapers called me the 'Monster of the Gorge', and were shrill in calling for my blood. The police, dismissing my story of the creature, felt they had enough evidence in the fact that Gideon had left me a large sum of money in his will.

In vain I protested that it was I, at God knows what cost to myself, who had fought my way through the snow to summon help. For the police, disbelievers in witchcraft (as indeed I had been before this), the answer was simple: I had killed my friend for money and then made up this tarradiddle about the creature in the mirror.

The evidence was too strongly against me and the uproar of the Press, fanning the flames of public opinion, sealed my fate. I was a monster and must be punished. So I was sentenced to death, to die beneath the blade of the guillotine. Dawn is not far away, and it is then that I am to die. I have whiled away the time writing down this story in the hope that anyone who reads it might believe me. I have never fancied death by the guillotine: it has always seemed to me to be a most barbarous means of putting a man to death. I am watched, of course, so I cannot cheat what the French, with macabre sense of humour, call 'the widow'. But I have been asked if I have a last request, and they have agreed to let me have a full-length mirror to dress myself for the occasion. I shall be interested to see what will happen.

Here the manuscript ended. Written underneath, in a different hand was the simple statement: *The prisoner was found dead in front of the mirror. Death was due to heart failure. Dr Lepître.*

The thunder outside was still tumultuous and the lightning lit up the room at intervals. I am not ashamed to say I went and hung a towel over the mirror on the dressing table. Then, picking up the bull-dog, I got back into bed and snuggled down with him.

BIOGRAPHICAL NOTES

1

'Leixlip Castle' by Charles R(obert) Maturin (1782–1824). First published in *The Literary Souvenir, or Cabinet of Poetry and Romance* (1825). Dublin-born, Maturin was ordained in the Church of Ireland and served as curate in Loughrea and Dublin. His romantic and gothic novels, *The Fatal Revenge* (1807), *The Wild Irish Boy* (1808), *The Milesian Chief* (1812—imitated by Walter Scott in *The Bride of Lammermoor*), *The Albigenses* (1824), and his masterpiece *Melmoth the Wanderer* (1820), were written as an imaginative escape from the terrible poverty and degradation surrounding him in his Dublin parish at St Peter's. 'Leixlip Castle' is his only surviving short story.

2

'The Dream' by Mary W(ollstonecraft) Shelley (1797–1851). First published in *The Keepsake, 1832* (for sale before Christmas 1831). Mary Shelley, only child of William Godwin (author of *Caleb Williams*) and the early female emancipator Mary Wollstonecraft, eloped with the poet Shelley in 1814 and married him in 1816, the same year they met with Byron and Polidori at Lake Geneva and challenged each other to write a horror story. Her novel *Frankenstein, or a Modern Prometheus* was first published in 1818; and several short stories, including some fantasies, were collected by Richard Garnett as *Tales and Stories* (1891).

3

'Metzengerstein' by Edgar Allan Poe (1809–49). First published in the *Baltimore Saturday Courier*, 14 January 1832; and reprinted in *Tales of the Grotesque and Arabesque* (1840). The unique Edgar Allan Poe was both the inventor of the realistic detective story, and the creator of a nightmare world of supernatural horror, macabre and fearful in its imagining—an inspiration to every subsequent writer in the genre. His grim tales, all closely based on his own phobias, notably 'The Premature Burial', 'The Fall of the House of Usher', 'Ligeia', and 'The Pit and the Pendulum', and immortal poems like *The Raven* (1845), made Poe the seminal bridge between ancient Gothic and modern horror.

4

'Master Sacristan Eberhart' by Sabine Baring-Gould (1834–1924). First published in the *Hurst Johnian*, December 1858, the magazine of St John's College, Hurst-pierpoint. The Revd Baring-Gould, squire-parson of Lew Trenchard, will

Biographical Notes

always be associated with the great hymns he wrote, especially 'Onward, Christian Soldiers', but he was amazingly prolific in other branches of literature, including novels, biographies, religious and travel books, and studies of folklore like *The Book of Were-Wolves: Being an Account of a Terrible Superstition* (1865). Several of his earliest literary works were Gothic supernatural tales such as 'Master Sacristan Eberhart' and 'The Dead Trumpeter of Hurst Castle'; and 'Margery of Quether' was among the most noteworthy of his later stories in this genre.

5

'Dickon the Devil' by J[oseph] Sheridan Le Fanu (1814–73). First published in the Christmas Number of *London Society*, December 1872 (where the author's name was misprinted as 'T. Sheridan Le Fanu'); and subsequently forgotten for over fifty years, until it was reprinted in M. R. James's selection *Madam Crowl's Ghost, and Other Tales of Mystery* (1923). Le Fanu was born in Dublin, and related to the dramatist Richard Brinsley Sheridan on his father's side. Several of his best ghost stories, and his greatest Gothic novel *Uncle Silas* (1864), were first published in the *Dublin University Magazine*, of which he was proprietor from 1861 to 1869.

6

'The Secret of the Growing Gold' by Bram Stoker (1847–1912). First published in *Black and White*, 23 January 1892, with illustrations by Paul Hardy; and reprinted in *Dracula's Guest, and Other Weird Stories* (1914). Best known for his immortal Gothic masterpiece, *Dracula* (1897), Stoker also used ancient castle settings in his later novels *The Lady of the Shroud* (1909) and *The Lair of the White Worm* (1911). His best short stories in the genre, notably 'The Burial of the Rats', 'The Squaw', 'The Secret of the Growing Gold', and 'The Judge's House' (closely inspired by Le Fanu, his fellow Dubliner), were all written during the late 1880s and early 1890s, while serving as manager to the actor Henry Irving.

7

'In Kropfsberg Keep' by Ralph Adams Cram (1863–1942). From *Black Spirits and White* (US: 1895; UK: 1896). Cram was the leading American authority on medieval architecture and an expert advocate of the Gothic style. Notable examples of his work are the All Saints Church in Boston (1894) and the Cathedral of St John the Divine in New York City (1911). He was also consultant architect for the Washington and San Francisco cathedrals. His many books include *The Ruined Abbeys of Great Britain* (1905), *The Gothic Quest* (1907), *Heart of Europe* (1915), and *The Substance of Gothic* (1916, Lowell Lectures); but the extraordinary *Black Spirits and White* was his only collection of Gothic ghost stories.

8

'The Dead Smile' by F[rancis] Marion Crawford (1854–1909). First published in *Ainslee's*, August 1899; reprinted in *Uncanny Tales* (1911; *Wandering Ghosts*, US 1911). Born in Italy, educated in the US and at Cambridge, Crawford became an accomplished linguist and Sanskrit scholar. *Mr Isaacs* (1882) was the first of forty-five romantic and historical novels, all immensely popular at the turn of the century—among them *With the Immortals* (1888), *The Witch of Prague* (1891), *Khaled* (1891), and *A Rose of Yesterday* (1897). He spent much of his later life in Italy. His classic macabre tales were posthumously collected as *Uncanny Tales* (1911).

9

'By One, By Two, and By Three' by Stephen Hall. First published in the *Strand* (American edition), March 1913, with six evocative illustrations by Thomas Somerfield. This story never appeared in the British edition of the *Strand*, prob- ably due to its horrific content. Earlier horror stories rejected by the British *Strand* include 'Lot No. 249' (1892) by Arthur Conan Doyle, and 'The Monkey's Paw' (1902) by W. W. Jacobs. These tales (both by *Strand* regulars) appeared in *Harper's Monthly* instead. 'By One, By Two, and By Three' seems to be the only story by the mysterious Stephen Hall, so it is tempting to assume this is a pseudonym of a writer better known for lighter non-Gothic fiction who wished to conceal his identity.

10

'The Buckross Ring' by L[eonard] A[nthony] G[eorge] Strong (1896–1958). First published in *The New Decameron, Volume IV*, edited by Blair (1925); and reprinted later the same year in Strong's collection *Doyle's Rock and other stories*. Both volumes were published in Oxford by Basil Blackwell. Strong was educated at Oxford, where he contributed to several magazines including *The Cherwell* and *The Oxford Outlook*. From 1920 to 1930 he was a schoolteacher in Oxford, a job he was able to abandon when *Dewer Rides* (1929) and *The Jealous Ghost* (1930) launched his career as a very successful novelist, poet, and children's writer.

11

'The Knocker at the Portico' by Basil Copper (born 1924). First published in August Derleth's anthology *Dark Things* (US: 1971); reprinted in *The Year's Best Horror Stories* (UK: 1972; US: 1974), and Copper's collection *Here Be Daemons* (1978). Basil Copper has been described as 'unquestionably one of the greatest living macabre writers', with six short-story collections and several fine Gothic novels—including *The Curse of the Fleers* (1976), *Necropolis* (1980), *The House of the Wolf* (1982), and *The Black Death* (1992)—to his credit. He has also written a series of over forty novels about private-detective Mike Faraday, and two critical studies of *The Vampire* (1973) and *The Werewolf: in Legend, Fact and Art* (1977).

12

'The Entrance' by Gerald Durrell (1925–94). From *The Picnic and Such Like Pandemonium* (1979). Born in India (like his elder brother Lawrence) and educated privately in several European countries, Gerald Durrell's childhood in Corfu was recorded in the trilogy *My Family and Other Animals* (1956), *Birds, Beasts and Relatives* (1969), and *The Garden of the Gods* (1978). His animal-collecting expeditions in three continents provided many stories for his immensely popular books including *The Overloaded Ark* (1953) and *Beasts in My Belfry* (1973).

ACKNOWLEDGEMENTS

The editor and publisher gratefully acknowledge permission to use the following copyright material:

B. Copper, 'The Knocker at the Portico' (1971), reprinted by permission of the author.

Gerald Durrell, 'The Entrance' from *The Picnic and Suchlike Pandemonium* (1979), reproduced with permission of Curtis Brown Ltd., London, on behalf of the estate of Gerald Durrell. Copyright Gerald Durrell 1979.

L. A. G. Strong, 'The Buckross Ring' from *Doyle's Rock and Other Stories* (Blackwell, 1925), reprinted by permission of The Peters Fraser & Dunlop Group Limited on behalf of the estate of L. A. G. Strong. Copyright © L. A. G. Strong 1925.

OXFORD

MORE OXFORD PAPERBACKS

This book is just one of nearly 1000 Oxford Paperbacks currently in print. If you would like details of other Oxford Paperbacks, including titles in the World's Classics, Oxford Reference, Oxford Books, OPUS, Past Masters, Oxford Authors, and Oxford Shakespeare series, please write to:

UK and Europe: Oxford Paperbacks Publicity Manager, Arts and Reference Publicity Department, Oxford University Press, Walton Street, Oxford OX2 6DP.

Customers in UK and Europe will find Oxford Paperbacks available in all good bookshops. But in case of difficulty please send orders to the Cash-with-Order Department, Oxford University Press Distribution Services, Saxon Way West, Corby, Northants NN18 9ES. Tel: 01536 741519; Fax: 01536 746337. Please send a cheque for the total cost of the books, plus £1.75 postage and packing for orders under £20; £2.75 for orders over £20. Customers outside the UK should add 10% of the cost of the books for postage and packing.

USA: Oxford Paperbacks Marketing Manager, Oxford University Press, Inc., 200 Madison Avenue, New York, N.Y. 10016.

Canada: Trade Department, Oxford University Press, 70 Wynford Drive, Don Mills, Ontario M3C 1J9.

Australia: Trade Marketing Manager, Oxford University Press, G.P.O. Box 2784Y, Melbourne 3001, Victoria.

South Africa: Oxford University Press, P.O. Box 1141, Cape Town 8000.

CLASSICS

Mary Beard and John Henderson

This *Very Short Introduction* to Classics links a haunting temple on a lonely mountainside to the glory of ancient Greece and the grandeur of Rome, and to Classics within modern culture—from Jefferson and Byron to Asterix and Ben-Hur.

'This little book should be in the hands of every student, and every tourist to the lands of the ancient world . . . a splendid piece of work'
Peter Wiseman
Author of *Talking to Virgil*

'an eminently readable and useful guide to many of the modern debates enlivening the field . . . the most up-to-date and accessible introduction available'
Edith Hall
Author of *Inventing the Barbarian*

'lively and up-to-date . . . it shows classics as a living enterprise, not a warehouse of relics'
New Statesman and Society

'nobody could fail to be informed and entertained—the accent of the book is provocative and stimulating'
Times Literary Supplement

POLITICS

Kenneth Minogue

Since politics is both complex and controversial it is easy to miss the wood for the trees. In this Very Short Introduction Kenneth Minogue has brought the many dimensions of politics into a single focus: he discusses both the everyday grind of democracy and the attraction of grand ideals such as freedom and justice.

'Kenneth Minogue is a very lively stylist who does not distort difficult ideas.'
Maurice Cranston

'a dazzling but unpretentious display of great scholarship and humane reflection'
Professor Neil O'Sullivan, University of Hull

'Minogue is an admirable choice for showing us the nuts and bolts of the subject.'
Nicholas Lezard, *Guardian*

'This is a fascinating book which sketches, in a very short space, one view of the nature of politics . . . the reader is challenged, provoked and stimulated by Minogue's trenchant views.'
Talking Politics

ARCHAEOLOGY

Paul Bahn

'Archaeology starts, really, at the point when the first recognizable 'artefacts' appear—on current evidence, that was in East Africa about 2.5 million years ago—and stretches right up to the present day. What you threw in the garbage yesterday, no matter how useless, disgusting, or potentially embarrassing, has now become part of the recent archaeological record.'

This Very Short Introduction reflects the enduring popularity of archaeology—a subject which appeals as a pastime, career, and academic discipline, encompasses the whole globe, and surveys 2.5 million years. From deserts to jungles, from deep caves to mountain-tops, from pebble tools to satellite photographs, from excavation to abstract theory, archaeology interacts with nearly every other discipline in its attempts to reconstruct the past.

'very lively indeed and remarkably perceptive . . . a quite brilliant and level-headed look at the curious world of archaeology'
Professor Barry Cunliffe,
University of Oxford

BUDDHISM

Damien Keown

'Karma can be either good or bad. Buddhists speak of good karma as "merit", and much effort is expended in acquiring it. Some picture it as a kind of spiritual capital—like money in a bank account—whereby credit is built up as the deposit on a heavenly rebirth.'

This Very Short Introduction introduces the reader both to the teachings of the Buddha and to the integration of Buddhism into daily life. What are the distinctive features of Buddhism? Who was the Buddha, and what are his teachings? How has Buddhist thought developed over the centuries, and how can contemporary dilemmas be faced from a Buddhist perspective?

'Damien Keown's book is a readable and wonderfully lucid introduction to one of mankind's most beautiful, profound, and compelling systems of wisdom. The rise of the East makes understanding and learning from Buddhism, a living doctrine, more urgent than ever before. Keown's impressive powers of explanation help us to come to terms with a vital contemporary reality.'
Bryan Appleyard

JUDAISM

Norman Solomon

'Norman Solomon has achieved the near impossible with his enlightened very short introduction to Judaism. Since it is well known that Judaism is almost impossible to summarize, and that there are as many different opinions about Jewish matters as there are Jews, this is a small masterpiece in its success in representing various shades of Jewish opinion, often mutually contradictory. Solomon also manages to keep the reader engaged, never patronizes, assumes little knowledge but a keen mind, and takes us through Jewish life and history with such gusto that one feels enlivened, rather than exhausted, at the end.'
Rabbi Julia Neuberger

'This book will serve a very useful purpose indeed. I'll use it myself to discuss, to teach, agree with, and disagree with, in the Jewish manner!'
Rabbi Lionel Blue

'A magnificent achievement. Dr Solomon's treatment, fresh, very readable, witty and stimulating, will delight everyone interested in religion in the modern world.'
Dr Louis Jacobs, University of Lancaster

THE OXFORD AUTHORS

General Editor: Frank Kermode

THE OXFORD AUTHORS is a series of authoritative editions of major English writers. Aimed at both students and general readers, each volume contains a generous selection of the best writings—poetry, prose, and letters—to give the essence of a writer's work and thinking. All the texts are complemented by essential notes, an introduction, chronology, and suggestions for further reading.

Matthew Arnold
William Blake
Lord Byron
John Clare
Samuel Taylor Coleridge
John Donne
John Dryden
Ralph Waldo Emerson
Thomas Hardy
George Herbert and Henry Vaughan
Gerard Manley Hopkins
Samuel Johnson
Ben Jonson
John Keats
Andrew Marvell
John Milton
Alexander Pope
Sir Philip Sidney
Oscar Wilde
William Wordsworth

THE OXFORD AUTHORS
SAMUEL TAYLOR COLERIDGE
Edited by H. J. Jackson

Samuel Taylor Coleridge, poet, critic, and radical thinker, exerted an enormous influence over contemporaries as different as Wordsworth, Southey, and Lamb. He was also a dedicated reformer, and set out to use his reputation as a public speaker and literary philosopher to change the course of English thought.

This collection represents the best of Coleridge's poetry from every period of his life, particularly his prolific early years, which produced *The Rime of the Ancient Mariner*, *Christabel*, and *Kubla Khan*. The central section of the book is devoted to his most significant critical work, *Biographia Literaria*, and reproduces it in full. It provides a vital background for both the poetry section which precedes it and for the shorter prose works which follow.

THE OXFORD AUTHORS

JOHN KEATS

Edited by Elizabeth Cook

This volume contains a full selection of Keats's poetry and prose works including *Endymion* in its entirety, the Odes, 'Lamia', and both versions of 'Hyperion'. The poetry is presented in order of composition illustrating the staggering speed with which Keats's work matured. Further valuable insight into his creative process is given by reproducing, in their original form, a number of poems that were not published in his lifetime. A large proportion of the prose section is devoted to Keats's letters, considered among the most remarkable ever written. They provide not only the best biographical detail available, but are also invaluable in shedding light on his poetry.

THE OXFORD AUTHORS
SIR PHILIP SIDNEY
Edited by Katherine Duncan-Jones

Born in 1554, Sir Philip Sidney was hailed as the perfect Renaissance patron, soldier, lover, and courtier, but it was only after his untimely death at the age of thirty-two that his literary achievements were truly recognized.

This collection ranges more widely through Sidney's works than any previous volume and includes substantial parts of both versions of the *Arcadia*, *A Defence of Poesy*, and the whole of the sonnet sequence *Astrophil and Stella*. Supplementary texts, such as his letters and the numerous elegies which appeared after his death, help to illustrate the wide spectrum of his achievements, and the admiration he inspired in his contemporaries.

THE OXFORD AUTHORS
JOHN MILTON

Edited by Stephen Orgel and Jonathan Goldberg

Milton's influence on English poetry and criticism has been incalculable, and his best-known works, *Paradise Lost, Paradise Regained*, and *Samson Agonistes* form a natural mainstay for this freshly edited and modernized selection of his writings. All the English and Italian verse, and most of the Latin and Greek, is included, as is a generous selection of his major prose works. The poems are arranged in order of publication, essential in enabling the reader to understand the progress of Milton's career in relation to the political and religious upheavals of his time.